Charlie QUINN Lets GO

Also by Jamie Varon

Main Character Energy

Charlie QUINN Lets GO

A NOVEL

JAMIE VARON

PARK ROW BOOKS

Recycling programs for this product may not exist in your area.

ISBN-13: 978-0-7783-6841-0

Charlie Quinn Lets Go

Copyright © 2025 by Jamie Varon

All rights reserved. No part of this book may be used or reproduced in any manner whatsoever without written permission.

Without limiting the author's and publisher's exclusive rights, any unauthorized use of this publication to train generative artificial intelligence (AI) technologies is expressly prohibited.

This is a work of fiction. Names, characters, places and incidents are either the product of the author's imagination or are used fictitiously. Any resemblance to actual persons, living or dead, businesses, companies, events or locales is entirely coincidental.

TM is a trademark of Harlequin Enterprises ULC.

Park Row Books
22 Adelaide St. West, 41st Floor
Toronto, Ontario M5H 4E3, Canada
ParkRowBooks.com

Printed in U.S.A.

To Mom and Dad: Your stories about living in Laurel Canyon in the '70s inspired so much of this book.

1

The worst part about the day I hit rock bottom was how blindsided I was. One moment, my Life Plan was perfectly on track, and the next, in one horrible swoop, everything imploded like a skyscraper stuffed with dynamite. *Boom.*

The hellscape day started off infuriatingly ordinary, which honestly just pisses me off. At the very least, there should have been warning signs. A heads-up. An ominous feeling. *Anything.*

Here's how it went: I woke up at 5:00 a.m. like usual, ate my bland oatmeal, had coffee, scrolled the news, briskly walked on a treadmill at the gym while listening to an audiobook on optimizing productivity, answered emails from my phone, and added several items to my to-do list. Then I showered, blew out my shoulder-length brown hair, put on a tasteful and professional amount of makeup, got dressed, then was out the door by 6:30 a.m.

As I walked to work, I remember stupidly thinking my life was pristinely going according to plan. I was smug. Smug! Steadily climbing the professional ladder, I had just been granted a promotion at the global consulting corporation I'd been working at since I graduated from Stanford. A couple weeks ago, we'd finally returned to the office after a year and a half of lockdown, and when we did, I had a brand-new title and role: Senior Project Manager.

My boyfriend, Josh, was going to propose soon, I could feel it. It was in my—no, *our*—Life Plan. Then, in two years or so, we would buy a house, split the down payment, and settle into the predictable, comfortable life I'd always dreamed of. No surprises. No risk. Security, dependability, safety.

The only thing out of the ordinary that morning was the fact that Josh was still asleep by the time I left our apartment. He never slept in, and I made a mental note to ask him about it later. Maybe he was coming down with something.

The walk to work was only ten minutes, but by the time I got to the office, I had already shed my light jacket. It was September in San Francisco and the weather was unpredictable. When the sun peeked out from the clouds, it started to scorch. I was in black slacks, sleek tennis shoes, and a white button-up rolled to the elbows. My daily uniform.

In the elevator up to the twelfth floor, I answered more emails and when the doors opened, I was satisfied to notice I was the first person to arrive. The floor was quiet and the lights clicked on automatically as I walked. My office was tiny and lacking personality, but it was "a room of one's own," as they say.

Before this promotion, I had an open-concept cubicle. Now I had a door, *and* a window that overlooked the city.

Pulling up my calendar to see my schedule, I noticed my boss's boss had requested a one-on-one for late afternoon. Quickly, I accepted it, but I wondered what it was about, since I typically didn't have much interaction with Francine Rosso.

A text then came in from Josh.

> you left already? on your birthday? i wanted to make you breakfast. happy birthday, babe!

> thank you! have a ton of stuff to do today, so wanted to get ahead of it.

> come home early. let's go to dinner tonight and celebrate. it's the big three-oh!

> we really don't have to. it's all good!

> come on, charlie. let's do something special. i want to take you out.

> i've got a busy day. i'll see what I can do.

I didn't want to go out for my birthday, considering I made a habit of ignoring this day altogether. When your dad leaves the day before your tenth birthday party without saying goodbye and you foolishly think he's going to come back the next day, and he doesn't, and, in fact, he *never* comes back—that might kill the birthday spirit for you once and for all.

Like usual, I wanted to stay at work until eight, eat the meal I prepped this weekend (grilled chicken, brown rice, and broccoli—balanced, easy, and devoid of choice), and fall asleep watching a comfort show like *Brooklyn Nine-Nine*.

While I was answering more emails, my little sister, Benny, and my mom both called me, and I ignored them. Who called someone at 10:00 a.m. on a Tuesday anyway? Only they would do that, forgetting that most people have real jobs. They lived in Los Angeles and seemed to exist on an entirely different planet.

I'd been tragically born into a family of optimists who trusted the Universe had their back, and regularly consulted with tarot cards and astrologists about what to do next, leaving every single thing up to chance and luck. The delusional gene had not been passed down to me, so you can only imagine the black sheep I was, working in corporate America, having a 401k, job security, a savings account.

The rest of the morning and afternoon passed in a frenetic blur of emails, meetings, spreadsheets, and a quick salad at my desk for lunch.

By the time I looked up, my eyes were burning and it was time to meet with Francine. She was on the twentieth floor with the rest of the C-suite and their spacious offices. Even though I had just received a promotion, I coveted that level. It always struck me as fascinating that whenever I hit one milestone, I was already hungry for the next one. My accomplishments never felt like enough, so I figured I just needed to work harder.

After a smooth elevator ride, the doors opened to a long desk and behind it was the receptionist, Chris, a blond twenty-two-year-old guy fresh out of a good college.

"Hi, Charlie," Chris said. "Francine is ready for you. I'll buzz you in."

"Thank you," I replied.

There was a sterile, shiny white door with no knob practically camouflaged into the large wall and when the light buzz sounded, I pushed my way through. The massive space was so quiet I could hear my shoes squeaking on the linoleum as I walked. The floor was surrounded by windows, giving a nearly complete view of San Francisco. It was minimalistic and lifeless, but I enjoyed the order of it, the lack of nonsense or frivolity.

Francine waved me into her office in the far corner. She was wearing a cream blazer over a black silk shirt and her red hair was a bit wild and curly. She looked strangely out of sorts, not as put-together as the last time I'd seen her a couple weeks ago when the offices reopened.

We said our hellos and then Francine's face dropped, along with my stomach.

"I don't know how best to say this, Charlie, so I'll just say it," she began. "We have to let you go."

My mind instantly was loud static, heat rising across my chest. I was certain I'd misheard her.

"Wait, what?" I asked, laughing uncomfortably. There was no possible way I was being fired. They had *just* promoted me. For seven years straight, I'd worked tirelessly for this company, first in and last out every day, no vacations, no sick days. I had done nothing *but* work since I got hired here straight out of college. This job was my entire life.

"The pandemic really changed things," Francine said, her tone apologetic. "You're not the only person being laid off. We need to do a thirty percent cut for our shareholders."

"But I work twelve hours a day. I work on the weekends. I've never had a bad performance review."

Francine had the decency to wince. "It's not about your performance," she explained. "You're a great employee. It's your role. We're absorbing it."

"Can I have the role I had *before* my promotion, then?" I asked desperately.

"I'm sorry," Francine said. "But, no. This is final. We're giving you a severance package. You should take a vacation. Enjoy some time off."

"A vacation?" I scoffed. "I don't want to go on a vacation. I want to work."

"There's nothing I can do." She shrugged uncomfortably. "My hands are tied. We're in a whole new world now, Charlie. Everyone is feeling it."

"I don't want a whole new world," I said, laughing. "I was fine with the old one."

"The pandemic didn't change you?" she asked, her voice dropping.

"Not really," I said.

"Oh." Francine started shuffling through a neat stack of papers to her right.

"Did it change *you*?" I asked a little nervously. Francine and I did not talk about personal matters, ever. We hardly even talked at all.

"I don't know," she said. She fidgeted and tucked her hair behind her ears, not quite meeting my eye. "Don't you ever wonder what we're all working so hard for?"

I reeled back. *No, Francine, I've never once wondered that.*

"No," I said. "It's just what you're supposed to do. You grow up, get a job, and work hard at it."

"But . . . why? What's the point?"

I was dumbstruck by the question, especially coming from someone at such a high level in a role I aspired to one day have, but before I could think of any kind of answer that made sense, she waved her hands in front of her face and said, "Never mind. Forget I said anything. I'm just in a mood over all this stuff. I hate laying people off."

"Okay," I replied, because I felt like I was floating, or drowning. What was I going to do now? All the work I'd put into this company and they drop me, just like that, as if I meant nothing at all? The promotion I'd been grinding for—*gone*. So much for job security!

"I'm sorry this is happening, but I really think you should take a vacation. You deserve one, Charlie. You work too hard."

I work *too hard*? Isn't that what they'd always asked of me? Wasn't that what I was told would be the only way for me to get ahead? Now my devotion to this job was suddenly "too much"?

Before lockdown, this company used to keep a list of people who left at five on the dot. They overtly celebrated "loyalty," which was just another word for "prioritizing work above all else." I had done everything they'd asked of me, and more. This was the thanks I got? Take a vacation? Fuck off and goodbye?

Francine stood up from her chair and motioned for the door, leading me out, and I walked robotically, not quite comprehending what was happening.

"HR will email some forms that you can sign digitally," she told me. "You'll also get information on your severance package and I'll write you a great recommendation letter."

"Okay," I said tonelessly.

"Try to enjoy some time off, Charlie. Have some fun."

"Okay," I repeated.

The quiet of the C-suite floor wasn't nearly as comforting as it had been twenty minutes earlier. I swayed on my feet and almost fell over before I righted myself, shook my head once to get my bearings, and headed back to the elevator with resolve. *I'll be fine*, I told myself. *I'll be completely fucking fine.*

My office now felt suffocating. Mind numb, body moving on autopilot, I gathered up my paltry number of personal items. I had very few people to say goodbye to. Before the pandemic, I had colleagues and we'd get lunch together, go to happy hour, complain about our bosses, but almost all of them had quit or been laid off at some point. Most of them hadn't wanted to return to the office when it reopened. They probably had lives outside of work, wanted to stay remote. Not really a thing I could relate to.

Francine had encouraged me to take time off? *Have some fun,* she said, like it was so easy.

Fun?

Fun was not really on my list of values.

It was still light when I left the office. Disoriented, I ambled out of the high-rise and started walking back to my apartment.

When your job is your entire identity, what the hell happens when you lose it?

2

Somehow, I arrived at my apartment building, nauseous and adrift, incapable of remembering a single turn I made to get myself there. I wouldn't tell Josh about being laid off. Not until I had a plan of action. Not until I could stop my head from pounding and I could manage a coherent thought again.

Josh would probably feel sorry for me and that's the last thing I needed. He was much more concerned about feelings than I was—it was one of very few points of contention between us. He always wanted me to "open up." *About what?* I'd ask him. As if indulging every feeling you have is going to get you *anywhere* in life. I didn't like self-pity or navel-gazing. Life sucks. You get on with it. What was there to discuss?

Two years ago, I was at a networking event and met Josh Randall, a marketing director at Google. He was dynamic, interesting, and, most importantly, stable. Dating him was like being in the low tide of a lazy river. Admittedly, there were no sparks, but I never worried if he would shatter my heart into a million pieces, and at the end of the day, that was what really mattered.

We wanted the same things, had the same boxes to check off. Date for a couple years, get engaged, get married, buy a house, begin the rest of our lives. Ever since I was a teenager, I'd wanted a clear, organized plan for my life, wanted that sense of knowing

I was doing things the right way. And I'd been checking that list off since then—finish high school, go to an impressive college, graduate, get a good job right out of the gate, build loyalty and a 401k, and keep climbing the ladder. Check, check, check.

My mom's favorite saying growing up was "embrace the chaos" and, for me, the resident control freak, you can imagine how much anxiety *that* motto inspired. Because my mom very much *embraced* the chaos. In fact, she instigated most of it.

One time during my junior year of high school, I was despondent to have received a B+ on an exam for one of my AP classes that would definitely lower my GPA, which would also hurt my chances at going to an Ivy League college.

When I told my mom about it, she was blasé and said, "Charlie baby, school is but a tool for conformity. Just relax and go with the flow." *Go with the flow?* I said back to her, incredulous.

Realizing for the hundredth time that my mom would be of no help to me in my life and the only path to success would be to do the opposite of whatever she was doing with hers, I sought out my AP teacher and begged for a retake on the test, studied while my mom had a group of musicians over late into the night, and then aced it.

When I walked into the foyer of my apartment, I resolved to get back on track and find a new job *immediately*.

I kicked off my shoes, uncorked a bottle of white wine, and poured myself a generous glass. After changing into comfortable clothes, I washed off the little makeup I had on my face, then sat down at my laptop, topping off my wine as I passed by the kitchen.

My résumé was ready, because I kept an updated one on my computer, just in case. Having a task was dulling out the buzzing in my head. *It'll be okay*, I told myself. *If I can just keep busy until I find a new job, I'll be fine.*

Just as I was getting into the zone of making a tidy to-do list for my job hunting, I heard Josh's key in the door.

When I looked up, he was dressed in a nice light blue shirt and tan slacks, holding a bouquet of colorful flowers in a large glass vase in front of his face.

His eyes widened when he saw me and his face lit up. "Oh. Wow, you're home early. That's great! Happy birthday!" He handed me the flowers once I stood up.

"Thank you," I said, setting the flowers on the kitchen counter. He pulled me in for a hug and kissed me on the cheek.

"How much time do you need to be ready?" he asked, turning away from me and pouring himself a glass of water.

"Ready for what?"

"I'm taking you to dinner," he said flatly. "I thought that's why you're home early. For your birthday."

"I said I didn't want to go to dinner," I told him. "I'm not really in the mood."

"You're never in the mood," he muttered. "Charlie, it's your birthday. The world has finally opened back up. Please, can we just go out and do something different for once?"

"I have the chicken, rice, and broccoli in the fridge," I said. "We can just have that."

"But we have that almost every night."

"Josh," I said, setting down my glass of wine. "I don't want to do anything for my birthday. I told you. Just change into your sweats. I'll start warming up dinner." I busied myself pulling out the glass containers from the fridge.

When I turned back around with the containers in hand, Josh was still watching me. He looked extraordinarily tired.

"I can't do this anymore," he whispered.

"Do what?" I asked.

"This," he said, gesturing to the space between us. "I can't, Charlie. I just can't."

The whole world seemed to stop at once, alarm bells blaring in my head.

"What are you saying right now?" I asked.

"I—" He paused and dropped his eyes to his hands and wrung them together. "I've been thinking about this for a while and I thought I could turn us around, but nothing is going to change. You don't even want to go to dinner for your birthday, Charlie. I don't know any other solution except . . ." He took a long breath in. "We need to break up."

"You're breaking up with me because I don't want to go to dinner? For my own birthday? *On* my birthday?"

"I'm breaking up with you because this isn't a *life*, Charlie."

My mind was whirling the same way it had in Francine's office only a few hours earlier.

"But, we were going to buy a house, get married one day. We had a *plan*."

"A plan?" he asked, wincing. "Charlie, do you even love me?"

"What do you mean? I thought we were on the same page."

"About what?"

"That we're not about passion or big love, but about two adults building a life together," I said.

My world was tilting on its axis, going haywire.

"Charlie, I never agreed to that," he said. "I don't want to live the same day over and over and call it a life."

"But, that's what you do, Josh," I shot back sharply. "It's called *growing up*."

"But, Charlie, I want to *live*. I don't want to just exist."

"Oh, come on. What does that even mean?"

"Why are you working so hard? Why am I? For what?"

"I . . . don't know." I felt like I was having déjà vu. First Francine, now Josh. Where did all the workaholics go?

"Don't you think we should know?" Josh asked. This was wild, considering how ambitious and driven Josh Randall was when I first met him. He was so work-obsessed I had to schedule our dates with his assistant. All we'd ever talked about was work. He was as singular-minded as me. Who was this new person? And when had he changed? And, more importantly, why hadn't I noticed?

"I guess . . ." I began. "That's what they tell you to do. Go to college. Get the good job. Get married. Get a house. Live happily ever after?"

"But are you? Are you happy? Is this our happily-ever-after? *This?* An hour at the end of the day for personal time and then working all weekend to catch up for the week? Really? Because the way I'm seeing it, we're going to keep doing that until we wake up and we've lost our whole life. What is the point?"

"Josh," I said, wanting this conversation to end immediately. It felt like I was pitched on the side of a cliff, and he was about to push me over it. "It's just what they tell you to do. It's what everyone does!"

"Do you ever feel like . . ." Josh started, his eyebrows stitched together ". . . like the pandemic changed you? Like you're trying to go back to your 2019 life and your 2019 ways of doing things and you just . . . can't? Your 2019 self is gone forever. That life is a distant dream. Everything is different now. Like maybe you're meant to do something else or be someone else entirely? Like you don't even know who you are anymore?"

My heartbeat picked up. The plan had been to get through lockdown by any means necessary and the minute it was done, put it behind me. I'd done that and moved on.

"I think you have too much time on your hands," I said. "You're overthinking it."

"I don't think I am, Charlie," he said back, voice low. "I actually think I've been massively *under*thinking it."

"Again. What does that even *mean?*"

"I don't know what it means. It just feels like I've been sleep-walking, trying to get from one thing to the next. Graduate high school. Graduate college. Get the good job. Get the next, the next, the next, that I've never stopped and thought about what I actually *want* and what might make me happy."

I robotically pulled the containers from the microwave, stirred them, put them back, and tried to absorb what Josh was saying.

"Is being happy the ultimate goal, though?" I asked.

Josh took a sharp inhale and when I turned to him, he looked stunned. "Are you serious? Of course being happy is the goal. That is the *only* goal."

"Oh," I said, fidgeting with the stem of my wineglass. "You've done everything right, Josh. All those things you've done and checked off, *that* should make you happy."

"But, you're not listening to me, Charlie. I'm not happy. They haven't made me happy."

"Then you need to do more. Gun for a promotion. Don't stay stagnant. We'll get a house. Keep moving up." *And I'll get a new, better job. That'll fix everything.*

He sighed, long and low.

"I don't think that's the answer," Josh said. "I've been trying to figure out a way to bring this up with you, but you never stop. I can only talk to you in the brief moments you have in between tasks. We never go on vacation. Remember we had that week before the offices were reopening and I wanted to take us somewhere? Anywhere you wanted to go. I know you don't like the beach, so I thought, okay, let's go to London, Italy, Paris, wherever. We can do something different. But you refused, Charlie. This isn't a life. I appreciate that you like working hard, but it has to be *for* something."

"Well, I'm sorry that I don't like traveling as much as everyone else," I snapped.

Josh stepped back like he was absorbing a blow.

"Charlie, remember when the Google offices were reopening and I told you I really didn't want to go back?"

"Yeah."

"You said I'd feel differently once I got there."

"Right."

"Well, I haven't felt different at all. Each day, I feel worse. I hate what I'm doing. It feels completely useless. I have meetings back-to-back all day. I never stop. And I don't know what I'm doing it all for."

"A paycheck," I said. "Stability. You get up, you go to work, and that's what you do."

"Well, maybe I don't want to do that anymore."

I scoffed. "Then, what else are you going to do?"

"Find something I care about. Find my purpose."

"Like what?"

"I don't know, but I want *more*. Don't you want to get out and see the world? A year and a half cooped up inside, I can't stand going into an office again. Maybe I'll start my own business. I can do anything. So can you, Charlie. This cannot be all there is to life."

"I don't want to do anything else," I said.

"I don't think I believe that," he countered. "You're running from something and I don't know what it is. I've been with you every single day for two years and I don't actually *know* you."

My limbs stiffened like I was turning from flesh to stone all at once.

"I'm sorry to disappoint," I said, heart beating loudly in my chest, face hot. "But this is who I am." This conversation felt like an indictment of all my flaws.

"But, who are you, Charlie? What do you like? What are your passions? What gets you up in the morning? What big hopes do you have for your life?"

"Passion?" I snorted. "*Please.* As if passions get you anywhere." I had followed my fickle passion once before and I'd *never* make that mistake again.

"I don't think you're being honest with yourself, Charlie."

"Yeah, I like routine. So what? I grew up with a mom who . . ." I stopped and Josh sat up straighter.

"A mom who what? Tell me. You never talk about your childhood."

"The past is not important," I spat out, harsher than I intended. "I like my life the way it is, Josh. I don't want anything to change."

"Well, then I don't know what to say. I *need* things to change. If you won't open up to me . . ." He threw his hands in the air like he was giving up. "I want to be happy, Charlie. *Alive.*"

I let out a dry laugh. "Well, not everybody can be happy all the time. That's not how life works."

He deflated like I'd popped a balloon he was holding. "That's a phenomenally sad thing to say."

"It's true. Who's *actually* happy? I'd rather be safe and stable than anything else."

He shook his head and I noticed his eyes were rimmed with red. "Charlie, I'm so sorry to upset the *plan* you've had, but I want to at least *try* to be happy. And I think you should, too. I think we're a little too young to already be giving up on that."

Now, that made me angry. "I'm not giving up on anything," I hurled back. "I'm being *realistic.*"

"Well maybe I don't want to be realistic anymore."

"Okay. So you found someone else? How cliché of you."

"No," he said resolutely. "I would never do that to you. Don't try to make me into the bad guy here. This isn't about someone else."

"Okay," was all I could say.

"Okay? Why does it feel like you're more upset by the plan changing than about losing me? You don't want to fight for us? Are you even sad?"

Sad? *No.* More like angry. My carefully constructed world was breaking off in pieces without my consent and I didn't like it, didn't enjoy feeling like I was careening into the air without a parachute. *That's* how I felt.

"Do you need me to be sad?" I asked him. "I'm not going to be shamed because I work hard. This isn't some Hallmark

Christmas movie where I discover the 'true' meaning of life or some bullshit."

He just let out a defeated sigh.

Then he quickly moved from the breakfast bar and came around to where I was standing in the kitchen, grazed his thumb gently across my cheek, and whispered, "If you really love me and want me to stay, I will. I will work on this with you. Just say the word."

A long tense silence stretched between us, Josh's eyes pleading, unblinking.

Taking a step back from him, I crossed my arms across my chest and said, "I'm not going to hold you hostage. And I won't beg. Go if you want to go."

His face contorted in pain and another pause stretched between us. Finally, in the strained quiet, he gave a nod that looked like surrender.

"I'm doing this for both of us," he whispered. "I hope you find what you really want."

I stifled the urge to roll my eyes, because I was perfectly fine and knew *exactly* what I wanted, unlike him. He'd clearly lost his edge.

"What should we do about the apartment?" I asked.

He exhaled long and hard, like my attention to detail and practicalities had finally worn him down to the bone. Well, good riddance, then.

"I'll stay with Marcus tonight," he said. "You can have the apartment. I can get my stuff whenever you're not here."

"Okay."

"Okay," he mimicked, looking like he was now on the verge of tears. Turning away from him, I poured another glass of wine, emptying the bottle. I listened to him pack a bag and then he left, wordlessly.

In the space of an hour we'd become strangers.

I sat down at my computer and stared at my résumé until the words blended together. For a moment, I felt alarmed by the fact that I wasn't sad. Josh was right, at least in one way—I'd just watched the plan of my life crumble and I mourned that much more than the man who left.

What did that say about me?

3

Remember that thing about rock bottom? *Well.* You're not going to believe that somehow this day gets worse!

Buckle up, babe!

I don't know how long I stood in the kitchen, staring into the abyss, eating flavorless chicken on autopilot, and trying to convince myself I could still stay on track, but it was long enough that the only thing that finally got me moving was a gurgling in my stomach and an unmistakable gag that had me flying to the toilet.

I got on my knees and stared at the water for approximately one second before throwing up so violently that I wondered if I should call 911. Tears leaked from my eyes as everything I had eaten for what seemed like a whole year projectile evacuated from my body. Was I in a horror film? Sure seemed like it!

Even me, stoic and collected Charlie, was rendered utterly helpless and totally pathetic by this sudden bout of food poisoning. The only noises echoing in the bathroom were my whimpers and gags. I'll save you the details about all that went down (and out), but after ten minutes, I didn't think there was anything left in my system, so I sat back against the bathroom wall only to get hit by a roiling nausea that sent my head right back into the toilet.

What the hell was happening?

After another ten minutes of dry heaving, my stomach clenching painfully, I began shaking, descending into a feverish state. My teeth chattered violently, and I was somehow both sweating and freezing. I could hardly move, but I managed to unclutch the toilet bowl and sit up on the soft bath mat, then pulled down a dry towel, and threw it over my shoulders to stop myself from shivering.

That took another ten minutes.

As if things couldn't get worse, once the convulsing stopped, I suddenly found myself *hysterically sobbing*, grasping at my cheeks in shock. I hadn't cried in seven years and I was terrified by the abrupt onset of it, the way I curled onto the cool tile of the bathroom and held myself like I was weak and fragile. What exactly I was even crying about, I had no clue.

I was like a two-year-old having an uncontrollable, irrational tantrum in the middle of a Target.

The most horrifying part was that I was completely incapable of stopping. I prided myself on being masterfully in control of my emotions, or pretending they just didn't exist.

My body started to shake, and I heard myself bawling even more, and I thought it might be nice to have a friend, or a neighbor, or even for Josh to breeze through the door and take it all back, press a warm compress to my forehead, keep the plan going, put life back in order again.

It was the type of unwieldy, out-of-control breakdown I'd sought to avoid with every single fiber of my being.

In between the panic that I may never stop crying was an unwanted ache of loneliness that seemed to howl its way through my bones. Like whatever was possessing me wasn't just emotional, but a physical, tangible pain.

My emotions were like a dam bursting and all I wanted to do was shove them back behind the crack, seal it up, and never let them come out again. Seven years in a riskless, safe life and still I ended up here, on the bathroom floor, whimpering uncontrollably?

What the fuck?

My phone started vibrating on the counter and I crawled for it. When I saw my little sister, Benny, FaceTiming me, all common sense drifted, because I answered it like she was a lifeline, desperate to see her, even while pathetic rivulets of tears streamed down my face. I hated being vulnerable, and I knew I had hit a new low if I was open to Benny, of all people, seeing me like this. She would try to fix it. That was just who she was.

"HAPPY BIRTH—" I heard Benny's singsong voice as the video loaded and when she saw me, her mouth opened into a shocked O-shape. Who could blame her? I looked like hell.

"Hi," I said weakly. My brown hair was plastered to my forehead, the ethereal golden brown of my eyes somehow made clearer by the tears *still* streaming down my cheeks.

Benny's face seemed to shift through several different emotions at once—concern, confusion, and a tiny gleeful grin that only a little sister would deliver while their sibling was clearly dying on the bathroom floor.

By the time Benny spoke, I had somewhat collected myself and was wiping my face with the towel I had over my shoulders.

"Please tell me you look like this because you partied too hard for your thirtieth birthday and have let loose for once in your goddamned perfect life?"

I cleared my throat, held up a finger, stood up on weak legs, gurgled with mouthwash, and sat back down on the floor, careful to stay near the toilet in case something else needed to be forcefully expelled from my body.

"That is the *exact* opposite of why I look like this," I croaked out.

"What happened?"

"Food poisoning."

"No!" Benny screamed. "Oh, my God. I'm driving up there with soup. This is too sad, even for you, Char. Food poisoning on your birthday? Where's Josh? If that man is not at CVS right now spending one hundred dollars on your well-being, I'm going to scream at him via text."

A long silence stretched between us as I became suddenly invested in my cuticle length.

"What?" Benny finally asked, impatiently (but, somehow, in a way I found charming). She was my exact opposite. Optimistic, fun-loving, free-spirited, warm. Where I came from was still a mystery.

"Josh is gone," I told Benny. "He broke up with me. And I lost my job. My whole life, poof, *gone*." I did a little implosion movement with my hand.

"Wait," Benny said. "Back the fuck up. Wait. You got fired and Josh broke up with you ON YOUR BIRTHDAY? I'm going to kill him. And your boss."

"Put the sword down, Benadette," I implored, even though my shoulders loosened with her fervent protection. "I got laid off, so not exactly *fired*, and Josh . . . Well, I don't know. He said the pandemic changed him. He's not happy."

"Are you devastated? What's going on? You seem calm."

I stiffened, and then lied. "Of course. You know me. I'm fine. Apart from the whole food-poisoning thing." I wasn't about to tell Benny that five seconds before she called I was howling out sobs like I was having a nervous breakdown (because I was planning on ignoring that entire debacle and blaming it on the vomiting, anyway). Food poisoning–induced hysteria or something.

"Damn, Char. You and I handle being broken up with in *vastly* different ways. I'm of the screaming, crying, throwing-up, listening-to-Taylor-Swift-for-hours-on-end variety. Well, actually, I guess you nailed the throwing-up part." She laughed and I shot her an annoyed look.

Benny had always lived with her emotions on the surface. Maybe it was because she was born into a totally different environment than I was—I didn't have an older sister protecting me like she did. By the time I was twelve years old, I was shielding Benny from Mom's unpredictability, picking up babysitting jobs, and storing money away in case Mom forgot to pay the electricity or we needed groceries.

Mom wasn't into drugs or anything. She was just flighty, an aspiring actress who never wanted a "normal" life and was *still* waiting on her big break. Bills seemed . . . optional to her. She wasn't a bad mom, just an infuriating one. And for Benny and her, it was so easy to be free-spirited when you had someone (me) doing all the worrying for you.

Mom was also my opposite in almost every single way. It was kind of cliché: the hippie mom with the neurotic daughter. It could be funny, if life were a sitcom, but instead, life was a bitch.

When I grew up, I was determined to check off all the boxes my mom never bothered to check and I'd spent almost a decade trying to prove to her (and, by extension, Benny) that my way was superior. That *they'd* been wrong, not me.

"What are you going to do about your apartment?" Benny asked. "And work? Your work is your life." She chuckled. "You're going to go crazy. What are you going to do *do* all day?"

"It all just happened," I said, ignoring the rising sense of cold dread. "I'll figure it out."

"Come home," Benny said quickly. "Stay with us! You always say no because you have to work. But you don't have a job, so you really have no excuse this time. At least come for a few days. Please?" Her tone was laced with that unmistakable little-sister insecurity. She asked me to come home almost every time we talked, and I'd grown tired of her pleading. I could hear the hesitation in her voice. She was definitely prepared for me to turn her down.

"We'll see in the morning," I told Benny.

"No, that's it. This ends now. You're in crisis. If you don't come here, we'll come there, and Mom will sage your apartment and make you see her favorite psychic in Oakland."

I nearly vomited again.

"You threatening me with my nightmare is not working in your favor."

"I know," Benny replied cheerily. "But, I'm forcing the prodigal daughter to finally come home by any means necessary."

It had been seven years since I'd been back in LA. I'd seen Benny and Mom during that time, sure, but only because they came up to San Francisco and planned around my schedule. I could handle my mom, but only in small doses. But now, facing the prospect of being alone in this apartment with nothing to do for however long it took to find another role in an uncertain market, I was actually considering it. I mean, I could still job hunt from my laptop, and drive back up if I found something.

So I surprised myself by saying, "Okay."

"EXCUSE ME!!!" Benny screamed. "Did you just say *okay*?! You're going to come? DON'T get my hopes up. You're really coming?"

"I'll come," I said, thinking I must be truly desperate if I was agreeing to go back to the mayhem of our Topanga Canyon home.

"I can't believe it. I truly *cannot* believe it. I am AWE-STRUCK. You have struck me with awe, Char Char!"

"I'm not coming if you call me Char Char."

"Fine," she said. "I'll sacrifice that. When will you come? Drive down tomorrow. Oh, my God, I'm going to lose my mind I'm so excited."

"I'll come day after tomorrow, okay? I need to recover." And I needed a buffer day to give me time to decide to back out or not.

"Hallelujah," Benny said. "We'll figure everything out together. I promise. Josh is an idiot."

"He's really not," I said. "Can I tell you about it when I get there? Please don't kill him before I drive down."

"So many rules," she said, pouting. "Fine. I will put a hold on killing Josh for now, but no promises after I hear the full story."

"I'll see you soon."

"I can't wait," Benny said. "I am so excited! Mom is going to flip out. Our baby is coming home!"

"Can you please calm down by the time I get there?" I asked, chuckling.

"Not a chance."

We said our goodbyes and I started to pack. Just one suitcase. Enough for three days, a week maximum. It was something to do. Somewhere to go. And it would make Benny happy. I had tomorrow to decide for sure. If I really didn't want to go, or more likely could not stomach the idea of going, I could say no. Benny would get over it.

After packing, I spent the rest of the night running back to the bathroom every few hours to vomit and then curl up in the fetal position, questioning my entire life.

The day I turned ten without my dad there followed by his wordless abandonment was the worst birthday ever. But this one—well, it was a real close second.

―

All it took was one day in my sterile apartment, alone, without any work, my stomach still cramping, pathetically dry heaving up saltine crackers to decide.

Fuck.

I was going home. Tomorrow, I'd be in LA, back to all the same people and places that had driven me out of there.

That's when I knew for sure.

I'd resolutely and definitively hit my rock bottom.

Welcome to your damn thirties, Charlie Quinn!

Ugh.

4

By the next morning at 7:00 a.m., I was on the road, armed with my suitcase and a large cold brew from my local coffee shop.

I tried to listen to an audiobook, some business tome, but couldn't manage the focus it required. Then, I put on a crime thriller and couldn't get into that, either. Only just across the Bay Bridge, I had already run out of material for the six-hour drive ahead of me. Turning on the radio, I drummed my fingers across the steering wheel to songs I didn't recognize.

It was still foggy over the Bay and the bridge wasn't congested. I tried to keep my mind busy, but there was nothing to distract me. My worst nightmare.

Don't judge me. You'd also be hesitant to listen to your thoughts and follow your impulses if the *one* time you'd let yourself go, you'd been left heart-shattered, alone, and furious you hadn't protected yourself better. My career was on the fritz, but at least it couldn't obliterate my heart the way love could.

There was so much I didn't like to think about. If I allowed my mind to start running, I'd be consumed by the very same emotions I worked so hard to control. Josh had always wanted me to "open up," and he was right that I never had. He was also right that he didn't know me. I didn't *want* him to know me. I never wanted another person to know me ever again.

Because when they know you, wow can they hurt you.

But it only took an hour of staving off the drift of my mind before the memories I avoided the most started pouring in. Memories that felt like they belonged to someone else, as if they existed in movie scenes—a fictional story, told in the third person, in which someone *else's* heart broke. It was so much safer to view it that way . . .

7 years ago, Stanford University

During her Introduction to Philosophy elective class that she'd avoided until her senior year, she sat front row and was the very picture of studious, writing notes by hand. She was on scholarships, grants, and hefty student loans at prestigious Stanford University; the last thing she'd ever do with her education was waste it.

He tapped her on the shoulder lightly, leaned forward before she'd had a chance to turn around, and whispered, "Never in my life have I seen anyone with such focus." She was not used to receiving compliments about her intensity, so the hairs on the back of her neck stood to attention and before she could see who the voice belonged to, the professor swept into the room and began the lecture, which she didn't miss a word of.

After it was over, the row behind her had cleared out save for just one man with black-rimmed glasses and a sideways smile, looking at her with his arms crossed over his chest, as if he had all the time in the world to wait.

"I'm Noah Hawthorne," he said, sticking his hand out.

"Charlie Quinn," she told him, and when she shook his hand, they both looked at each other wide-eyed at the literal spark that transferred between them.

"So, how do you do it?" Noah asked. He wore a loose denim jacket over a faded black shirt and gray sweats. It should have looked rumpled and careless, but he wore it with breezy confidence, and she felt that unmistakable, rare flutter of immediate attraction. He shifted, blushed

slightly at the top of his cheeks, like he noticed her noticing him. He ran his hands through his thick brown hair and adjusted his glasses, which covered brown eyes offset by dark eyelashes.

"Do what?" she asked.

"Focus on something as mind-numbingly boring as Mr. Pratt's lectures."

"Oh, that's easy," she said, shaking her head. "I am tragically and debilitatingly addicted to being a straight-A student. If I don't receive an A in this class, I may actually die."

He let out a loud guffaw. "Brutally honest," he said. "I like that."

"Brutal, being the operative word."

"High standards?" he asked.

"Impossibly."

"Your parents?"

"No, worse," she said, a hint of a smile playing across her mouth. "My own."

"Aaah," he said, clicking his tongue. "I have the opposite problem."

"Let me guess." She made a show of assessing him up and down while his eyes sparkled with mischief. "Rich parents. Old money. A father that never made his own way, so he takes it out on you?"

"Check."

"High ambitions for their golden boy?"

"Check."

"You resent them for it, have zero expectations for yourself, and are a chronic underachiever just to spite them even though you are intelligent and capable?"

He stood up and softly clapped. "Check, check, check." He picked up his simple hunter green backpack, and slung it over his shoulder. "Honestly I'd be impressed but I'm too forlorn about being so predictable."

"Don't be," she said, gathering up her own backpack and following him out to the lecture hall aisle. "I'm really just that smart and perceptive."

He laughed that uninhibited booming laugh again and her heart actually fluttered.

"I bet you have wonderfully supportive parents, don't you?"

"Parent. Singular," she said, turning to watch him walk up the stairs. He was tall and long-limbed, but he was matching her pace and footfalls. "Funny enough, my mom is extremely free-spirited and I am the uptight, responsible one who hates emotions. Let's just say, she isn't quite as enamored with my focus as you apparently are."

"You hate emotions?" he asked, wide-eyed.

"Yes, they're very distracting."

"I'm a Pisces. I'm just one big emotion all the time."

"I'm a Virgo. I like order."

"We're hanging out at the extremes. I'm all feelings. You're all to-do lists."

She laughed. "I can't tell which is healthier."

"Neither," he said. "I fear you are emotionally repressed and I am emotionally fragile. A terrible combination. We should never fall in love."

"God," she said, too quickly. "I should hope not."

He went wide-eyed again. They were at the doorway and she was going to be late for her next class if she didn't leave in one minute.

"I'm that unlovable?" he asked in that teasing, but also sensitive way she now associated with him.

"No," she said, walking off and waving. Over her shoulder she added, "I am."

The scene faded to black when my phone blared through the car speakers. It was Benny. I shook myself off like I was coming to from a daze.

"Are you on the road yet?" she asked, in lieu of a greeting.

"Of course."

"Thank God," she said. "I thought for sure you were going to tell me you weren't coming. I had a speech planned. It was quite moving." She paused. "Well, it was more of a guilt trip. Or a threat. If you weren't coming down, I was bringing Mom and coming up and forcing ourselves into your apartment armed with your astrological chart and a full breakdown of the emotional journey of your next ten years, which you would have hated, so it's a good thing you're on the road."

"Are you done now?" I asked, laughing.

"Yes," she replied, and I could hear her yawn through the phone. It was ten in the morning. Just another difference between Benny, Mom, and me. They were both night owls. "I couldn't sleep I was so excited. I'm going to clean. Are you at the Grapevine yet?"

I smiled, despite myself. The Grapevine. That brought back memories. It was the last long highway before you hit Los Angeles and when I used to come home from college, Benny would always ask that: *Are you at the Grapevine yet?* And for some reason, that question made me feel loved. Like she was waiting for me. That was before everything happened, though. Before I stopped coming home altogether.

"Not yet," I said. "Maybe another hour."

"What road trip snacks do you have?"

"I just have coffee."

"Charlie!" she practically screeched into the phone. "Pull over right now and get snacks. Who are you? You cannot road trip without *snacks*. God, we have a *lot* of work to do."

I laughed, because Benny could warm even the coldest heart. She had that unflappable ability to never let you get too serious. Sometimes I avoided her because of it, even though I felt guilty doing so.

"Okay, jeez, calm down," I said. "I'm exiting. What should I get?" I never ate junk food. Not because I didn't like it, but because I wouldn't allow myself. I wasn't sure why I had that rule. Or all the rules I had. Probably because it was easier to follow them instead of leaving anything up to chance. Certainly, it wasn't because I hated my body or was on a diet. Mom always said, *Hating yourself is a gift to the patriarchy, Charlie baby. My own mother was a slave to her body and counted my calories. It drove me crazy, her obsession with thinness. It was like she truly believed the only* thing she could offer this world was her ability to fit into a size four. I promised myself if I ever had daughters, I'd teach them what self-love looks like. Probably the only words of her wisdom I still heeded.

"What should you get?" Benny asked. "Wrong question. More like, what *shouldn't* you get? Don't get anything healthy. I swear, if you get some raw-almond-trail-mix shit, I'm going to be so upset. I need photographic proof of what you buy, Charlotte. I don't trust you to your own devices. You need Flamin' Hot Cheetos, obviously. Cool Ranch Doritos. Chex Mix. Red Vines. Do they have gummi bears?"

I couldn't help giggling. She was absurd in the best way. "I'm not even there yet! You're like a junk-food sommelier."

"I am," she said, tone serious. "I could practically see her nodding wisely into the phone. "Thank you for noticing."

At the one lone gas station at a random exit off the 5, I pulled my car into a parking spot. The bell chimed above the door and Benny said, "Oh, you're inside now. Yes. The road-trip-shopping excursion is very important, Charlie. Smell the smells. The burnt coffee, the hot dogs that have been slow roasting for twenty-four hours, the distinct aroma of either a Subway or McDonald's that's attached to the gas station. Use the restroom. There will not be any toilet paper in it and the soap will be out. Get a massive fountain Diet Coke. This is all part of the *experience*."

"You are honestly ridiculous," I whispered, but I found myself noticing everything that she was describing. It did smell like burnt coffee. The hot dogs were at the counter, wilting and roasting. There was even a Subway in the back.

"Am I wrong?" she asked, like she was right there next to me, pointing and saying *I told you so*.

I went into the restroom and into a stall. "There's toilet paper, though."

"Oh, you stopped at a *fancy* gas station."

The restroom smelled terrible. "Fancy is a stretch, Ben."

She laughed. "Okay, gather your supplies. Cheetos, Chex Mix, Cool Ranch. The three big C's. Don't forget the fourth, though—Diet Coke."

"I don't even drink soda."

"Why does *that* matter? You're on a road trip, Charlie. You are out of bounds of your normal life. Road Trip Charlie drinks fountain Diet Coke and eats Cheetos until her stomach hurts. You better feel like crap when you get here. You need to be dehydrated and lacking nutrients. *That's* how you road trip."

"Okay, okay," I relented. "I am just easing my digestive system back from food poisoning, but what does that matter?"

"How are you doing by the way?"

"Fine, thank you for your *immediate* concern."

She snorted.

"Sorry," she said. "I'm just excited you're coming. Are you okay, though?"

"Surprisingly, I feel fine."

"Good. Now, what music are you listening to?"

"An audiobook? The radio?"

She let out a comically loud sigh as I filled up a thirty-two ounce cup with ice and Diet Coke. "Charlotte Ruby Quinn. The radio? I can't believe this. No sister of mine is listening to the radio on a *road trip.*"

"You are so demanding."

"I had no idea how much I had to teach you, damn."

"What should I listen to, then?"

"Just click the link I sent you. It's a playlist. Listen to the whole thing. Do not skip. This is the beginning of your education."

"What education is this?"

"How to Actually Have Fun in Life."

I rolled my eyes, but I could feel the smile creeping in. "I have fun."

"No, you don't," Benny said. "You know I'm psychic. I just

got a hit. You're coming to LA and I've decided that the Universe wants me to teach you how to be absolutely fucking delighted by life."

"Okay, tell the Universe I'm going back to San Francisco."

She let out a loud cackle.

"Don't forget the gummi bears!" she called out. "Drive safe! See you soon. Love you!" And then the phone disconnected and I stood in the aisle looking for Cheetos and wondering what I'd gotten myself into.

5

By the time I hit the Grapevine, whatever magic Benny seemed to possess had started to rub off on me, because the music was hitting and the snacks were giving me a dopamine rush I hadn't felt in a very long time. It was so silly and simple, but crunching on Chex Mix while avoiding the pretzels, sipping on an ice-cold Diet Coke, and blasting pop songs I somehow knew the lyrics to without ever consciously listening to them—I was admittedly having . . . a little tiny bit of fun. Like I was a kid again. Like that incessant pressure I usually felt was lifted for a stretch of an hour. There wasn't a militant-style voice in my head saying I needed to *work harder, be more productive, never stop, keep going, never give up, go, go, go.* I hadn't realized my internal chatter was so punishing until it stopped for sixty minutes.

Without my defenses up, another scene played in my mind—again, the movie of someone else's life. The scene before it all changes, before the main character becomes irreparable.

> what a cliffhanger. why do you think you're unlovable?

The Facebook message pinged in on her laptop later that night while she was studying, aglow in the soft light of a desk lamp. Hours earlier, he'd requested to be her friend and she'd stared at the Accept button for ten minutes, smiling like an idiot, debating if she should just deny it, because she was not the type of person to smile like this at just a person's name on a computer screen. But she had accepted it and spent the whole night pretending like she didn't care if he acted on her acquiescence into her digital space.

Charlie had been out to dinner with friends and had some homework to finish before classes the next day. Her life at Stanford had been the most understood she'd ever felt. Other high-achieving students who worked hard and didn't think she was strange for being competitive and put-together. The past four years had been a reprieve and though she often saw Benny and her mom, she was better able to appreciate them now that she had her own life that existed outside of them.

who is this? she typed back, knowing exactly who he was, smiling despite herself. She was not a romantic by any stretch and never found herself giddy, waiting for the typing bubble to produce a response, but that's exactly how she felt.

ha. ha. ha. is what he wrote back and that smile she was trying to conceal spread across her face like honey on the tongue. i demand answers with that wry and unexpected honesty of yours.

are you consulting a thesaurus right now?

i'll have you know I have a robust vocabulary. and don't change the subject.

She laughed and then threw a hand over her mouth, looking to make sure she hadn't woken her roommate up.

okay, maybe i'm not exactly "unlovable" . . .

okay. i am intrigued, enthralled, and riveted by the use of ellipsis. you do know how to leave a guy hanging.

close the thesaurus!

i can't. i'm trying to impress this really smart girl who believes she is unlovable. it's confounding to me.

you're impossible.

impossibly lovable?

i'm shaking my head right now.

i bet you look ADORABLE doing that.

i don't.

well, beauty is really in the eye of the beholder. and i have beholded you so . . .

beholded is not a word.

unlovable? back to subject at hand? god, she's brutally honest but changes a subject like a pro.

rolling my eyes, she typed, *rolling her eyes through a smile.*

your eyes are very pretty. i beheld them.

now who's changing the subject? hmmm?

proceed . . .

i think I'm hard to love. and i don't love love. or romance. it's distracting. i'm cynical. not a hopeless romantic.

jeez. who hurt you?

She wasn't quite sure why she decided to tell the truth, but she typed it without thinking and then sent it; something about Noah made her want to spill out her guts and reveal them to him.

> a dad that left without saying goodbye and a mom that doesn't live in reality. take your pick. i've been an adult since i was ten. not a big fan of risk and hope. i like to know how things end. safer that way.

> this honesty is extremely hot, charlie, just so you know. so, you're maybe more emotionally avoidant than repressed?

She shivered at the "hot" comment and her body alighted like a match thrown onto gasoline.

> i'm an overachiever so i'd say both.

> well, you may need to change your stance. a life without risk isn't much of a life at all.

> sounds like something my mom would have stitched on a pillow.

> i like her already. btw, i'm a big hit with moms.

> i bet you are.

> not like that!

> lol anyway, why do you care?

> i already told you. i find you intriguing, enthralling, and riveting.

All the air in her small dorm room seemed to shrink down to right in front of her. She should have logged off. She thought about that turning point for years afterward. If only she would have blocked him and not risked anything . . .

But she couldn't. For some reason, against all her better judgments and everything she thought she knew about herself, she typed back and said, well if that's true, then you have great taste.

There was a long pause before she saw him typing again and she thought she'd lost him. It made her stomach plummet. She already liked the idea of him being in her life a little too much. She'd spent her entire collegiate experience at Stanford single. Of course, she'd hooked up casually, but she was not some wide-eyed romantic looking for Prince Charming, that's for sure. She had a career to begin, and she'd only ever felt strongly about one guy back in high school who'd left her feeling rejected, so what was the point? Best to avoid love altogether was her philosophy. (No surprise, her mom's philosophy was to throw oneself into love, life, and anything else, with as much abandon as possible. Charlie was . . . not a fan of that.)

But, damn it, when the typing dots appeared, she audibly sighed with relief. Her heart was a traitor.

> :) I understand you believe you are hard to love and do not possess any romantic inclinations but you do eat, yes? have dinner with me tomorrow night?

By that point, there was no other answer possible except yes.

Anger rose within me like a volcanic eruption and I slammed the music off, pushed the junk food away, and felt nausea creeping in. This was why I never let go of myself. Whatever Benny thought she was going to achieve when I got to LA, it wouldn't work. I had to keep myself in control. Why was I driving all this way? I should be in San Francisco lining up job interviews.

Once I was over the Grapevine and only thirty minutes out from the house, I pulled over, and called the headhunter who had secured me the job I'd just lost.

She answered quickly. Georgia Wallace was one of the best headhunters and most people in Silicon Valley swore by her.

"Hi, Georgia," I said. "It's Charlotte Quinn."

"Oh, hi, Charlotte," she said, clipped and efficient. "Don't tell me you got laid off."

"Well," I said. "Yeah, that's why I'm calling."

"Damn it. I'm sorry to hear that. The layoffs lately have been vicious."

"Yeah. Gave my whole life to this company only for them to lay me off like I was nothing."

"Awful," she said. "You want me to put some feelers out there for you?"

That volcanic anger noticeably dissipated, like water thrown on a fire, hissing out to ash. Finally, someone that didn't make me feel bad for actually wanting to work.

"You read my mind," I said.

"I'm on it."

"Also, wouldn't hurt to throw in some tech options. I'm open."

"What kind of work are you interested in? Any new passions?"

"I don't care," I said. "I just need to stay busy. Good pay, stable, long hours, I'll take it."

"I'll see what I can put together. The landscape has changed a lot, though, just a heads-up. Since the price of everything has increased, lots of places are having hiring freezes. There are more layoffs than open positions right now. Just wanted you to be aware. If it were me, I'd manage my expectations. The pandemic changed everything."

The nausea roiled back in.

"Easier said than done," I said. "Thank you for the heads-up."

"I'll still see what I can find out for you."

"Thanks, Georgia."

"Of course. Call me anytime."

Back on the 5, car silent, I inched forward in mind-numbing LA traffic. It wasn't even rush hour, but that didn't matter here. I remembered getting my first car at sixteen years old, the feeling of buying it in cash that I'd made from working random jobs for years. It was a dingy little light blue Honda Accord, but it was mine, and it was freedom. All around me, kids were gifted brand new luxury cars on their sixteenth birthday, paid for by rich parents. LA was not a great place to grow up without money, especially when everyone around you had so much of it.

But, I had put my nose to the ground and worked, saving up every dollar I could, until I put a stack of bills into the hand of the used car salesman on my sixteenth birthday. I bought it alone, paid for it on my own, and drove it off the lot, my hair whipping behind me by the open window. It was a moment I never forgot—what it felt like to sustain and rely entirely on myself.

But now, a hundred thousand dollars of student loans paid off to one of the best colleges in the country and I was out on my ass with nothing else lined up. I had done every single thing right to avoid this anxious sense of being untethered. Just yesterday morning, my life was exactly how I wanted it to be. Now, it seemed like I had nothing to show for two decades of ceaseless focus. *What a joke.*

I turned the playlist up to blaring. My car screen told me it was an Olivia Rodrigo song called "brutal" with a refrain that started "All I did was try my best // This the kind of thanks I get." It was angry and intense and I liked it immediately.

6

The bungalow surrounded by trees where I grew up looked exactly as I'd left it. Driving here had been rote and automatic. I hadn't even thought about it and suddenly I was on the curved road up into Topanga Canyon and outside the wood-paneled two-story home with the large brick chimney.

Once you got up here into the Canyon, the homes were much more spread out and it felt like you were removed from whatever madness was happening down there in the sprawl of Los Angeles.

The house was surrounded by towering oak trees, nestled into a lush hillside, tucked away off the road, and overlooking so much forestry it felt like you were pitched on the cliff itself. Which, in a way, you were, because on one side of the house it was held up by stilts of wood planted directly into the earth.

I parked at the rocky driveway and looked up toward the wooden staircase that would take me to "Quinn Canyon," the name Mom gave the house and the land when Benny and I were kids.

The house was still deeper into the trees and there was a large river rock landing that overlooked the sweeping canyon. I stopped and took in a sharp breath. There was a circle of Adirondack chairs placed around a firepit filled with ash. All through my childhood, we'd spent as much time out here as we did inside the house, a rotating cast of characters telling interesting stories or playing songs they had just written, some future big star on the cusp right here at the bonfire of Quinn Canyon.

It had been both thrilling and painful. People with big audacious, creative dreams that my mom nurtured, while she always told me to chill out, take a break, stop worrying so much about school. Her excitement over my accomplishments never quite reached her glee over some new actress making it big or a director about to get their break.

She so obviously wanted me to follow in her artistic footsteps in some way, and I often wished she could have been able to hide that better. It would have been nice to not feel like I was disappointing her by being studious and then paying my way at Stanford.

As I walked on, I took notice of some changes, like the multiple strings of fairy lights cast across the trees, lit up and twinkling even though it was still the afternoon. The trees never allowed too much sunlight into the house, so there was always a dimness about the space, an intimacy. It felt as though you were shrouded and concealed. The quiet here was . . . quieter.

Other minor improvements had been made to the house. It looked like all the non-wood surfaces had been painted somewhat recently and the roof had been redone. The shabbiness that I'd always associated with the house seemed to be gone, the carelessness that had been a result of not having enough money to keep it up properly.

This house was Mom's only asset and it had been a gift from an actor—and Mom's best friend—who had died seven months before I was born.

A part of me wanted to slink away, not go inside. There was a pounding in my chest, and when I lifted my hands, they were noticeably trembling. My mind was thundering at me to *run*,

run, run, and I might have—I really might have got back in my car—if right at that moment, the heavy wood door with its arched and intricate peekaboo window hadn't swung open.

Benny, unflappable and gorgeous, stood in the doorway with the widest, most genuine smile on her face.

"You're here," she squealed and ran to me, practically tackling me to the ground with a fierce hug. All the frustration I'd felt with her before vanished and I hugged her back, hard.

As she released me, I placed my hands on her shoulders and said, "Okay, let me get a good look at my beautiful little sister."

She beamed and tipped her chin up. The least self-conscious person I'd ever known, Benny was so wholly herself. She changed her hair constantly and somehow looked good with every variation, style, length, and color her adventurous hair stylist threw her way. Right now, it was cut to her shoulders, wavy and thick. Her messy bangs were electric blue and the rest of it was onyx black. Skin was pale, freckled, offset by the same ethereal golden-brown eyes we both shared with my mom—a distinctly Quinn women feature. She wore an oversized gray sweatshirt over jean shorts and white bunched crew socks, and she smelled like cinnamon and vanilla.

As much as she could get under my skin, she was my favorite person in the world.

"She's gorgeous," I said, after assessing her. She smiled and nodded, like she knew she was. Which was probably true. She didn't have an ounce of doubt in her body. Benny grew up with a love for herself that was something rare to witness. She never counted calories or tried to lose weight or keep up with trends. I'd never heard her say a single bad word against herself. I had to admit Mom had taught us both well.

Anybody who stepped into Quinn Canyon was not allowed to harshly criticize themselves. They were especially not allowed to bond over hating their bodies. It was a Jackie Quinn rule. One time when I was fifteen, she literally kicked an aspiring actress out of the house for ten minutes because she refused to eat bread and kept lamenting about turning thirty-nine, declaring she lied about her age to casting directors. Jackie threw her out until her "energy" could be cleared from the space.

That actress said those ten minutes changed her life. She went on to win an Emmy and thanked Jackie Quinn in her acceptance speech, never lied about her age again, and still works to this day. I may have had problems with Mom, but other people did not. They flocked to her like she was their safe haven in a harsh world. Maybe if I had been more like them, Mom could have been my safe haven, too.

"You're gorgeous back," Benny said, and snuck in another squeeze.

"Well, I don't have blue bangs."

Her eyebrow peaked. "We could arrange that . . ."

"No, we definitely could not."

She slung her arm over my shoulder and led me toward the door.

"Just one teeny-tiny makeover," she pleaded.

"Oh, wow, so I need a makeover?" I quipped. "I thought you said I was *soooo* gorgeous."

"You are gorgeous always and forever, but makeovers are fun."

"For who . . . ?"

"For me."

I smiled. "Maybe."

"I'll take it. It's hope!"

We walked through the doorway and as soon as the smell of sage and pine hit me, I traveled back in time. I was five years old again and I had a dad. He was crouched in front of me, placing a packed lunch in my little backpack, humming a Beatles song, telling me to have a great first day at school, and that Mom would be happy again soon, that she'd lost the role she wanted, that she wished she could have been there to see me off. I'd asked him, in my little kid voice, if I should go up there and make her feel better. He shook his head, told me she'd be okay.

That was when I was still feeling responsible for my mom, when all I wanted was for her to be okay. My dad always brought home trinkets from his travels, and even though being a dad was a very inconsistent part-time role for him, it never mattered to me. It was only when I got older that those memories turned bittersweet, when I realized that he wasn't just some fun uncle that was allowed to come and go. He was never around for long. And then, he was gone for good.

"Is Mom—"

"Mom's on her way," Benny finished. Then, she grinned conspiratorially. "I didn't tell her you were coming."

"Benadette Ruby Quinn." Yes, we had the same middle name. The same as Mom's. Jacqueline Ruby Quinn. *All my little gems*, she used to say.

"I wanted to surprise her," Benny whined.

I shook my head and stopped in the entryway, now even more uncertain that I wanted to be here.

I knew Benny meant well, but surprising Mom meant surprising me, too. What if she was angry that I'd stayed away for so long?

Before I moved out, we had been Triple Quinn, known throughout Mom's eclectic group of friends and wider acquaintance circle. There was never one of us without the other, not after Benny was born. It was the kind of childhood that seemed idyllic when you're a kid, but then you become an adult yourself and your memories shift. You realize maybe being your mom's life coach and confidante and shoulder to cry on wasn't very healthy.

"Come on," Benny said. "It'll be fine. Come into the kitchen. I'll make hot chocolate." She walked forward down the entryway and disappeared beyond it, but I continued on slowly, seeing my childhood home through fresh eyes. Everything almost looked the same. High dark wood beam ceilings, crisscrossed to a peak at the top. The staircase to my right would lead to three bedrooms, and lining the wall all the way up was an array of bohemian artwork, meticulously placed so there was hardly any space left for anything else. The staircase was intricate and the stairs were lined with Moroccan-style carpeting.

The living room had always been the focal point and in true canyon style, it was about half of the first floor of the house, perfect for entertaining a large group of people, which this house had done all throughout the years since it had been built in the '70s by a young movie star named James Carlyle who wanted a haven for other outsiders like himself.

James had been too gorgeous for his own good, and was discovered at seventeen, thrust into fame, but then forced to hide his sexuality. When twenty-year-old Jackie Quinn had been in Los Angeles for four years trying to make it as an actress, she met James and they became fast and best friends. Then, later, when James needed a beard to accompany him to various events, he asked my mom and she said yes.

When he died tragically five years after that, Mom was twenty-five and had just found out she was pregnant with me, wondering what the hell she was going to do, living in a dingy Hollywood apartment with four roommates. She got a call from an estate lawyer that James had miraculously left her one of his properties: the tucked-away bungalow in Topanga Canyon, a place that Jackie loved and had spent many evenings in with musicians, artists, actors, and all sorts of wildly creative and interesting people.

In that living room, she'd listened to early acoustic versions of songs that later became worldwide sensations. She'd talked to actresses who lamented the fact that they were still waiting to hear back from auditions and then she'd seen their faces on billboards on Sunset Boulevard the next year. She kept hope alive that her dreams would come true in the same way.

They hadn't.

They still hadn't.

But she was out there, trying, even now, at age fifty-five.

If you weren't her daughter, you may have been inspired.

But if you *were* her daughter, you may have wanted stability and a mom that was around, not chasing auditions and then devolving into misery whenever she didn't get a part.

Jackie Quinn wanted to be our best friend a lot more than she wanted to be our mother. And when I was fourteen years old and charmed by no bedtimes and "jam sessions" in the living room until midnight on a random Wednesday, I wanted to be her best friend, too. And then I grew up and realized it's much better to have a mother than a friend.

The James Carlyle experience defined Jackie Quinn's life. At the eleventh hour, she was taken care of. When I'd remind her it was luck, she'd swoop her arm around the bungalow and say, "If it's only luck, how did I end up here?" "One stroke of luck!" I'd say, exasperated. "Well, it sure hasn't run out yet!" she'd scream back. And I'd storm off petulantly. She lived on a dangerous edge. She called it her intuition. I called it madness. And guess who would have to be there when her "luck" ran out? Me. I was *always* her backup plan. She just didn't realize it.

The infamous living room had gathered more kitsch since I'd been there, but all the furniture was the same. There was a large worn-in dark green sectional couch and four deep-set chairs facing it. Behind the chairs was a window that stretched the length of the room and overlooked the canyon, all greenery and mountain in the distance. On the wall facing the front of the house was a massive collection of books and records that James had left behind in built-in wooden shelves. My mom had added to this collection over the years and it now spilled over to the dining room. There was an acoustic guitar on a stand next to a brown leather pouf.

The style was so '70s bohemian that it really did feel like

time had stood still. Which is exactly what my mom wanted. It was such a far cry from my place in San Francisco. When Mom had first seen my minimalist apartment, she'd gasped and said, "Charlie, how do you live like this? It's so sad!" It had infuriated me.

The long entryway next to the staircase had a worn Persian rug over the original hardwood floors and the walls were filled with more books and records.

When I finally got to the kitchen, the place that used to be my favorite room of the house, Benny looked up while holding a mint-green teakettle in her hand and said, "Marshmallows or no?"

"Sure," I said. I felt a little bewildered and out of sorts, beaten down by an assault of memories I'd long repressed. It took me a moment to realize I'd held back the good parts, too. Suddenly, a flood of happy memories in this kitchen came over me. I used to love cooking, and I'd baked so much good bread in here. I had a special touch with the dough and I'd serve it with butter I made myself to my mom's friends. They always requested full loaves. Baking was the only time my mind felt still. *Why did I ever stop?*

Never mind, I remembered why I stopped.

The kitchen was a collection of different types of wood. The same high-beamed ceilings as the rest of the house. Two tall windows overlooking greenery in the corner. Dark cabinets and a wooden island in the middle. Red clay floors with another massive rug to cover the area. The stove had been updated to a stainless steel, and so had the refrigerator. There were intricate pots with an array of plants above the wood cabinetry. Herbs sat in the windowsill. There was nothing sterile about the space. Nothing minimalist. It was *alive*. My hands suddenly itched to knead something, just for the hell of it. It was a strange feeling; I couldn't remember the last time I wanted to do anything other than work.

I sat down on the stool and Benny placed a heavy handmade mug in front of me. The top of the hot chocolate was covered in little floating marshmallows. When I took a sip, I heard the front door open. My heart leaped, and I kicked the stool out from under me and stood up.

Mom was home.

7

"Benny," Mom called out, while I heard her shuffling in the doorway, out of breath. "I had the strangest feeling just now that Charlie is coming to visit."

Benny's face lit up and she grinned. "She's psychic."

"She saw my car, Benny."

"Oh, yeah?" Benny whispered. "She was at Petra's house, which is up the road, not down it. So, *there*. She couldn't have even *seen* your car." Benny crossed her arms in front of her chest and gave me a searing look.

"She probably picked up on your excitement, then."

Her eyebrows pinched together and she dropped her smile. "Why do you always have to be so hard on Mom?" Benny shook her head then and turned away from me before I could answer, and whatever was roiling around in my stomach turned to lead.

"Ben—" I started and then Mom was in the doorway.

"You're already here," she said, flatly, staring at me.

I shrugged.

She narrowed her eyes and assessed me, looking like she could read my thoughts. My heartbeat picked up.

But then, her face broke into a sunbeam and she came toward me, arms outstretched. "My baby is home!" She hugged me tightly and her sweet fruity scent hurtled me back to childhood, when I'd crawl into bed and try to console her, curling myself up in the crook of her neck, hoping I could make her feel better, that I could bring her back to herself after yet another rejection.

She wouldn't let me go; she just kept hugging and hugging me, until Benny yelled, "Hey, I feel left out!" and wrapped her arms around us both and rocked until Mom laughed out loud and I tried not to feel suffocated.

They finally released me and Mom went around the small island and leaned against the sink, the golden light streaming in through the trees and onto the blond of her long hair. She was radiant. She had always *been* radiant. The kind of beauty that was truly effortless. A comfort in her skin that never wavered. She never had Botox, or a single cosmetic procedure on her face. Never restricted food or decried carbs one year or gone fat-free. She held herself and her body like it was sacred, like she was *worthy* of existing. It was no wonder she always had a bevy of friends and suitors, just waiting for her attention. A true cornucopia of admirers. Benny had that, too. Maybe I did as well. I made it a point not to notice anything like that now.

Mom continued to watch me from her vantage point, all while being highlighted by the sun streaming in through the windows. She was in comfortably worn loose jeans and a thick oatmeal-colored sweater. Her blond hair was wavy and past her shoulders. It was expertly highlighted, weaving through her natural white with darker blond tones. Her hair had always been the one thing she put real effort into.

"Happy birthday, by the way," she said. "You didn't return my call, so I didn't have a chance to say it to your face. Not that you have to return my call, of course. I'm sure you were busy. I hope it was a great birthday." She was talking quickly, almost nervously. I looked up from my fidgeting hands, confused by the unfamiliar self-consciousness that was emanating off her. She started biting her lip.

"Is everything okay?" I asked. Benny was standing off to my right, where built-in shelves were housing an impressive collection of what seemed to be every cookbook ever published in the entire world. A strange sight, given the fact that my mom had never cooked when I was growing up. If anything, I was the chef in the family.

"Everything's fine," Mom said, fingering the long crystal pendant at her breast. "Well, it's just—I don't want to scare you off again. I can't believe you're here. I don't want to say the wrong thing. I don't want you to leave again and not come back for years."

"Oh," I said.

"I don't say that to make you feel guilty, Charlie baby," she said. "You took what time you needed for whatever reasons you needed. I get that. One day, maybe you'll tell me why. I just, I'm really happy to see you, here in our home, the three of us back together again. I'm trying not to cry right now. I missed you, that's all. We both did."

"Oh," I repeated.

"I know you hate big displays of emotions and all kinds of feelings, so I'm done now. But, I love you and I'm so grateful you're here. That's it." She wiped at her golden eyes and made a show of shaking herself off dramatically and then smiled. "What's for dinner, then? Pizza?"

8

"Pizza!" Benny yelled out. "I'll get my shoes."

Mom looked at me and asked, "Pizza, Charlie baby? You in? Our usual place?"

I shrugged. "Sure."

Mom clapped her hands together and headed for the door, and I followed closely behind.

I knew exactly where we were going, a little tucked-away spot near Laurel Canyon where we'd gone hundreds of times in the past. Benny and Mom for sure had been going on their own. Double Quinn, not Triple. I ignored some strange pang that echoed in my chest.

"We can get ice cream at McConnell's after," Mom said when we reached the doorway, craning our necks up to see if Benny was coming down yet. "They have a new peanut butter flavor that you'll die for. I know how much you love peanut butter." She reached over and gave me a side hug, squeezing me tightly across the shoulders, and planted a soft kiss on the crown of my head. I noticed how I leaned into it, transfixed, and when Benny came ambling down the stairs, I straightened and angled my body away so Mom's arms would fall.

The problem with my mom was that it had always been hard for me to stay mad at her and keep my distance. It was part of the reason I hadn't been home in so long. When anger takes the place of pain, all you want to do is hold on to that rage by any means necessary.

Benny led the way outside. At Quinn Canyon, it was as if nothing else existed in the entire world, a cocoon of nearly pure darkness. I had to watch my step on the uneven rocks and down the shoddy staircase to where our cars were parked. Benny and Mom sped up ahead, obviously used to traversing this part of the land more than I was, and were waiting for me in Mom's old Jeep with the headlights on by the time I caught up.

When I climbed into the front seat, Benny was already in the back in the middle, her body leaning forward like she was sitting between us, just like she used to. It was so familiar. Strange, how quickly and effortlessly we fell back into automatic patterns.

About ten minutes into the drive, "Dreams" by Fleetwood Mac started playing and I knew Mom was about to turn it up and sing out every word. While she lived for change and novelty, she could also be quite predictable. She reached for the knob and the song erupted through the speakers. Her voice was stunning. There was so much untapped talent within my mom and I spent too much of my childhood watching her heart break because nobody noticed it. I guess it broke my heart a little bit, too.

I had a sudden ugly urge to shut off the music and ruin her moment. Mom's showmanship grated on me. Benny always loved it, because her feelings toward Mom were entirely uncomplicated. She idolized her. When Mom was finished, Benny clapped and screamed, "Well done!" and I just kept my eyes fixed on the road.

We were finally driving down Ventura Boulevard, and the intensity and vibrancy of the city hit all my senses at once. It was blaring loud, and frenetic with activity, and the brightness of the lights almost hurt my eyes. But it was also beautiful. Tall, towering palm trees and warm, dry evening air. Back when

I loved movies, I used to pretend I was in one every time I coasted down Ventura with the windows down.

A few minutes later, Mom pulled into a strip mall. In LA, and especially in the Valley, you knew to never underestimate a strip mall because it likely held the gems—sushi, taco, pizza spots that looked like holes-in-the-wall but actually served some of the best food in the city. The greatest spicy tuna with crispy rice you'd ever had in your life might be found between a pet shop and a postal annex.

The familiar smell of Rocco's Pizzeria wafted toward me the moment I stepped out of the car and my stomach growled—actually, *roared*—in response. It was strange, but I'd forgotten how much I loved food. It was another part of childhood with Mom and Benny that I'd left behind. Dinners out with Triple Quinn had been legendary and, eventually, I'd written them off as irresponsible. Mom never had enough money to be taking us out every other night. I started cooking us meals at home simply because I was so terrified that one day we'd go completely broke and lose our house.

Sometimes it takes getting out of a situation to realize how stressed you were in it. When I left LA, I felt like I could finally put everything in order, take control, and stop worrying that Mom's spontaneity would eventually ruin our entire life.

Rocco's Pizzeria was a true hole-in-the-wall. There were two outdoor tables on the sidewalk in front of the tiny restaurant. Well, "restaurant" was generous. The space consisted of one long counter and a wood-fired oven, pizzas made to order, and a line out the door.

When the tables outside were taken, people would sit on the curb in the parking lot, eating from cardboard boxes. It wasn't that busy tonight, so we only had a few people in front of us. It didn't take much for the line to be out the door, but at peak times, it would stretch all the way to the pawn shop four doors down.

A couple people ordered and then we were inside the little place and I felt like I was thirteen again. Every open space on the wall was filled with either newspaper and magazine clippings of Rocco's esteemed history or celebrity pictures with their arms around Ali, the owner and master pizza maker. Everyone mistakenly called him Rocco, assuming he had named the spot after himself. He had movie-star looks—tall, dark, handsome, olive skin offset by deep brown eyes. By now, he must have been in his mid-fifties. His Tunisian-born father, the actual Rocco, studied pizza-making in Italy before he moved to the US, and when he died, he handed the business to Ali. Before he fell in love with running Rocco's, Ali had wanted to be an actor.

"Charlie Quinn, as I live and breathe," he said when we made it to the counter. "It's been a long time."

I smiled. "It has, Ali. Good to see you. How are things? How's business? How's Miriam? And the twins?"

He beamed. "Miriam is good. She's running our second location now. We opened one in Silverlake. Rocco's in Silverlake. Can you imagine? Adam and Aya are about to graduate high school. Next year is college. Unbelievable how fast time goes."

"It is. I'm glad to hear all is well, though. What are the kids going to study?"

"Adam wants to be a graphic designer. Aya is going to business school. I can't believe it, but she loves the pizzeria. She wants to open more locations. I just want my little pizza shop, but she's got big dreams, that one."

"She always did," I said, remembering the plucky and curious little girl from when she was just a kid. She was always here at the shop with her dad, doing homework on a stool in the corner. "Tell them I said hello, will you?"

"Of course. How long are you in town for? They're usually in on the weekend."

Mom and Benny both stared at me, clearly eager to hear my answer.

"I'm not sure," I said.

Quickly changing the subject, I turned to Mom and Benny. "Are we doing the usual?"

"We have a different usual now," Benny said. "But no worries. It's been a while since we had the original usual." She laughed.

"Remind me what it was?" Ali asked. I felt a twinge in my chest about the fact that he had forgotten. That Mom and Benny had a new usual and I didn't know what it was.

"An extra-large pizza with pepperoni, sausage, roasted garlic, mushrooms, and double pineapple," I said. One thing about the Quinn girls, we loved pineapple. All three of us. Or, at least, we used to.

Ali wrote down our order.

"You got it," he said. "Coming right up."

We started shuffling to the door, excusing our way through what was now a pretty long line.

"Hey, Charlie?" Ali called.

I turned back around to face him. People understood his generosity of spirit, so nobody seemed especially put out that they were waiting while he conducted personal conversations. Half the reason you came to Rocco's was for Ali. The pizza was incredible, but he was the real draw.

"Yeah?" I said.

"I'm really glad you're home," he said. "Everyone missed you. Don't stay away so long next time."

Taking a sharp breath in, I muttered a tight-lipped, "Thanks."

Then, I lightly shoved through the crowd, suddenly feeling claustrophobic.

Mom and Benny were consumed in deep conversation with their heads bent together when I joined them. They'd probably been to Rocco's last week, if not the other day. I knew that their life had continued on without me and I had made the choice to not come back. So why did their heads bent together cause my throat to burn?

When I sat down, the two of them stopped talking and drew me back in.

"This place hasn't changed at all," I said.

"Ali was so grumpy about opening a new one in Silverlake," Mom said, laughing. "He vented to us about it several times. It was Aya's idea. The kid's got vision."

"He was very get-off-my-lawn about it," Benny said. "He said, 'Those hipsters are going to turn Rocco's into a Ticky-Tocky joint.'"

"TickyTocky? That's Ali-speak for TikTok I'm guessing?" I couldn't help but laugh.

"Of course," Benny said. "I've never seen anyone hate phones and social media more than that man. One time, I was picking up a pizza and he kicked someone out for filming him. Of course, everyone thought it was hilarious. And his grumpy rant went viral on TikTok. He hated it. Rocco's was flooded with tourists for like a full month before he put up signs saying no phones allowed."

"Yeah, I noticed those," I said. They were all over the front of the shop, phones with a massive red prohibited symbol through them. Unfortunately, they only added to the charm. I'd already seen several people surreptitiously take pictures of the shop and the signs in the window.

"Does he still close up when he gets a call to be an extra on a show?" I asked. That was common back in the day. You would show up on a Tuesday afternoon for pizza and there would be a sign in the window that said Gone Filmin' on a wood plank. Only in LA would a restaurant close so the owner could go stand in the background of a scene in *The Nanny*.

"He doesn't do it as much as he did, but yeah, sometimes," Mom said. "We actually had a job together a couple years back on *Grey's Anatomy*. We were car crash victims and had to be in makeup for hours to get bloodied and bruised up. We had the best time."

Benny looked at Mom adoringly and I stifled the hum of my irritation. Mom was still taking work as an extra? What the hell was she going to do when she got older? Who was going to take care of her? What about saving money? Retirement? How long could she keep this up? I could understand sticking with your dreams, but at this point, Mom was just being delusional. I was reminded once again that the only person here who would be able to bail Mom out would be me. And now I didn't even have a job.

Benny and Mom discussed some house repair project and I listened, trying to keep my mouth shut. Benny was talking about a job she'd wanted to book that had fallen through. The photography business she was trying to get going wasn't exactly thriving as she'd hoped it would, but the only person that seemed to be bothered by that was me.

Yet again, I felt like the only adult in the room. What I said next seemed to fly out of my mouth.

"So, how do you pay the bills, Mom?" I asked sharply.

"Charlie," Benny whispered at me, like a warning. Mom waved her off.

"Oh, don't start, Charlotte," Mom said, chuckling. "I get a job whenever I need money. Extra work, commercial spots, odd catering jobs that come in from old friends. You know I am a master manifester."

"Or you're just very lucky," I said. "Don't you think it's time to get a real job and grow up?"

"Why should I grow up?" Mom quipped. "Where's the fun in that?"

"It's not about *having fun*."

"Then what *is* it about, Charlotte?"

Benny's head was pinging between us.

"Responsibility," I replied. "Preparing for your future. What will you do when you get older and can't book extra spots and commercials?"

"I'm going to make it, Charlotte. I know you don't see the vision. But I do."

"You're right. I don't. I've heard you saying that for my entire life and I keep wondering when your luck is going to run out. Who's going to take care of you when this doesn't work in your favor? Do you have money saved? Do you have an emergency fund? A backup plan? I feel like I'm the only responsible one in this family."

"Is that what you think?" Mom asked. "You've spent your life afraid that something bad would happen, and it never has. I'm really sorry for that, but have I ever asked you for money? You may not believe this because it doesn't look the way you expected, but I've always had things under control. Everything was taken care of. You worried for nothing, and it was hard to watch, all that anxiety in my little girl. But I think you just wanted a reason to leave for good. You were a stressed-out kid and I just wanted to give you peace, but apparently all I did was cause you more angst."

I didn't know what to say to that, but Mom wasn't looking for a response and I felt thoroughly chastised.

"Besides, I abandoned my home and my entire family to become an actress," Mom added calmly. "As you know, my parents vehemently disapproved of me moving to LA to act and told me I needed to get one of those 'real jobs' you talk about or marry some boring guy who could take care of me. I lived my whole childhood with people who thought they knew better than me, until I finally left. Do you think I can just give up that easily? I have to make that decision to leave mean something."

"Charlie," Benny chimed in. "Mom has a lot of auditions lined up. Her big break is coming."

"Sure," I said in a sarcastic tone, my cynicism a well-worn habit that I couldn't shake off.

"Charlotte, I love that you're skeptical," Mom said. "I really do. You're ever the pragmatic Virgo and I am the fiery Sagittarius, meant for big things. Every single astrological reading I've done has told me I will come into my career later in life. I know you think that's foolish to believe in, but I think it's just as foolish to be whoever everyone wants you to be and make a plan that will never be certain. I'd rather have my big—and to you, unrealistic—dreams. Personally, I don't love being overly realistic. Your grandparents were so prudent they hardly *lived* at all. They died without ever doing a single thing outside their comfort zone or their responsibilities. I promised myself I'd never do the same, even if it meant disappointing them, which I did. They cast me out for following my dreams, refused to have a relationship with their grandbabies. Those were the kinds of people I grew up with. Your skepticism doesn't ruffle me, Charlotte. But it worries me. I don't want you to be so practical that you don't have a life at all."

I sat back in my chair, deflated, trying to figure out a reply. I was the uptight Virgo, her the big-dreamer Sagittarius, Benny the peacekeeper Libra—I'd been hearing it since I was a kid, Mom using astrology to excuse herself from being a responsible person. Like you could just tell your electric company you're a Sagittarius who was meant for stardom and couldn't pay your bill. Sure, that would work *perfectly*.

But before I could retort, in cinematically perfect timing, Ali dropped our pizza on the table right at the end of Mom's audition-worthy soliloquy. She really was a very good actress.

"Enjoy!" Ali called out as he ran back to the counter.

Mom just looked at me, eyes bright, and said, "Let's dig in, girls."

And that was that. Conversation over.

9

There was only one way to describe the vibe of dinner: tense. I stayed quiet while Mom and Benny discussed various details of their life together, like who needed to go to Whole Foods and if they should have a party for Halloween. They didn't ask me whether I'd be here for it. It was clear they assumed I'd be leaving soon, which I was definitely now planning on.

After devouring our pizza and saying a quick goodbye to Ali, Benny took the front seat and I sat in the back behind her. Mom turned up the volume on her playlist and didn't sing.

"Should we get ice cream?" I asked, the first thing I'd said in maybe twenty minutes. We'd just passed by McConnell's.

"I'm full," Benny said back, tonelessly.

"Me, too," Mom said.

Okay.

The rest of the drive up the canyon was silent, save for the music. The dark got even darker as Mom drove up through the winding road. The only thing that signaled we'd made it to the house was the twinkling string lights. When she parked at the end of the gravel drive, she shut off the car and walked off quickly without saying anything. Benny did the same and I stayed behind at the driveway, trying to figure out when I should go back to San Francisco—tonight, or tomorrow morning.

When I finally made it to the landing with the Adirondack chairs, Mom was sitting on one next to a guy that couldn't have been older than twenty-five and who looked like he'd stepped off the pages of a magazine spread. He had light brown skin and curly hair and wore an oversized pastel pink hoodie. His head was dipped with Mom's, deep in conversation.

Passing by them both, I went inside the house and through to the kitchen where I could hear Benny loudly opening and closing cabinet doors.

"Who's that guy out there?" I asked. Her back was to me and she was at the sink, filling the teakettle.

She didn't turn around when she said, "That's Jasper."

It didn't surprise me that people still did that—show up here unannounced. It had been happening since I was a kid.

"Who is he?" I asked.

"He's an actor," Benny said. "He comes over to ask Mom for advice. *Some* people think she's amazing. *Some* people would kill for a mom like her."

"Okay," I said, picking up on the subtext.

Benny put the teakettle on the stove and ignited the gas. When it was set, she finally whipped around toward me and glared. "What was that, by the way? At pizza?"

"What?" I knew exactly what.

"You haven't been home in years and the very first thing you do is insult Mom. I mean, really, Charlie, just because you're miserable, doesn't mean everyone else should be, too."

The words hit me like a slap and I doubled back.

"What's going on with you?" she continued, her voice rising with each proclamation. "What *has* been going on with you? Are you okay? Is this about Noah? I still think you should tell Mom what happened. She has no idea. And you asking me to keep this big secret from her hasn't been easy, but I've given you as much space as possible. But that wasn't just a bad breakup,

Charlie. You need to talk about it. For years, you've been making excuses, saying you can't come here because of work. Is that really it? You've been busy? Or is there more to it? I hoped that all the work you were doing made you happy. But you're not happy, are you? And apparently you don't think anyone else should be, either. We had a *good* childhood, Charlie. Mom was loving and encouraging to us. Why did you even come here if all you're going to do is criticize?"

I stood there, frozen, wordless. My mind was a blaring siren and I couldn't figure out if it was telling me to leave or if Benny's words had hit the bull's-eye.

"You know what?" Benny finally said when I had no reply. She turned back around to turn off the stove. "Never mind. I can't even look at you right now, Charlie."

Benny had never once been mad at me before.

She walked out of the kitchen and I heard her footsteps on the old stairs. My breathing was labored and that siren was even more pronounced now. Gripping the kitchen island tightly, I tried to stop a fresh scene from playing out, but it was too late.

"I'm not like other girls," Charlie said, and then added quickly, "And I don't mean that in a derogatory way against other girls. I mean it only in a derogatory way against myself. I am prickly, guarded, and biting. I get irritated very easily. I never get over anything. I want to be right too much. I'm not easygoing or upbeat. I'm the killjoy of my family, like the black cat that crosses your path and you groan because it's supposed to be bad luck. My sister . . ." She trailed off, and finally met eyes with him, thinking he'd be cringing, but he had his hands cradling his face, watching her, rapt.

"Your sister, what?" Noah asked, like she was about to reveal the end of a mystery novel, all eagerness and interest.

"She's one of those girls. She's a Golden Retriever or like a Pomeranian.

And I love her. I do. But it's like she took all the fairy tale for both of us."

"But surely it's not just about believing in fairy tales, right? That's not a flaw. One might venture that it's a good thing . . ."

"I'm saying this all wrong."

"No you're not."

"I am. That's what I do."

"You're way too hard on yourself."

Her laugh was sharp, and too loud for the restaurant. She cleared her throat. "Overstatement of the century." She thought her words would come out light and self-deprecating, but instead they tasted bitter on her tongue. "Okay, here's a stupid example. My mom and my sister could be out for hours shopping for clothes, hair stuff, makeup and then come home and obsess over new outfits."

"They wouldn't invite you?"

"Oh, they would, but I'd be miserable, so I'd tell them no."

"What do you like to do instead?"

She bit her lip. "Read books. Study. Listen to music on long walks." She wondered if she should say the next thing out loud, even though it wasn't that revealing. But to her, it was. "I . . . well . . . I like to bake."

"Like cakes?"

"No, like bread. When they'd finally leave, I'd have the whole kitchen to myself, listening to music, waiting for the bread to proof, getting the crust just right. I liked being alone."

"Your face just brightened when you talked about baking bread."

She touched her cheeks. "Did it?"

"It sounds like you felt like your true self was rejected by your family."

"They don't mean to!"

"You love them."

"I really do." She paused, and he gave her space to say more, like he was acutely attuned to her emotional landscape already. "I just didn't feel seen, I guess. It was lonely."

"I mean, what you haven't considered is that maybe all the things *you think aren't like other people or your sister and therefore aren't good enough are the things that make you unique and interesting?"*

"I don't dislike myself. Actually, I think I'm pretty great. It's everyone else . . ."

"I know."

"I just feel . . ."

"Like an outsider? Like the black sheep of your family? Like the one that doesn't fit?"

Her eyes met his with recognition. It made her rib cage expand to ten times its normal size, like someone was forcefully pumping air into her lungs.

"It's not like I can relate or anything," he said, laughing sharply.

"Yeah . . ." She shook her head. "What am I doing?" It was a whisper to herself. "I never talk like this. I don't like to feel sorry for myself."

"You don't?" he asked, with a charming sideways smile. "Oh, I do. My pity parties are incredible!"

She laughed.

"It's fascinating," she said. "I grew up with the cheeriest mom you could ever find and I'm frequently in a bad mood. You grew up with withdrawn and harsh parents and seem to always be in a good mood."

He nodded.

"Maybe we're all just doomed to want to be the opposite of our parents."

"Not my sister. She's my mom's best friend."

"Older or younger?"

"Younger, by about five years actually."

"Aha," he said, like eureka. "She got the reformed mom."

She stopped, gripped by fear for a moment.

"What is it?" he asked. It was an intimate question for what could only be described as a first date. He was reading her feelings, which she painstakingly tried to hide.

"It's nothing," she replied, trying to mitigate the intimacy. She played with the napkin on the table, wondering why it was taking ages to get their drink order.

"It's something," he said as he stilled her hand with his. She hadn't even noticed he'd reached for her, and his hand was so warm and soft and achingly pleasant over hers. She was awfully aware that it had been a long time since she'd been touched so gently like this. "You can tell me. I will protect your secrets as if they're my own."

She took a long breath in. "I was a pretty anxious kid and when Benny came along, Mom seemed much happier to have an easygoing child. Or maybe that's my perception of things. I guess I carry that with me. That I'm too much for everyone. Not easy enough. Not lovable enough?"

His eyes softened. "Thank you for telling me that." He paused. "I seem to like you exactly as you are. I think you're just enough, if that helps."

Her heart rate pattered senselessly. She needed to change the subject.

"Do you have secrets?" She threw her other arm up in an open-wide gesture. "By all means . . . feel free to make yourself vulnerable."

"Do you want that?"

She wasn't expecting her wry sarcasm to be met with such earnestness. He was arresting in that way, not falling into her little tricks of avoidance. His hand was still in hers, torturously small strokes of his thumb on hers. The feeling went straight to her core, where something switched on like a pilot light.

"Want what?" she asked, a little breathlessly.

"Me, to be vulnerable with you?" His voice was so low that his words sent a flush of heat all the way down her body.

"I guess?" she rasped out. The stroke of his thumb slowed down, and he added a purposeful amount of pressure, almost as though he were imagining the skin of her hand was something else entirely.

"I'll be vulnerable with you, if you'll be the same with me." She could hardly look at him and when she finally did, he was leaning forward across the table, brown eyes darkened.

"We just met each other," she said, and pulled her hand from his and set it on her lap.

"It doesn't feel like that to me. Does it feel like that to you?"

He was asking questions he already knew the answer to.

"I don't do this," Charlie insisted.

"Do what?"

"Open up. Fall for people." She'd only had one big crush before, but it had been unrequited and painful. Alex, in high school, and that one had hurt. That was before she knew how to protect herself.

"You're falling for me?" Noah asked, his words brittle and hopeful.

She stammered, and wanted to lie, but she couldn't. "There's a connection. I'll give you that."

"A connection? That's what you call this? I feel like I've been hit by lightning."

Charlie couldn't help but melt. "You say that to all the girls," she quipped.

"No, I really don't," he said, so serious she couldn't do anything but believe him.

With a grunt, I pushed myself off the kitchen island quickly and found the downstairs bathroom. I doused my face in cold water, trying to escape the story, the movie, the scenes that I pretended didn't exist. When I lifted my eyes to the mirror and dried my face with a hand towel, I noticed the flurry of Post-it notes stuck onto the glass.

You are magic.

Have faith.

You are lucky.

Believe.

Everything always works out in your favor.

Prepare for the best-case scenario.

I almost screamed at their proclamations, but instead I ripped them down one by one, bundled them into a ball, and threw them in the trash. Immediately, though, I felt bad about it, and I pulled them out and tried to smooth them, but they wouldn't re-stick.

There was no way I would sleep tonight—it wasn't even worth trying and the idea of being in my head for hours only made me panicked. Tomorrow, I told myself, I would go home. It was too late in the evening to leave now, even as I itched to escape.

Instead, I ventured back into the kitchen, turned the teakettle on, and pulled down a mug. When I went in search for the teas—the kitchen had been rearranged at some point over the years—I found a pantry full of baking supplies. My hands reached for the bread flour automatically. Without thinking, I placed kosher salt, flour, yeast, and a large glass bowl on the counter next to the hunter green electric mixer. Making the dough was as natural to me as breathing, even though it had been a long time since I'd done it.

The evening passed with me in a trancelike state. By the time the dough had been rested, proofed, scored, and placed into the oven, the sun was coming up through the trees and I could see just the smallest hint of a burnt orange sunrise through the windows.

I cleaned up the kitchen and did the dishes and when I was finished, the timer pinged and I pulled the perfect country loaf out of the Dutch oven, tapping the crust to make sure it was crunchy and stiff.

When I looked up, I saw Mom and Benny in the doorway in their pajamas, their hair messy and eyes still half-closed with sleep. They were both up earlier than expected. My heart yearned, like I was twelve years old again and waiting for them to wake up so we could go on our next adventure. There were so many good times. It was terrifying how easy it was to forget them, when all you've done is hold on to your resentments.

I decided I'd try an olive branch, in the form of carbs.

"I made bread," I whispered. It was still too early to speak normally, like nothing and nobody had woken up yet, like time was outside of us. "And whipped up some honey butter. Does anybody want some?"

Mom and Benny exchanged a look, like a silent conversation.

"I could make French toast," Benny said.

"And I'll French press some coffee," Mom added.

"How very French of us," I said, tentatively, like me being in on the joke was a truce for now.

"Oui," Mom said, with a flourish. *"Très bien!"* Her accent was flawless. Ever the actress.

"Charlie, can you get the eggs out?" Benny asked. Mom set to work on the coffee, and I fetched the eggs, and for that morning at least, Triple Quinn was at peace.

10

Honestly, even *I* realize how sad this next statement is going to sound but . . . I had completely forgotten that food could be . . . good? Josh used to say I had no taste for life, and at the beginning of our relationship, it was a compliment. We met as workaholics and he would often lament people who would get distracted by silly things like vacations and weekends. He didn't believe in having fun, was as laser-focused as I was. He never took his eye off the ball.

Until, of course, the pandemic hit. Now I can see what the red flags were. *Can't we order in tonight? Can't we watch a funny movie tonight? Can't we take some time off, go on a road trip? Do you think working this much is good for us?* I dodged his questions, but now they were all I kept hearing. At the time, I didn't have any answers for him, so I did what I always did—worked more. Threw myself into the job. Gunned after a promotion like my life depended on it.

But now I couldn't remember the last time I ate anything as good as honey butter on French toast made with homemade bread. All I'd been consuming for years was grilled chicken breast and plain brown rice and steamed vegetables and bland oatmeal and tasteless salads. Like any taste of pleasure, however small, might make me hunger for life again.

All the carbs and sugar hit me at once and I abruptly remembered I hadn't slept all night. It was unheard of for me to ever go back to bed while it was still morning, but I was exhausted, and I could leave LA that afternoon, get a nap in first. It was better for all of us if I just left, took the black cat of my personality and thrust it into the shadows yet again.

"I think I'm going to get in bed," I said to Mom and Benny, yawning. "I didn't sleep last night." Mom was reading a book, as she typically did in the mornings, even when I was young. She nodded. Benny was on her phone scrolling. She'd taken a gorgeous picture of our breakfast spread with the morning light streaming in and when she had shown it to me, I started to see the beauty through her eyes. She was very talented.

Benny put her phone down as I was standing up and said, "Take a walk with me first, will you? Then sleep."

"I'm pretty tired . . ."

"Please?"

"Okay," I said. "Fine. Let me get my sneakers."

We met at the door. It was already a cloudless and dry day, the heat of the sun scorching its way across the city, so I stayed in my short-sleeved shirt and sweats and we headed out.

There was a well-worn trail near the house that I knew we'd take. Through the thicket of trees and greenery, after twenty minutes, we'd pop out to a wide view of Los Angeles. We used to walk this almost every day. One thing I never stopped doing that Mom encouraged was walking. It was one of the few pieces of our life I didn't leave behind, even if my walk was on a treadmill, which Mom would think was ludicrous. She'd say, "Why walk on a treadmill when you could be outside, in nature?"

Benny picked up a long stick and whacked at invisible branches in our path. It wasn't overgrown, but it was still rattlesnake season. We didn't take our chances.

Trailing behind Benny, I kicked up dirt and dust. She slowed so I could catch up to her and then put her arm around me and squeezed.

"I'm sorry I called you miserable." She sighed. "That's a

shitty thing to say to someone who just got broken up with and lost her job and had violent food poisoning—on her *birthday*."

"Do you really think I'm miserable?" I asked, my voice so quiet I could hardly hear myself.

She paused, bit her lip.

"Not miserable. That was harsh. But not exactly . . . happy."

"What's with everyone?" I asked, suddenly irritated. "When did it all become about being happy?"

"For me, always," Benny said, laughing, throwing her hands up. "But for the rest of the world, I think the pandemic opened a lot of eyes. People were just on autopilot, working and working, not experiencing any enjoyment. Like, why do anything if you don't enjoy your life at least sometimes?"

God, she really sounded like Mom.

"That's what Josh blamed the breakup on," I said, staring down at my shoes, which were now covered in brown dust. "The pandemic."

"Tell me what he said."

I didn't want to tell her, but I did. It wasn't hard to remember—Josh's words were replaying in my head already. They still stung.

When I finished, Benny said, "Huh," and I waited for more from her as we walked to the end of the trail. When we made it to the clearing, the smog wasn't too bad and we could see all the way through to the mountains, past the sprawl of the city.

Benny turned to me and said, "That's maybe the kindest breakup ever."

"Kind? Benny, whose side are you on?"

"I have never been on anyone's side other than yours, Char, but I want you to be happy. It sounds like Josh wanted the same thing for you and for himself. I mean, hey, I'm the first one to think men are the *worst*, but Josh was a good one. And Charlie, you don't see yourself like I do. I have to be honest. You are so . . . clenched. You smile, sure, but it never reaches your eyes.

You seem . . . afraid of life. I'm always here for you. But, as your sister who loves you more than life itself, it's . . ." She winced, like she didn't want to continue, and her eyes veered to the skyline. "Honestly, it's hard to see you like this."

"Maybe it's just *easy* for you to be happy."

"It's really not, Charlie. I work at it."

I guffawed. "You do not."

"I do. I get low, too. You're not around me all the time anymore. You don't have all the information. But here's how I see it. Okay, I lost this photography job to someone else, right? I *really* wanted it. Big centerfold spread for a cool online magazine. Would have raised my profile. I was disappointed. But I also came to the conclusion that it must not have been meant for me. Something better is coming. It's all going to work out. But if you had lost that job, you would have thought the world was against you and you were doomed. Who's right? How do you know? You're only seeing things through your chosen worldview and filter.

"Now, think of this. Maybe you thought you needed to force that job and fight for it. Maybe you would have been persistent. Maybe eventually you would have gotten it through sheer tenacity. But then the job is horrible. And nothing goes right. And because you were so busy fighting for something that should have never been yours, you don't have time to take the call for the job that would have been beautiful and amazing and exciting. So, I choose to believe it's all working out for me, and to be okay with letting things go."

I rolled my eyes. "You sound like Mom."

Benny bumped me hard on the shoulder. "What's so wrong with being like Mom? Mom is going toward what she loves. You're afraid of becoming her, but all that means is that you aren't her. Then, who are you? What are you going *toward*, Charlie? What do you love?"

I didn't really know what to say to that.

But Benny didn't want an answer. She already knew I didn't have one.

She just sighed again and kept talking. "This skepticism and negativity and cynicism and pessimism you're holding on to sucks, Charlie. I'm sorry, but it does. It's like you don't even want to *try* to enjoy life. You need to let loose. You don't have a job right now. You have some free time to do whatever you want. And here you are, sulking around and acting like the world is against you."

There was absolutely no dressing down like the one a little sister could give.

"Most people *want* to be happy, Charlie. You know that? I actually don't even think you want that for yourself and I can't for the life of me understand why. I know what happened with Noah was hard on you, but does that mean you never live your life again?"

"Happiness is just unrealistic, okay?" I blurted out. "It's not safe. You make stupid decisions. I *understand* responsibility. I understand control and plans. I understand working hard." I stalked off quickly and heard Benny clambering after me.

"Hey," she said, when she finally reached me. She put her hand on my shoulder and I turned around to face her. "You know what, Charlie? Honestly, you're perfect. I love you no matter what. I don't want to change you. You are so talented, and I love your work ethic and frankly, I could probably use some of it. I could stand to be more responsible, to actually stick with a plan. But I think you can be all of this, and you can, I don't know . . . *lighten up* a little."

"I don't know *how*, okay, Benny?" Words were coming out of my mouth before I had a chance to stop them.

Benny softened and hooked her arm into the crook of mine as we began our way out of the trail and back to the road.

After a few moments of silence, she said, "I have an idea. You're going to hate it."

"Great introduction," I said, laughing. "Really selling it, Ben."

"I'm just preparing you."

"Okay, I'm prepared."

"So, when was the last time you did nothing?"

"Nothing?" I shivered at the thought. "Never," I added. "Yeah, never."

"You have some money saved, right? Please don't tell me you have been working since you were like a toddler and you don't have money saved."

I laughed. "I have money saved, Benny. It's me. Come on. Of course I do."

"Okay, good. I was about to send you to Petra's brother, the big-time financial advisor who lives in Chicago. He's famous around here. All the artists who are terrible with managing their finances go to Apollo."

"I still cannot believe his name is Apollo."

"Have you seen him lately? Literal Greek god. He really grew into the name."

"That family and their genes."

Petra, former model, Mom's best friend, and the closest neighbor to Quinn Canyon. Petra was effervescent and lovely and had practically raised us alongside Mom.

"How is Petra?" I asked.

"She's good. She'll come over soon. Don't change the subject." She clapped her hands together. "Okay, my idea."

"You're the one drooling over Apollo," I retorted. "Now, back to your terrible idea I'm going to hate."

"Hey, it's a *great* idea! The *idea* is not the problem."

"Let me guess. The problem is me?"

"Ding, ding," Benny chimed.

"Okay. Go. Tell me your idea."

She took a long and deep inhale and started speaking on the exhale.

"You need a month of *yes*," she said, like I was supposed to understand what that meant.

"What the heck is a month of yes, Benadette?"

"Nothing," she said. "I'm making it up. I figure you've had a lot of years of saying no. No to coming to LA. No to vacations. No to time off. No. No. No. So, what do you do? You do the opposite for a month. A month of yes."

"I really want to say no right now, but I feel like it's playing right into your hand."

She double-tapped her nose like, *exactly*.

"I'm thinking out loud," she said, gathering steam and excitement. "I think you should stay here for a month, obviously. Do nothing responsible. Wake up every single day and just go where it sounds delightful and fun and surprising. The more surprising the better, because it's outside your norm. No overthinking. Do and say the opposite of what you'd normally do and say. Follow your urges. End up somewhere interesting. Just go where the wind takes you. No plans. No projects. Bake your bread. Discover new parts of the city. Go to great restaurants. Spend some of that damn money you worked so hard for." She caught her breath and added, "And, you have to say yes to anything I request. If I want to take you shopping or for a makeover or do a photo shoot with you or make you go to the Getty Villa to look at art in the middle of a Tuesday afternoon, you *must* say yes. To any request."

"Anything?!"

"Anything."

"You need to really commit, too," Benny added, voice dropping to indicate her seriousness. "Throw yourself into it. One month. If you hate it, you can go back to your life as a drill sergeant workaholic and never listen to another one of my wild ideas again."

Now, *that* intrigued me. Could this get her off my back, once and for all? Could this prove to her that living in this way—by whimsy and chance and luck—was a recipe for disaster?

"And if I don't say yes to everything you request?"

"Honestly, Charlie, this isn't some unrealistic movie where I give you a high-stakes ultimatum. This is real life. Do it or not. I'm just saying it might actually be good for you. I'm not going to *force* you."

I shot her a grin. "You're not even going to make a bet with me?" I asked. We were standing by our cars, waiting to go up the stairs to Quinn Canyon.

"A bet?" Benny asked wryly. "Okay, fine." She thought for a moment and then her eyes brightened. "If you don't stay through the month and do what I say, you have to pay me ten thousand dollars."

I choked. "Ten thousand dollars? For what?"

She shrugged. "The drama."

"Benny Ruby Quinn, my darling little sister, why in the world would I agree to this?"

"Because, Charlie Ruby Quinn, my impossible older sister, I think somewhere real deep down—and I mean, *reallllll* deep down—you want to be happy."

11

My stomach roiled and churned, but I didn't say no. That shocked me the most. I didn't immediately tell her no.

"Ten grand," I finally said. "Really?"

"Hey, you're the one that wanted to make a bet."

"I was *joking*."

Benny shook her head. "You want some real stakes to liven this up, then? Here's the truth that only a sister will tell you, Charlie. If you keep going like this, you're going to wake up one day twenty-five years from now and you're going to regret it. Do you need higher stakes than that? Do you want to waste your life being afraid and cynical? I'm not even fully convinced you loved your job. I just think you never stopped working long enough to evaluate if you were happy or not."

"I can't end up like Mom," I whispered.

"We'd all be lucky to end up like Mom," Benny said, hand on her hip. "She is living her life on her own terms. She is more alive than most thirty-year-olds in this city. I think ending up like Mom would be a gift."

"Hmmm," was all I said.

"Okay," Benny countered, and clapped her hands together. "I read about this woman Bronnie Ware who worked as a palliative nurse caring for the dying. She said people had five main regrets on their deathbed. You want to know what they are, Charlie?"

"Not really."

"It's a good thing our bet hasn't started, because you'd already owe me ten grand. This is a request. You have to listen to me."

I smiled despite myself and rolled my eyes. "Fine. Tell me."

"I have them memorized," she stated and started listing the regrets off on her fingers. "One, I wish I'd had the courage to live a life true to myself, not the life others expected of me. Two, I wish I hadn't worked so hard." At that one, she pointed her finger at me so hard it hit my breastbone. "Three, I wish I'd had the courage to express my feelings. Four, I wish I had stayed in touch with my friends. And five, I wish I had let myself be happier. You're failing four out of five. And, not to be harsh, but if you had any friends to stay in touch *with*, you'd be five for five, babe."

"Jeez," I breathed out. "You can be honest, Benny, but you don't have to be cruel."

"I am *never* this honest. I am very uncomfortable right now. You know I hate confrontation. But I think you need an intervention. Nothing changes if nothing changes."

I had never met a single soul in the world that could deny Benny Quinn, because even her worst ideas sounded pretty good when she was passionate like this.

Also, I trusted her with my life. She had never wanted anything but the best for me. Over the years, she'd asked so little of me. Even though I knew this wouldn't work or change anything, I wanted to say yes just so this would finally prove to Benny and Mom that they'd be better off if they were more realistic and practical.

"Fine," I said to Benny.

Benny jumped back, eyes wide. "You're saying yes?"

"I'm saying yes. I think it's crazy and it's definitely not going to work, but I'll commit. I'll give it my best try."

"And the bet? You want to risk the 10-K or you'll take your chances dying with all five regrets?"

"Gosh, when did you become so morbid?"

"I think the only way to really live is to embrace the fact that one day you die," she opined.

I laughed. "Let's make it interesting, then. We'll do both. I'll risk dying with regrets and the ten grand. You can hold both over me to get me to comply."

"This is too much power, Charlie," Benny said, holding her hands in front of her body like she was about to turn into a superhero villain. "I'm going to be drunk with it."

"You already are," I said, putting my arm around her as we finally started the ascent to the house. "But I have one request of my own before I agree."

"What's that?" Benny asked skeptically, like this one request was about to foil everything.

"No more talking about Noah."

Her head whipped toward me, and I saw her narrowing her eyes in my peripheral vision.

"Fine," she finally agreed. "But I want it on the record that I think *not* talking about Noah is a mistake and you *should*—nay, probably *need* to—talk about it, but I'll relent for the sake of the month of yes."

"Okay, then I'm in."

She stuck her hand out. "Shake on it."

I grabbed her hand and shook. "There."

She clutched my hand in hers. "One whole month. You have to listen to me. You have to do something delightful every day. You have to say yes, inhabit the energy of possibility. If you don't, you give me ten grand and die with all your regrets and never have to listen to me again."

I nodded and shook her hand hard with my whole arm. She smiled like a kid.

"This is the weirdest thing I've ever agreed to," I said.

"It's going to be great."

"For you maybe."

"I already have my first request," she said while we were right outside the door to the house.

"I just got nervous," I revealed, and it was true. My stomach flipped.

"I'm doing this for your own good," she said. "It's not like I'm going to make you eat cockroaches or something."

"I may prefer that to some of the things you're going to request."

Benny narrowed her eyes and said, "You have to be nice to Mom and give her a chance and actually spend time with her."

"*Ugh*. Can I eat the cockroaches instead?"

"Charlie," Benny replied like a warning.

"Fine," I said. *"Fine."*

I had packed for three days in LA and was planning on leaving in mere hours. Now I was going to be here all month. Benny Quinn was a witch, because what the hell had she just gotten me to agree to?

12

When we entered the house, Mom was descending the staircase looking so beautiful my breath caught in my throat. She was in wide-legged pants the color of silky cream and a coral bodysuit that set off her features perfectly. She lit up a room the way she lit up a screen.

I remembered running lines with her every week, transfixed by the way she could embody any character at will. I used to believe she'd become a star; it just felt inevitable. It was as much my dream as it was hers. And, so, every "no" broke my heart, too. Maybe I was too young to learn that even if you believed in yourself, you still might not make it. That sometimes no matter how much you want something, it could still be elusive.

"You will not believe what Charlie just agreed to, Mom," Benny said, as all three of us ambled into the living room. Benny and I fell into the chairs facing the couch where Mom sat in the middle, legs crossed, arms sprawled across the back, like she was a queen on her throne. This was the Triple Quinn configuration.

"Tell me," Mom said, smiling. "I just have to leave to meet my agents in Beverly Hills in thirty minutes."

"Well, first, some context," Benny said. "Charlie is now single. Josh broke up with her on her birthday of all days. And she lost her job on her birthday, too. Isn't that messed up?"

"What?" Mom said, sitting up straight and looking directly at me. "Why didn't you say, Charlie? I'm so sorry about Josh. His loss. And I know how much you loved your job and how hard you work. What happened? You gave everything to that damn company. How are you doing?"

"I'm fine," I said quickly. "I'll find another job." Even to my own ears, I didn't sound that convincing. My voice was too high-pitched and fast, like I needed the reassurance more than Mom did.

"Not many people would be fine after all of that," she said, sounding skeptical of me. "And it's okay if you're not."

"I'm fine," I said again. Mom knowing the predictable life I'd built had just fallen apart in one fell swoop was already too much. Me being upset about it would only give her the satisfaction I never wanted her to have.

"Okay," she replied. "Why didn't you tell me all of this when you got here?"

"I didn't want to hear how everything works out in the end in my favor." I tried to keep the mocking to a minimum, but the way Benny was staring daggers into me, I could tell I had failed.

Mom didn't notice my tone. She simply asked, "And what's so wrong with having faith that it's all going to work out? Isn't that a *good* thing?"

"Because not everything works out, Mom," I retorted. "Not everything happens for a reason. Terrible things happen every single day and we have no way to stop them. *That's* reality."

Mom looked at me a little too long, like she was waiting me out, and then she turned to Benny and said, "Well, what did our Charlie agree to, then?"

"Oh," Benny said, slapping her hand on her knee. "Right. Yes. So, first, she's agreed to stay here all month. Yay! Second, I've demanded she take time off, do nothing, go find something delightful or surprising every day, to follow her whims, AND she has to do *anything* I request. All month. It's her month of yes."

Mom let out a laugh and then turned her attention back to me. "You agreed to this? *You?* Are we in the multiverse? Did we change timelines? When's the last time you took a month off? Never?" She wasn't being mean-spirited; she was genuinely shocked.

"It's only for a month," I quipped. "I think I can survive one month without working."

"You can?" Mom asked, smiling. "Well, I had no idea."

"I'm going to make her say yes to life," Benny said, crossing her arms. "If it's the last thing I do."

Already, my annoyance was rising like a pot of water set to boil.

"Well, I think it's a lovely idea and I am thrilled you're going to be here for a month, Charlie. If I had it my way, you'd stay forever. Or, at the very least, you'd come home way more often. It's so much brighter when you're here."

That surprised me. It was?

"Well, I'm off," Mom said, standing up. "I'll see you girls tonight. Don't wait up. I'm having dinner out."

And then she was gone, and Benny and me were left in the living room.

"Go take a nap," Benny said. "But when you're up, let the games begin. I have a whole plan for today."

"Oh, God, what is it?" A cold sweat started to break out on my neck.

"Answer me this, what color would you *never* dye your hair? And what hairstyle would you *never* get?"

"Blond," I said. "Bangs." Two things that required maintenance and were that specific type of "girlie" I never felt I could pull off. Frivolous. That's what it was. Blond with bangs was frivolous.

"Great," Benny said, typing something into her phone, then sliding it into her back pocket. "I made an appointment with my stylist, Mari. You'll be going blonde and getting bangs."

I shook my head and laughed. "Great," I said, mock-sweet. I mean hey, if I agreed to this, I guess I was going all in. That would be the only way to prove them both wrong. They thought they knew better than me? Then yeah, *game on*.

"After, we're going to get you new clothes, which you'll wear to this tapas restaurant tucked away in Malibu that I've heard great things about. You're paying."

I laughed again. "Alright, then," I said. "You're the boss."

"Oh, I like that."

"I thought you would."

"Go sleep. You have two hours before our appointment."

"Pretty efficient for someone who isn't very organized."

"I learned from the best," she said, and she patted me on the top of my head before I stood and headed for the stairs.

I hadn't even been to my old room yet. When I opened the door, I thought for sure it would have been changed, but it looked exactly the same. It was like stepping into an old identity. There was my white linen duvet, freshly washed. There was my little bunny stuffed animal I could never seem to part with. There were my school awards and even my diploma from Stanford, framed and set above my little desk where I'd done countless hours of homework. There were pictures of me, Benny, and Mom with people who were now famous, who passed through Quinn Canyon on their way to superstardom.

There were a handful of pictures with old high school friends, people I'd since lost touch with. Benny had always been my best friend, but I used to have other people, in high school and college. I used to have . . . a life. There were posters for movies and bands I loved. When had I stopped watching movies? Why didn't I even listen to music? That was all I ever wanted to do when I was younger. Mom, Benny, and I would have marathon movie days. The house used to be filled with music. It was like everything I once loved had dried up.

Flinging myself on the bed, I stared up at the ceiling. There was no possible way to be confronted with the things I used to love without another scene playing through my mind, and I had nothing but time to let it roll.

13

"This was the best first date I've ever had," Noah said, as they left the funky Thai restaurant and strolled down the street. She lived close by, and he had parked at her apartment before they walked over.

He took her hand in his and she didn't pull it away. It sent a feeling of pure warmth and light through her—his long fingers entwined with hers. She was only two months away from graduating and going out into the world. The last thing she needed was a distraction.

But Noah was irresistible to her. She squeezed his hand, and bravely leaned into him. Instinctually, as if they'd done this a hundred times, he put his arm around her shoulder and tugged her in.

It was later than she thought it was, because the street was mostly empty. Noah removed his arm and faced her. He tucked a strand of wavy brunette hair behind her ear and cupped her face. She closed her eyes and softly moaned at the intimacy.

"Have you ever been in love, Charlotte?"

"No," she said. He traced circles on her collarbone while goose bumps popped up on her arms. "Fundamentally unlovable, remember?" There had only ever been one other person that she'd responded to this strongly—Alex. But she had been a rash and unpredictable teenager then, and nothing had ever happened. It hadn't been love, she was almost sure of that.

"I'm not convinced of this unlovable thing," Noah insisted.

"Have you?"

"Loved you? No, not yet."

Her stomach jumped at the yet. She wanted him but she didn't want to want him. She felt herself drawn to him recklessly, like she could forget herself too easily if she wasn't careful.

"Have you ever been in love, with someone, I meant."

"No," he revealed. "Crushes. Lust. But nothing real. Nothing like—no, nothing real."

He didn't need to say "nothing like this" because it hung between them.

"This is happening very fast," *she said to him. His hand was now on the back of her neck, under her hair, tentative and heated. She wanted him to pull her closer. He couldn't stop looking at her mouth.*

"Too fast?" *he murmured, leaning in.*

"Yes. No. I don't know."

"I really need to kiss you right now," *he whispered.* "Can I?"

Her breath caught in her throat and for once, she wasn't thinking. Or guarding. Or keeping herself at a distance from everything and everyone. She simply nodded, because she needed the same thing.

He took his time with her. Stroked his hand across her cheek, trailed a fingertip down her neck, caught her eyes in his and she matched the intensity.

He placed both of his hands on her face and when he kissed her, it was so delicate and urgent that she melted into him. She had kissed people before, but not like this. This was the type of kiss where the world stopped turning, when you realized that nothing you've ever experienced in your life ever felt as good as this man's lips on yours. She groaned into his mouth and he kissed across her cheek and whispered, "Those little sounds of yours are going to kill me."

She giggled—giggled!—and felt like she had become an entirely different version of herself in the space of one dinner. This was why people wrote love songs. This was why people set their life on fire for love. This was passion. This was the type of passion her mom had been telling her about her entire life. She'd never felt it before. Never understood it. Until now.

She put her arms around Noah's neck and kissed him even more intensely, swept her tongue into his mouth, and this time he was the one making those little sounds. She wanted him. She wanted him more than she'd ever wanted anything before.

"Careful," he said, breathless, but staying close. She could feel him talking on her lips. "I may have to prove you wrong."

"About what?" she asked, raspy, low.

"You, being unlovable."

She heard more than felt her gasp.

"Who are you?" she asked, because she suddenly couldn't understand how she got here. He was a stranger merely days before, but now she couldn't imagine her life without him. Didn't want to imagine it.

"Who are you?" he asked back. "This is so weird. I feel like I'm one kiss away from being completely in love with you. And I don't know you. But I feel like I've known you my whole life." He was watching her now, their faces so close together, and she wanted to tell him she didn't feel the same, but she couldn't. She couldn't lie.

"I don't understand this," she said. "Because that's how I feel, too. And I'm not even a romantic person."

He smiled wryly. "I'm beginning to think you don't know yourself that well. Unlovable? No. Romantic? Yes."

"I am not this person who gets swept away."

"Or maybe you just haven't let yourself."

"What about your flaws, then?" she asked, hands on her hips now. The moment had cooled, but a heat still reverberated between them. He started walking, and grabbed her hand again.

"I am a hopeless romantic stuck in a nightmare," he said.

"Dramatic."

"No, really," he replied. "I want the adventure. I want a surprising and unpredictable life. But, the moment I graduate, my dad wants me back home so he can train me to take over the family business. He does the kind of soulless investment banking that I am vehemently opposed to. He says he'll cut me out of both the family and my trust fund if I don't

comply. But all I want to do is to go travel. See the world. Do it on the cheap. Stay in hostels, go by bus or train, eat from food stalls, whatever."

She had no idea what came over her, or why she didn't stop herself, but she said, "Can I come?" She had never wanted to do anything but get a corporate or start-up job out of school, but suddenly the idea of traveling around the world with just a backpack and Noah sounded like the greatest idea ever. It was reckless. And ridiculous. And exactly the kind of thing Jackie Quinn would encourage. It made her feel close to her mom, like she was actually her daughter, after all. Like she had some of her mom's courage within her. Like she wasn't the black sheep she'd always worried she was.

Sliding off the armor of control and responsibility was surprisingly easy.

"You want to?" he asked. "I'll go if you go."

"Will your parents allow it?"

"I doubt it," he said.

She couldn't imagine being in the position he was in. She had no inheritance, nothing to really lose. It would seem callous to tell him not to care about his father's approval or about money that would rightfully be his, even if she felt he didn't need it and could make his own way if he wanted to. He certainly had the determination needed to make it. But it wasn't her place to dictate how he interacted with his family. She knew firsthand that family dynamics were much more complicated than black-and-white, right or wrong. She knew you could love people who hurt you, too.

"Where would we go first?" she asked instead.

"Italy," he answered, quickly, like he knew the itinerary already. "No, Japan! Wait, maybe Portugal. Or, God, what about Brazil? Australia? New Zealand?" He was getting more animated and she was smiling up at him, adoringly. "How do you choose, Charlie? There's so much to experience!"

She had promised she was not the type of person to be swept away, but she was swept up in Noah. Swept up in his infectious way of seeing the world as one big adventure to explore. He had a punishing father and a virtually absent mother and experienced a lonely childhood, but here he was, dreaming of places he wanted to go with her.

"We'll go everywhere," she said. "Every single place we want to go."

"You mean it? Don't you want to get a job after college?"

"A job can wait."

"What would your mom think?"

She laughed. "My mom would tell me to go and never look back."

"Ugh," he said. "That makes me a little jealous."

Huh, she thought. Maybe she hadn't appreciated her mom enough. "I'll share her with you," she told him, and he beamed.

"When we get married," he joked, but she could tell he was serious about it, too.

Surprisingly the thought of marrying him didn't make her feel claustrophobic.

"Yes," she joked back. "When we get married."

It felt natural to her. She had no idea why, or how, but she supposed she had to admit that she was predisposed to believing in soulmates and fated meetings, simply because her mom had instructed her on it over and over.

And now, here was her chance to meet fate and let herself finally live.

I was still on my bed, staring up at the ceiling, and for the first time since these scenes had started making their way back into the forefront of my mind, they weren't just making me upset. It was nice, even for a moment, to remember the good times, too. To remember who I used to be, even if that version of myself had been fleeting and was now gone forever.

14

"Holy shit."

Benny's eyes were wide as Mari swung me around toward the mirror for the big reveal. The salon was bathed in natural light, accented in gold, and had a resident dachshund named Freddie who could be seen asking for head pats from clients or lounging on a curved velvet green sofa near the window.

"Does it look bad?" I asked, cringing, keeping my eyes closed.

"Let me repeat—holy shit," Benny said.

"Okay, holy shit can mean bad or good, Benadette," I jokingly barked at her.

"Just open your eyes, Charlotte."

I did, opening them one at a time, squinting.

"Holy shit," I cried out. "Is that me?"

I stared into the mirror at my own reflection. My hair wasn't bleached blond like I'd worried it would be. Mari had given me a perfect beachy dirty blond blended with precision that offset my golden eyes in a way I could have never dreamed of. The haircut looked almost too cool for me and my new bangs were effortless across my forehead. A makeup artist named Iris had come by and spent thirty minutes dusting my face with various brushes while I had a head full of foils, and the application was flawless. It looked natural, like every color Iris added just subtly but perfectly illuminated my features.

"You. Look. So. Hot." Benny's voice was guttural she was so giddy. "Mari, I've said it before and I'll say it again, you are a hair genius."

Mari did a little curtsy, pulling her black dress to the sides to reveal chunky loafers with a gold buckle. She had light pink hair and wore scarlet lipstick and I'd been a little wary of her to begin with. I wanted subtle and Mari was . . . not a subtle person. But, I had to admit, she was damn good at her job.

"Hair genius," I agreed. "Thank you. I love it."

Mari fiddled with my bangs. "You'll need a touch-up in three or four months. Don't go to anyone else. Come back here."

I laughed. "Okay." I turned back to the mirror, still in awe. "And I need to buy everything Iris used on my face. It looks so good."

At the register, I paid quite a lot of money for both the haircut, color, and makeup, tipping Iris and Mari generously. I never spent my money. It felt a little thrilling to drop that much on something as impractical as new hair and a bunch of makeup.

"Come on," Benny said, after she hugged Mari goodbye. "We have to go shopping now."

"I feel like I'm in a movie," I said, as we walked down Ventura Boulevard toward my car.

"A makeover might be silly and unnecessary but sometimes you just have to embrace the silly and unnecessary in life," Benny declared. She watched me. "Your energy is different. You're even walking differently."

"Am I?" I asked. "Is this why people get their hair and makeup done?"

"Yeah, because it *feels* good. And it's fun." She shook her head playfully. "I have *so* much to teach you, Charlie. Sometimes people do things *solely* because it feels good to do them, not because it's productive or useful. It's called self-care. Can you even imagine?"

"No," I deadpanned.

Benny howled.

We got to the car while Benny was still laughing and when we were inside, she immediately plugged her phone in so she could direct the music, just like she had on the ride over here.

"I mean, sure, it could be considered superficial to get your hair and makeup done, and to go shopping for anything other than pure necessity, but where's the fun in all that? I really think feeling good about how you look changes your whole experience. You are kinder, you attract more. Not because everyone is superficial, but because when you feel good about yourself, the Universe responds."

"Oh, here we go with the Universe."

"Charlie, new request," she said. "You and the Universe need a truce."

"I just don't think the Universe cares." I pulled out of the parking spot.

"So everything is just random?" Benny asked. "Oh, stop at a coffee shop. We need a little treat."

"Okay," I said. "And I don't know. Maybe everything *is* random."

"So you really don't think there are fated meetings or soulmates or experiences you attract through your energy or manifesting or anything like that? What do you believe in?"

"Nothing," I said. "I guess I don't believe in anything."

"Gosh, that's boring." She pointed to the left of the street at a modern building. "There. Go through the drive-through. I'm about to teach you the art of the 'little treat.'"

"And what's that?"

"When you want a little treat, you get a little treat."

I chuckled. "I'm not a little-treat person."

"Sure, that's what you believe. I just think you've never let yourself have the little treat."

"Fine, get me whatever you're getting."

"Good," she said. We got behind a row of five other cars.

"I think if you really look at your life, you'll see that very little has been random. That you've been led to certain places to meet certain people to have certain experiences. If you think everything is random, then that means nothing has meaning, not even our own lives. That just doesn't make sense, Charlie."

"Alright, how's this?" I began. "If the Universe wants my trust so bad, I'll take a sign. An undeniable one. Something that really can't be explained. Lead me somewhere I would never expect."

"Make it magical, Universe!" Benny cried, raising her face to the sky.

"I'm open," I said. "I'm open for a very limited time."

Benny laughed. "I honestly love your skepticism," she said. "It'll make it even better when the Universe brings you something like the love of your life or a whole new career. Wouldn't that be crazy?"

"Yeah," I scoffed. "Yeah, right."

"Be careful what you wish for, Char Char."

I shook my head at her.

"Don't call me that."

"Hey, I'm the boss of this month of yes. New request. I get to call you Char Char whenever I want. Is me *not* calling you Char Char worth ten grand to you?"

I shook my head at her even harder.

"Fine," I muttered.

She shot me a *very* annoying smirk of utmost satisfaction.

When we got to the window a moment later, Benny leaned over me and screamed out her order of what sounded like two extremely sweet and decadent iced coffees. I paid, and at the second window, the barista handed us two concoctions with a massive swirl of whipped cream at the top.

When I pulled away from the drive-through, Benny started up a playlist and said, "To the mall! Drink your little treat! Sing along if you know the words!"

Not wanting to encourage her, I resisted for a moment, but then I did exactly what she said and damn it, that drink was one of the best things I'd tasted in a long time and somehow I knew every single word to all the songs.

By the time we got to the mall and parked, we were both spent with laughter. We slurped up the last dregs of our drinks and walked arm in arm toward the stores.

15

Benny led the way through the mall that smelled like cinnamon rolls and was packed full of people, despite the fact that it was the middle of the week.

She stopped me in front of a store I'd never set foot in.

"Here's the deal," she said. "You're going to go inside and you're going to pick out a bunch of things you would never wear and would never have even considered trying on before. Nothing you could wear to work. The more impractical the better. Got it?"

She was so serious I had to smile. "Got it, boss."

"And you have to try on anything I bring you," she said.

"Okay," I told her.

Benny narrowed her eyes. "I'm a little suspicious by how easygoing you're being. Like, you know your hair is blond now, right? That I'm going to make you wear something really tight and revealing and in colors besides beige and gray?"

"Benny," I said. "I'm going along with your schemes."

"I just expected a lot more resistance."

"The day is young."

She shook her head, laughing. "Let's go."

An hour later, I was at the register with a pile of admittedly beautiful clothes that I would never have picked out for myself. Per Benny's request, I had changed into something new. I was wearing a staggeringly short burgundy dress that seemed to accent every single part of my body I liked, but never revealed. Benny made me pair it with leather knee-high black boots, even though I protested, only to be served a disapproving look so intense I just zipped up the boots and complied.

Even Kit, the woman that helped us, whistled when I came out wearing the outfit. It was the very definition of impractical and I, unfortunately, and against my better judgment, felt extremely sexy while wearing it.

I grabbed my bags and Benny dragged me over to another store where, within the space of an hour, I had another pile of new clothes and swiped my credit card once again.

"We didn't get everything," Benny said, holding up all the bags in her hands. "But this will last you for a bit. We have to get to dinner."

"Where are we going?"

"It's this tapas place called Wavy that Jasper's friend Sophia told me about. She said it's amazing and like one of those hole-in-the-wall spots that the tourists haven't taken over yet."

"And it's in Malibu?"

"Sort of," Benny said. "I'll put it in the GPS. It's up in the hills where Zuma Beach is. The restaurant is a converted house. Super cool."

"Is it new?" I asked.

"No, but the executive chef is, and he totally reworked the menu. Apparently, he's off to Chicago soon to open a new restaurant, though, so Sophia said to go while he's still cooking there."

"Sounds interesting."

"We have to hurry, though," she said, picking up her pace. "Traffic is terrible and we have a reservation."

When we got to the car, she held her hand out for the keys. "I'm driving. You're too slow and you forgot how to drive in LA. We need aggressive right now."

"Fine," I agreed. We loaded the bags in the trunk and I got in the passenger seat. Benny hooked up her phone, got the GPS onto the screen, put music on, and then pulled out of the parking spot so fast the tires squealed.

"My God," I said.

"Hold on," Benny replied.

And I just shook my head, fastened my seat belt, and clutched the armrest so tightly my hand almost cramped.

16

As Benny took a very sharp right turn off the PCH, I could hear the crash of the waves on the shore of Zuma Beach. It was considerably cooler by the water, and I liked the smell of the salty air through the open window. When Benny stopped at the small valet station behind another car, I pulled down the mirror and freshened up my bangs, still a bit overwhelmed and amazed by how different I looked.

The restaurant was a one-story white house covered in ivy with large bright pink bougainvillea vines surrounding the oak wood front door. It didn't have a view of the water. It was just a little spot tucked away within some greenery. It was modest, but no doubt an expensive piece of real estate. There was a white sign in a handwritten script that said Wavy that I noticed once the valet had taken my car and driven off to park it in some discreet location.

"Are we cool enough for this place?" I asked, tugging my dress down, even though it wouldn't budge. Somehow it felt shorter than when I had bought it forty-five minutes earlier.

"If we decide we're cool enough for this place, then we are," Benny said, like a wise sage. "Reality is just responding to our energy, anyway."

"Good lord," I replied, rolling my eyes, and Benny just smiled and shrugged like my pessimism wasn't going to affect her one bit.

"Wait," she said, before she opened the door. "I forgot to add one more thing for this whole experiment."

"Oh, God, *what?*"

"This one you might actually like," she said, grinning. "You've been such a Goody Two-shoes for so long, Charlie. I think you need to embrace the bad girl inside. Just give in. You know you want to. It's one month of debauchery. Embrace pleasure. Sow your wild oats. Take on an alter ego. Be Charlize, not Charlotte. Charlize would get up to some trouble."

I shook my head. "Has anyone ever told you that you're a bad influence?"

She thrust her finger in my face. "You know, depending on the way you look at it, one might say I'm a *great* influence, because I just saw some light come back into your eyes. So, you like the idea of being a little bad."

"Sure, why not," I told her. "I'll see what I can do." I wasn't backing down now. She wanted to keep adding tasks, I'd keep agreeing.

"I mean, don't go rob a bank," Benny said. "Be reasonable."

"Yeah, Benny, like I was about to go pull off a heist."

"Well, shit, Charlie, in that case, take me with you. I always thought I could be a great addition to a heist."

"*Such* a bad influence," I teased.

Benny batted her eyelashes. "I'm an angel."

"An angel of chaos, maybe."

"Thank you," she said. "I'll take that as the highest compliment."

"You would."

"Let's go inside," Benny said, twirling around.

The hostess stand was in the entryway and the entirety of the house was bathed in dim, flickering light. It looked like walls had been knocked down to create one large dining area where there were a handful of tables, all full, save for one. It was an exceedingly cool place that had charm and novelty in equal measure.

Each mid-century modern table was adorned with a single yellow rose, cut short and in a mismatched glass vase, along with a triplet of flickering candles. The hostess handed Benny and me menus when she sat us at our reserved table.

It was one long list of dishes, fifteen in total. They were all small plates, and the menu had a note that recommended four to five dishes for two people. It was an array of cuisines, from pizza with shaved brussels sprouts and bacon to shrimp and corn grits with house-made hot sauce and fennel and grapefruit salad. On the back of the menu were the drink options. It was sparse and curated.

There was a time before everything happened, before Noah, that I loved discovering new restaurants. I even considered going to culinary school, but instead chose to get a business degree from Stanford. Taking in the menu, I wanted *everything*, wanted to taste every single dish. For the first time in years, I felt ravenous.

Our server swung over to our table with a flourish. She was in all black and a dusty blue apron with Wavy written in that same handwriting from the sign outside, and tattoos up and down both her arms.

She took our drink order of a large bottle of sparkling water. Benny and my mom didn't drink. I hadn't had a drink since the night of my birthday and it felt good to be clear-headed right now. Before the pandemic, I drank a few nights a week, but during lockdown, Josh and me were putting away bottles by the night.

The server started walking away, but I called back to her.

"Can I put our food order in, too?" I asked.

"But, I—" Benny cut in and I stilled her with my hand.

"We're going to order everything," I said. "One of every single thing on the menu."

Benny's smile was so wide her mouth was hanging open.

"I love it," she cried, nearly panting. "One of everything!"

The server nodded her head. "What a decadent choice."

"Thank you," I said.

When the server walked off, Benny looked at me and said, "The student has become the master. Good work, Charlize."

I just smiled and told her, "Let the games begin?"

"Oh, they have *begun*," Benny replied, as she sat back in her chair, arms crossed, looking a little too gratified for someone I was hell-bent on proving wrong.

17

Benny and I were mid-conversation when our waitress and three other servers descended upon our table with a bevy of dishes placed on trays.

"Incoming," Benny said, her eyes lighting up, as we both watched fifteen small plates cover our table, the servers using Tetris-like skill to fit them all on. We were seated in the middle of the small dining area and everyone else in the room quieted down to a hush as they watched us. I felt the strangest sensation of pure delight crawl its way up my body and once it reached my mouth, I broke into a smile so big my cheeks pushed my eyes into a squint.

"There! *That's* a real smile," Benny cried, pointing at me over the table. "That one reached your eyes."

Before I could respond, we heard a deep voice behind the servers. "You know," he said, "I always wondered when someone was going to order everything on the menu at once, but it hadn't happened until now. I had to come out and say hello."

When the servers finally departed, there stood a man in chef whites, giving us both a friendly smile, hands behind his back. It was dim in the restaurant and he for sure hadn't seen us yet, but my mouth dropped open, and I let out a little surprised gasp. I would recognize the figment of all my teenage fantasies from anywhere. He was somehow even more beautiful than I remembered.

"Alex?" I said. "Alex Perry?"

His hands dropped and his face lost its smile as he stepped forward, scanning. Once he stepped into the light, and recognized us, his green eyes went wide.

"Benny and Charlie Quinn? No fucking way," he said, steadying himself on the back of the empty chair between Benny and me. He pulled it out and sat down, shaking his head in disbelief.

He looked excessively gorgeous and I could feel the nerve endings on my skin flame to attention like he was holding a magnet and I was tipping toward him involuntarily. His dark brown hair was grown out, slightly curled, and it offset the unique moss color of his eyes. He had a five-o'clock shadow, and his body had filled out, his height no longer making him lanky, but instead—*fuck*, he was a grown man now. I did a hard swallow, rendered almost wordless. My heart was yammering in my chest so hard I thought for sure he'd hear it.

When I looked to Benny, she had her hands under her chin, elbows on the table, watching us both with pure mischief in her eyes. She knew damn well I'd spent most of my teenage years violently crushing on Alex Perry.

"You're the executive chef here?" I asked, eyes wide, voice hoarse. "I didn't even know you were back in LA."

"And here I thought you were in the Bay Area," he replied. "I ran into your mom's old boyfriend Lukas and he said you were at some big job in San Francisco and never came home. You're not on social media, either." My body nearly shook with pleasure. He'd *asked* about me? He'd *looked* for me? Alex Perry *remembered* me?

"I came to visit a few days ago," I said to him. "I'm here for the month. I'm kind of doing this whole say-yes-to-life experiment. Hence, ordering everything on the menu."

I could feel Benny practically bouncing with energy beside him.

"And the hair," Alex said, tipping his head up toward me. "You look good blonde. But you know, you're you. You always looked good."

"Did I?" I asked without thinking, so caught off guard that Alex Perry was sitting next to me right now I didn't have my usual defenses up.

Alex laughed, then his voice deepened as he said like a matter of fact, "You were my unrequited teenage crush. I was, um . . ." he gave me a shy smile, looked up at me through darkened lashes ". . . pretty damn obsessed with you, Quinn."

My whole entire face erupted into a blush and I was grateful for dim lighting and makeup. I coughed, not knowing how to respond to that.

"Funny," Benny said, cutting in. "Not so unrequited actually. You were also Charlie's crush."

"Benny," I whispered hard, throwing her an I'm-going-to-kill-you look.

"Hey, we're all adults here," Benny said, grinning. "It's ancient history." Then she shrugged and added, looking between Alex and me pointedly, "Or . . . is it?"

"Benny, weren't you saying you needed to use the restroom?" I retorted.

"No—" she started, then nodded curtly, finally understanding my subtext. "Yeah, you're right. I need the restroom."

Alex pointed toward a door and said, "To the left, all the way back."

Benny whispered to me as she walked by, all smug, "You believe in the Universe yet?"

Even though I shot her a look, I couldn't deny this was quite a coincidence. I hadn't seen Alex since he abruptly moved away our senior year.

Once Benny was gone, Alex leaned in closer toward me. "You had a crush on me, Quinn?"

I tried to look away, but his eyes were caught on mine. "Don't mess with me, Perry. You knew."

"I never knew for sure," he said. "I don't know if you know this about yourself, but you're very hard to read. And I was shy back then."

"And now?" I asked.

"Not nearly as shy," he whispered, leaning even closer to me. "So, what's this say-yes-to-life thing? I could have some fun with that . . ."

Warmth flooded me and something long dormant flipped on with unmistakable intensity.

"See, if you had flirted with me like this in high school . . ."

"I've grown up since then."

"Yeah," I said, sighing. "I can tell."

"We came close that one night," Alex said, and his eyes pointedly dropped to my lips.

"I remember."

"I never forgot," he said, raggedly, dragging his gaze back up to my eyes.

"I thought I imagined it, honestly," I said, pulling back. Because the truth was, I did think Alex was into me back then. At least, I hoped he was. But then he left LA and it wasn't until months later I found out it was because his mom had unexpectedly and tragically passed away from an aggressive cancer. *God*, life was heartbreaking. I never tried to find him. It was a moment in time at that party when I thought we almost kissed, but I didn't have any claim to him. I couldn't even believe he could talk about that time of his life without it shattering him, but he seemed bright and excited to see me.

"Yeah, I thought I imagined it, too," he said, low. "It was the worst timing. How I left. When I left." He stroked his face with his long tapered fingers and I watched the movement like it was erotic.

"I should have tried to get in touch," I said. "I'm so sorry, Alex."

"How could you have gotten in touch? Nobody had phones back then. I was unreachable, trust me. I wanted to be unreachable. But I thought about you."

When his eyes found mine again, they were laced with vulnerability. It made me take a breath in just to steady my heart.

"Did you ever think about me?" he asked.

The heat between us was so high already I couldn't take my eyes off him. Nothing else existed in this restaurant—just him and me, like years hadn't passed between us.

"Of course," I told him.

"Here's an idea," he said. "Pick up where we left off? You said you're here a month? My last day at Wavy is on Sunday and then I'm taking a new job in Chicago in a month. Hang out? I can say yes to things, too."

I was about to answer that I didn't think it was a good idea to get entangled only to have it end in a month, but a woman in a black chef uniform came to the table and whispered in his ear. He nodded and said to her, "I'm coming."

He turned back to me. "I need to go, and your food is getting cold." He pulled a pen from his pocket and grabbed the napkin under my sparkling water glass. "Write your number down." He handed me the pen and his eyes trained on mine again. "Please." His voice was a pleading whisper and I couldn't say no, even if my gut was telling me this was not a good idea.

I wrote my number down, and when he picked up the napkin, he folded it up and pressed it into his inside pocket with a pat of his hand like it really meant something to him.

"I'll text you," he said, smiling and standing up. "Charlie Quinn. Wow."

Right as he was leaving, Benny joined the table and said, "Bye, Alex. Good to see you."

"Bye, Benny," he said behind his shoulder. "You, too."

Benny placed her black napkin on her lap, speared a perfectly roasted wedge of a potato covered in a spicy pesto. She looked up at me, popped it in her mouth, and said, "So, you still don't believe in signs? Of all the restaurants in all of LA, we walk into the only one where Alex Perry works and lo and behold, he came out from the kitchen just to find us here. You asked for a sign. This is a pretty big one, don't you think? How else do you explain it?"

"Coincidence?" I said, even though I didn't fully believe that. She shook her head. "Oh, you're impossible, Char Char."

18

"I am the most full I've ever been in my entire life," Benny cried as I drove the PCH back to Topanga Canyon. She was clutching her stomach.

"We definitely did not have to eat every single thing we ordered," I said.

"Plus the dessert that Alex sent out for us."

"Or those special little cheese bread puffs he had our server bring."

We both laughed and then groaned.

"I need TUMS," Benny said.

"And ginger ale," I added.

"Stop at a gas station before we burst."

I pulled into a place with a mini-mart and Benny and I strode in, going right for the aisle with travel-sized packets of medicine.

"Remember all our late-night runs to the 7-Eleven on Magnolia?" Benny asked, her arm laced in mine as we scanned the shelves. "We should get Mom some Red Vines."

"Mom lived for a late-night run—and Red Vines," I said, letting the memory stay fond and not laced with the realization that maybe taking your kids to a convenience store at ten o'clock on a school night wasn't the best parenting move. They *were* good memories. Mom would look at us both and declare we needed ice cream or chips or a baked hand pie and we'd squeal with delight as we loaded ourselves into the back seat of the car.

I'd be tired at school the next day, or Mom would let me skip, and that was the kind of lack of discipline and responsibility that eventually brought me late-onset resentment. You couldn't live like that forever, unless you were Jackie Quinn, apparently. As a kid, I vacillated between loving that spontaneity and also feeling stressed by it.

Benny found the TUMS and Red Vines and I got two fizzy bottles of ginger ale while lost in memories. As we walked up to the counter to pay, my phone pinged and when I saw who texted, the inside of my body felt like someone had shaken up a soda in there and let it all loose at once.

"Oh, my God," I whispered under my breath, before I could stop myself. Benny heard and whipped around.

"What?" she asked, alarmed.

"Alex texted."

"Daaaaaamn, that was quick," she said, giddy and loud. "Well, what did he say?"

"It's private." I didn't want to show her, because I knew what she would do: make me say yes to him.

"Charlotte. Show me. Oh, my God. It's a request."

"Fine," I said.

We both leaned over my phone and read the text from Alex.

> i'm not wasting any more time when it comes to you, quinn. unfortunately i work this weekend. but, monday? please tell me you're free.

"That's so fucking hot," Benny said, lifting her palms up. "Alex Perry wants you. He wants you bad and he wants you to know it. You're going for it. I can already tell you want to say no. I can already see you denying yourself this. It's *Alex Perry*. You're saying yes or you're paying me ten grand and living to regret not getting with Alex when you could. That'll haunt you on your deathbed."

"He's going to Chicago in a month, Benny."

"So? Have fun for a month. Enjoy yourself, *Charlize*."

"It's not worth it."

"Charlie," Benny said, grabbing me by the shoulders. "Are you afraid you're going to develop feelings for him? I thought you didn't 'get' feelings." Her eyes were wide and she was grinning.

"I'm not. I don't. I won't."

"You're totally afraid. Look at you."

"I'm not going to fall in love with him."

"Love?!" Her jaw practically unhinged. "Who said anything about falling in *love*?"

"I'm just saying," I cried, flustered. "It's an expression."

"No, it's not."

"It's not a good idea, Benny. Don't I get a veto on your requests?"

"Not unless you want to owe me ten grand and die regretting not getting with Alex after you pined over him for years."

"Fine," I said, through clenched teeth. "I'll say yes. Charlize would say yes."

"Exactly. Charlize would take the opportunity and run."

An alter ego could work. Charlize would be able to do everything I was too afraid to do and when it was time to go back to San Francisco, I could shrug her off like a coat. No entanglements. No strings. No risk.

Benny and I walked back to the car and as we got in, she said, "Alex looked really good. Like, better than he used to."

I sighed, like a lovelorn teenager staring up into the eyes of a boy band poster. "So damn good."

"I want all the details. That's a *big* request."

"You know what, Benny?" I said, playfully. "Tomorrow, I'm going to grill you on all *your* conquests, get every detail out of *your* love life. We're going to sit down and discuss your career.

I'm going to tell you all *your* flaws that you need to work on. That's what you've been doing with me. Meddling. Prying. Intervening. How does that sound?"

"I know you think you're threatening me," Benny said, laughing. "But I think it sounds fun. I can't wait! I love talking about myself. And you know how much I live for your attention. I'm your little sister. I'll take anything I can get from you! Should we get coffee while we're at it? Make a day of it?"

"Oh, my God," I said, pulling out of the parking spot and easing my way onto the PCH again. "You're impossible."

"That makes two of us I guess," she said. And I didn't even have to look over at her to know she was grinning.

19

The bonfire was aglow when we got up to the landing of Quinn Canyon. Mom was sitting on one of the chairs, with Petra next to her, then the guy Jasper from the other night who I hadn't met yet, and a young woman holding an acoustic guitar across her lap. Mom was a night owl. Always had been. She could stay up until the sunrise and sleep all day. She used to say that's what Stevie Nicks did, and she idolized her. She thought Stevie was the perfect example of a woman who lived her life on her own terms and didn't let a single external opinion dictate what she did.

She also loved to tell the story of when Stevie breezed into Quinn Canyon with her "coven" one night (Stevie was friends with one of Mom's friends at the time) when I was only two years old and Stevie had—as legend has it—held and rocked me to sleep, which Jackie always believed to be the most magical thing that ever happened to her, not least because I was a fussy child and getting me to sleep was apparently very hard for Mom to do. Stevie had sung "Landslide" to me like a lullaby. Of course I have no recollection of it, but the amount of times Mom has told the story, it's almost as if I could remember it myself.

"Charlie," Petra called out, already out of her chair and barreling toward me. Petra was tall and slim, with long straight brown hair laced with gray. She'd once been a supermodel, but had left those days behind years before. I always expected her to carry with her remnants of superficiality, but she never did. She let her hair go gray, didn't wear much makeup, and heartily didn't believe in cosmetic procedures. She used to say all those years of caring about her appearance made her never want to spend another second of her one life fixated on how she looked.

"Petra!" I held my arms out for a hug.

She smelled the same as she used to—a slight hint of the lavender oil that she pressed to her wrists and temples every morning.

"We've missed you," she said, grabbing me by the shoulders and kissing me on the cheek. She touched a few strands of my hair. "And when did you go blonde?"

"Blonde?" Mom asked, and shot to her feet and joined us. Her face broke into a wide smile. "How unlike you. I love it. It looks perfect on you."

"You did this today?" Petra asked.

"Yes, and today was *quite* the adventure," Benny said, cutting in and throwing her arms around Petra and me. I shot her a look, but I knew Benny was going to do what Benny does best and give them all a detailed account of every single thing that happened. There was no stopping her, so I just accepted it.

"Don't leave us out," the woman with the guitar said, loudly enough for us to hear. "Jasper and I need to hear the story, too."

"Of course you do," Mom said. "Jasper and Willow, this is my daughter, Charlie."

I went over and shook their hands, then Benny and I sat in the two empty chairs across from the four of them.

"Jasper is a very talented actor who just got his first starring role in a Netflix series," Mom said. "And Willow is talking to Capitol about signing a record deal. She's amazing."

"Your mom collects all the best people," Willow said, her voice a melodic lilt. "You're so lucky." She was ethereally beautiful and had straight chestnut hair that hung past her shoulders.

"For real," Jasper said. "I would never have navigated this whole audition process without your mom."

I sat there, not quite sure what to say, because being friends with Jackie Quinn, or having her as some sort of temporary mentor, was one thing. Having her as a mom was much more complicated.

"We got you Red Vines," Benny said, pulling the package from the bag and handing it to Mom.

She ripped into them immediately and passed around the container.

When Willow handed it to Benny, she mimed vomiting and said, "We are so full we may actually burst. We ordered every single thing on the menu at Wavy, Jasper. Tell Sophia it's as amazing as she said."

"I will," Jasper told Benny.

"Before that, I took Charlie for her makeover. Doesn't her hair look incredible? We also went shopping, and Charlie had to buy a bunch of things she wouldn't normally wear." Benny stopped and looked at me. "We forgot the bags in the car by the way."

"I'll get them in the morning," I said.

"You all went shopping without me?" Mom asked. "You know, I want in on this little experiment of yours."

"What experiment?" Jasper asked.

Benny made a whole show of explaining the experiment again, detailing my workaholism and cataloging all the ways in which I was doing life wrong. At this point, I just laughed.

"That sounds *so* fun," Willow said.

"Lovely," Petra agreed. "I want to come with. What's next?"

"Well," Benny said, kicking up the flourish again. "Mom and Petra, you're going to die when I tell you who the executive chef of Wavy is and, Willow and Jasper, you're going to have to take my word for it—this is juicy."

"I'm so glad I decided to come over tonight," Jasper said, laughing.

"Alex Perry," Benny said, dropping it into the conversation like it was a bomb and letting it hang there.

"No way," Mom gasped. "Charlie, baby, you were so into him."

"Beyond," Petra agreed.

"Well, apparently, as we found out tonight, Alex Perry was into Charlie right back."

Mom let out an actual squeal while Willow and Jasper burst into laughter.

"Are you dying right now?" Mom asked me. "He liked you back? Teenage you would have dropped dead."

"Thirty-year-old me kind of wants to right now," I said back wryly as Willow snorted.

"Charlie is going on a date with him," Benny said. "On Monday. And he's so hot. Like, he got hotter."

"Stop," Petra exclaimed.

"I am giddy," Mom said. "I'm actually giddy over this, Petra!"

"I am, too!" Petra said back.

"I hate this," I quipped and all five of them laughed even harder, as if I were joking.

"You did text him back, right?" Benny asked me.

"Not yet," I told her. I'd been driving us back and then I was here. I hadn't had a moment alone to even process that text, to let my body feel it the way it wanted to, to savor it, to lie on my childhood bed in disbelief that Alex Perry was somehow in LA and wanted to see me. It was one of those things you just wanted to exist with for a moment before talking about it.

"He's probably checking his phone every second after that text," Benny said, aghast. "You have to text him back. He's positively *desperate* for you to."

"The drama in this family," I said. "It's been like thirty minutes."

"Inquiring minds want to know what the text said," Jasper chimed in.

"Inquiring minds, yes please," Willow repeated.

Benny didn't even wait for me to take my phone out. She just recited it back to them, almost word for word. The four of them reacted at once.

"He's down bad." Jasper.

"You *have* to text him back." Willow.

"I'm living vicariously through this." Petra.

"I'm losing it!" Mom.

"I'm going to text him back," I said, trying to calm them all. "Give me a minute."

"He doesn't want to waste any time," Petra said. "You dazzled him."

"Alright, alright," I said. "Let's take it down a notch." But inside, I was bubbling up, like champagne fizzing away in my body.

"Wait, didn't he move away?" Mom asked. "Like to Michigan or something?"

"Yeah, during our senior year," I said. "A few months before graduation."

"Oh, God," she said, hand over her mouth. "Now I remember."

"What?" Willow asked, fully invested.

"Alex's parents had a production company and they had become incredibly successful," I explained. "But during his senior year, his mom was diagnosed with pancreatic cancer and within the span of a few weeks, she was gone. It was so unexpected. And the Perry family was honestly one of the best—the kindest, happiest people. Alex's mom and dad were so in love. And his dad was devastated. He moved the whole family to Michigan to be closer to his parents. It was all so sudden."

I didn't say anything about the weekend before Alex left school, when I was out at a party and he showed up, and we spent the entire night in someone's backyard, talking. We were two seconds from what seemed to be a kiss when the cops showed up and we had to run to disburse into the neighborhood.

That moment had been years in the making. Alex and I always had classes together. We'd attended the same elementary, middle, and high school, but hung out in separate groups. Sometimes we talked during class or when our groups of friends got together, but I was always too afraid of getting rejected to take it any further. I started going to parties the last semester of my senior year when I'd received early acceptance to Stanford and could relax for a minute before college began.

Of course, I always hoped I might run into him at those parties. But after that night, it was Monday at school, and he didn't show up. He left without saying anything, and I didn't find out why until months later. It wasn't enough to stay in touch. It's not like we were dating. But, what could I do? Hold it against him? Never. But it definitely hurt, before I found out about his mom and why he left. That night had seemed like it was a beginning, but instead he became my last unguarded crush. I learned to protect myself because of Alex Perry.

The first to say anything was Jasper. "That is heartbreaking."

"They were the good ones," Petra added. "Cindy and Scott Perry. They were the best of the best people. *God*. I haven't thought about them in a long time. I wonder how Scott is now. And their daughter. I forget her name."

"Amber," I replied. "Amber and Alex. They were only eighteen months apart. Irish twins."

"Give him our best," Mom said. "Poor things. That was such a tragedy around here. We all loved Cindy. Everybody did."

I felt the tension in the circle. No one knew what to say.

"That was heavy," I said, attempting to break it with a bit of levity. "Anyone else want to divulge their personal details for the bonfire circle fodder? I mean, I know I just met you, Willow, but please do tell if you've reconnected with any of your high school crushes recently. Jasper? Care to take the spotlight off me for a bit?"

They all laughed.

"Actually," Willow said. "I'm in the middle of a real-life love triangle. That's good fodder."

"Do tell," I said, and rested my elbows on my thighs and leaned in as Willow told us about the guy and the woman she was dating at the same time, who knew about each other, but both were now asking her to choose between them.

"It's a real bi dilemma," Willow said, laughing.

"Well, you could always try polyamory," Petra said, as if that fixed everything.

"My personal philosophy is have the cake and eat it, too," Mom said.

"Yeah," Benny said. "Doesn't sound like a dilemma. More like a delicious opportunity."

"This has not been helpful," Willow said, laughing.

My phone vibrated in my pocket. Just the thought of it being a text from Alex sent a flush of heat through me.

"I'm going in," I said, standing up. "Really nice to meet you, Jasper and Willow." I squeezed Mom's shoulder, kissed her cheek, and did the same to Petra. "So good to see you, Petra."

I rushed up to my bedroom, fell on the bed, and opened my phone, hoping, hoping, hoping, that it was another text from Alex, even though I felt ridiculous.

Just seeing his name made me feel almost dizzy.

I waited to read the text, relished the heady anticipation, held the phone to my chest like I was sixteen again.

> yeah, i can't play it cool. i've been staring at my phone wondering if you're going to text back. i can't stop thinking about you. about that party. that night. we almost did. do you ever think about it?

I replied back quickly, putting him out of his apparent misery.

> i made it a point a long time ago to never think about it, but it's all i'm thinking about now. monday. i'm in, perry.

> thank god. i worried i got you back only to lose you again. monday. i will be thinking of nothing else until then, quinn.

Lying on my bed, I felt as if I could levitate off it as I reread the texts ten more times just to believe they were real, just to keep feeling that fizzy sense of disbelief pinballing its way inside of me. After I hearted his text, I heard Benny calling me from downstairs. I found her, Petra, Willow, and Jasper in the living room, all furniture moved back, and Mom connecting her phone to a massive Bluetooth speaker. The lights were pink now. Mom had apparently installed colored light bulbs.

"We're having a dance party," Mom told me. "Come on, Charlie, like old times."

"No," I relented, shaking my head. "No, thanks. You all enjoy." I started walking toward the kitchen to get a snack when I felt Benny's hand on my shoulder.

"Charlotte, this is a request," she commanded. "You. Dance. Now."

I turned around and sighed in her direction heavily. She didn't even let me answer, just pulled me by the hands into the middle of the room.

"Dancing Queen" by ABBA—the quintessential Quinn dance party kickoff song—rang through the speaker and I was transported back two decades. I started swaying, because once upon a time, I really did love this. Benny, Mom, and I used to dance for hours. Often just the three of us, or sometimes a big impromptu dance party with whoever was at the house that night.

Petra put her arms around my shoulders and we moved together, eyes closed. Mom was on my other side now, and I was in the middle of them both, lost in the music.

When Cyndi Lauper's "Time After Time" started playing, we all suddenly began singing so dramatically and intensely while seemingly line dancing across the room, we kept doubling over in laughter, Jasper and Willow both a little shell-shocked at how seriously Triple Quinn plus Petra took this. After that, "Ob-La-Di, Ob-La-Da" by The Beatles went off and Benny, Mom, and I shrieked because if there was any song that was *our* song, it was that one. We screamed the chorus, and rocked back and forth like we were singing an Irish drinking song in the middle of a Dublin pub.

Then, it was "Landslide" by Fleetwood Mac and that's when Jasper and Willow joined in the absurdity and couldn't keep from singing along to one of the greatest songs ever written. Mom could never listen to "Landslide" without having to inexplicably also listen to "Not Ready to Make Nice" by The Chicks and let all her feminine fury out, to which all of us—even poor Jasper who was very outnumbered at the moment—absolutely belted every word, making good use of our vocal cords at the "I'm still mad as hell" line.

The six of us were breathless and wild just five songs in.

Reckless abandon was a contagious thing.

Mom always said people needed permission from others to let loose and that's what Quinn Canyon represented. Permission to be free. Mom was always the first to give in, to show everyone how it's done.

The lights were so dim it was practically dark in the bungalow and the music was so loud I couldn't quite stop myself from giving in. Soon, I was jumping with my hands in the air, hair whipped across my face, rivulets of sweat rushing down the sides of my neck.

When Whitney's "I Have Nothing" started playing—Mom devising the perfect playlist and the perfect moment for a ballad—I didn't even think twice before performing my own karaoke rendition of it. This was one of my favorite songs ever, and Benny, Mom, and Petra knew it. I sang the song like I *was* Whitney Houston. My eyes were closed and I could feel them all laughing with me, swaying, and being my backup vocalists. I couldn't believe I still remembered every word to this song.

The moment I was done, we all devolved into carefree laughter and I did a silly little bow.

"A bit pitchy, but overall not bad," Benny joked, and that made us all laugh even more.

Mom pulled me into a hug before I could stop her and I melted into it.

Then the playlist clicked into The Police and then to Prince and then to Harry Styles and then to Dolly Parton and then to Donna Summer and then to The Cure and on and on and on like a Quinn Canyon soundtrack.

We all bounced around the room and hugged and danced and didn't stop until it was very late and we were sweating and dehydrated and starving and flushed and could hardly stand upright.

It usually took me hours to fall asleep without melatonin and/or several glasses of wine, but the moment my head hit the pillow I was out, until suddenly I startled awake with a gasp at 3:12 a.m., gripped, yet again, by those damn memories I worked so hard to suppress.

20

They were dancing slowly in a circle to one of Charlie's favorite songs, "I Have Nothing" by Whitney Houston. Noah teased her that the song was pretty angsty for someone who said she wasn't that romantic. She'd laughed with him, and said she was reexamining her self-assessment. Maybe she was a romantic, after all. It certainly seemed like it.

She'd begun to rediscover the music of her childhood, the records that played endlessly in Quinn Canyon—Fleetwood Mac, Whitney, The Beatles, Elton John, ABBA. She'd enjoyed playing them for Noah, each night dancing together after she told him stories about Triple Quinn. Charlie felt like she'd stepped into the pages of a romance novel.

They spent most of their time alone, caught in the delicious web of their intimacy, but sometimes they met up with friends—introducing each other to their people, doing trivia nights at the bar downtown, going mini-golfing with Charlie's good friend Heidi and her boyfriend.

Charlie had finally told Benny about Noah. She made Benny promise not to tell their mom. Not yet. She wanted to be more sure that Noah was in this before she let Jackie get excited. Noah had to go home, tell his parents he was off to travel the world with her, disappoint them, upset his entire life. Charlie didn't know how that would play out yet, and she wasn't about to tell her mom this grand plan only to take it back. Every single minute with Noah felt fragile.

Even her childhood seemed to soften in the glow of her and Noah.

When she spoke of it, she spoke with equanimity and understanding. Noah loved every story. Through his eyes, her childhood was idyllic. He couldn't wait to see Quinn Canyon. He was dying to meet Jackie and Benny and frequently asked if he could be a "Bonus Quinn" and the thought of bringing Noah into the fold of her little family made her so inexplicably happy that it terrified her. Love could lift you to perilous heights, holding only the hand of a fallible human being, who could any day decide to change their mind and walk out the door.

It had happened once before to Charlie with her dad and she remembered it all too well, but being with Noah was about trusting that lightning doesn't strike you twice.

They had their big trip mostly planned, but wanted to embrace spontaneity. They'd leave right after graduation, spend at least a year abroad. Noah's dad had an internship lined up for him at a bank, something that would funnel Noah directly into his business. He hadn't told his parents yet, that he was going with her, that he didn't want that life.

She worried about it constantly. She was in love with him. It had been two months, and they didn't spend a day, or night, apart.

He was going home to discuss his plans with his parents. She offered to go with him, but he thought it might be better if he braved it alone. She didn't tell him how fearful she was that he'd lose his will. She was scared of losing her own nerve, but more scared that he'd buckle and fold to the demands of his overbearing dad.

She hated that sense of insecurity. She didn't doubt Noah's love for her. She doubted his ability to be able to withstand his alienation from his family, and to be ripped from all the comforts he had known and grown up with. Even though she would never voluntarily give up Noah, she hated the vulnerability it inspired within her.

Just the thought of not being with him devastated her. She used to feel strong, impenetrable. But now she was gooey, malleable, always craving his touch. They met during classes, and those hours between seeing Noah would be endless—the waiting, the wanting, the needing him. She had never felt anything like it, and part of her resented it. She was unfocused.

She was bubblegum and heart eyes, when all she'd ever wanted was to be a fortress.

They lay in bed together after they made love, and she let her mind wander and go blank, the feel of his fingertip tracing the curve of her skin like a nerve ending set on fire. He was staring at her longingly, and she never got tired of the way he looked when he looked at her. He kissed her neck and ran his soft lips down until he hit her collarbone.

"You're my drug," he said, low. "I don't know how to get enough of you."

"Just imagine doing this in Paris," she whispered. "Or in Vienna, Prague, or Tokyo."

"I want to go now. Not even tell my parents. Just go."

"They'd send out the National Guard for you."

"I wouldn't even make it onto the plane."

They were two weeks out from their first flight. They'd land in Lisbon and then, wherever they decided they wanted to go next. Noah was using money at his disposal for now, but she was funding it all on credit cards. Maddeningly irresponsible, but she had to do it. She was an adult, but it was the first time she'd felt truly young.

"So, you go tomorrow for three days," she said, already missing him before he'd even left for Connecticut.

"If I can even last three days," he said. "With them. Without you." He kissed her, long and slow, his tongue languid against hers, his warm hands roving her body, and she was breathless by the time they stopped.

Her head was swimming, but she tried to find the thread of their conversation.

"Play nice," she said. "Maybe they'll be reasonable."

He laughed. "You haven't met my parents. Reasonable is not who they are."

"Just pretend you'll be whoever they want after the year abroad. And then we'll deal with them when we're back."

"We will?" he asked, his eyes glinting. "I like the sound of we."

"I'll go with you," she said, something desperate in her voice. "If you want me to go. I will."

"If you go with me, there's no chance," he said. "At least if I can talk to them alone, I may be able to figure it out."

"Okay," she said. "It's all going to work out." She had let so many of her mom's words leak into this relationship. She believed in soulmates, fate, the Universe, everything. She wanted the certainty her mom had. That it was all going to work out for them. That she and Noah were meant to be. The life they'd sketched out—the traveling and then the return together—it was what she never knew she wanted. She had always been skeptical of people who came from rich families, but Noah was different.

"What if they don't agree?" she asked. She'd been avoiding this question for a long time now.

"Then, we'll go anyway," Noah replied.

"But you'll lose everything."

"Not everything," he said, and kissed her so tenderly on the lips she melted into him, forgetting all previous worries. "It's easy, Charlie. I choose you."

"But what if . . ."

"What if, what?"

"Noah, don't make me say it."

"What if, what?" he repeated.

"What if we break up? It's only been two months. What if this doesn't last? Then you've given up too much for me."

"We won't break up," he said, without a hint of doubt. "And I don't know how many more times I can say that the money doesn't matter."

"The only people who say the money doesn't matter are the ones that have it."

"You're being too practical here."

"And maybe you're not being practical enough."

"Charlie," he said, stilling her. "You want the truth?"

Her breathing stopped. "Yeah."

"Even if we break up, and I can't imagine that happening, I'd still be happy I chose what I wanted to do. If these are their terms and they're going to stick to them, then it's best I make my own way. Money *is not worth being under my dad's control. The money is tainted. That is not love. I won't miss that. I'm giving them one more chance to be good parents."*

She let out a breath, finally relaxed.

"My heart's on the line here, Noah," she said. "Like, it's really on the line."

He nodded, cupped her face with his palm. "Mine, too," he said. "I can't lose you. I can't imagine a life without you now."

"Me, either."

"And, if you remember correctly, I'm the one who should be worried. You said you're not romantic. Or lovable."

She laughed. "You proved me wrong."

"Good," he said, and kissed her cheek, shifted to his back, and she laid her head on his chest, like she had every other night for the past sixty nights.

Charlie would tell her mom about everything once Noah was back. Then she would be sure. She felt excited at the prospect of surprising her mom with this wonderful man and the grand adventure that lay before her. Mom would be so excited for her. Even without her mom knowing about this whole plan, Charlie felt like she finally belonged with Triple Quinn, like she was actually one of them.

It was as sweet a feeling as falling in love with Noah was.

Snapping out of the scene was harsh, and I kicked the covers off me, panting and sweating. This was why Alex was a bad idea. I'd felt this intoxicating sense of warmth before, drawn to someone despite all my inner protestations.

And it hadn't ended well.

In fact, it had ended with total, brutal, life-shattering heartbreak.

21

When I woke up again, it was late morning and my body felt spent from being seized all night, jaw sore, a headache forming at my temples.

I had to get out of this house and keep busy, and the ocean popped into my head. Benny's month of yes meant I had to follow the urges I had, so when I went downstairs and suggested brunch and a walk on The Strand in Manhattan Beach, Benny was already up the stairs getting ready and Mom was begging to tag along. We were out the door and in the car within twenty minutes.

"See what incredible things you can do when you're not always thinking about work and getting the next promotion and trying to get ahead?" Benny crooned from the back seat. "Eggs Benny on the beach on a beautiful Saturday. What would you be doing back in San Francisco?"

"If I were back home, I'd be working. That's what I did on the weekend. I caught up on work."

"Well, you must have really loved your job," Mom said. "I'm sorry you got laid off. You'll find something else you love. I'm certain of it."

Had I loved my job? That never mattered to me. Following your passions was a way to be broke and starving. I watched Mom try to be an artist and fail, so that never appealed to me. Sure, we were never destitute and Mom really did handle it, but I never could get over my fear that, one day, it would all fall apart. So, I simply figured out what practical work I could be good at that was also lucrative. I didn't want to struggle and I wanted to achieve so much that I never needed to worry again, safely ensconced in the embrace of financial solvency and a plan that left nothing up to chance. Loving my job wasn't part of that equation.

It never occurred to me that even the most certain bets were still a gamble. Here I was, jobless and single, holding up the scraps of a Life Plan that had fallen apart just as easily as a life of risk and chance and luck and passion.

"I just like working," I told them, my identity so well-worn and grooved I couldn't seem to shift it. "That's all. I don't think I'm doing anything wrong by wanting to be responsible and hardworking."

"There is absolutely nothing wrong with that," Mom said. We were stuck in bumper-to-bumper traffic on the 405, inching forward with everyone else who wanted to head south on a cloudless, sunny Saturday morning. "Have I ever made you feel like that was wrong?"

"I don't know," I said. "Maybe?"

"I only wanted to lighten you up sometimes, Charlie," Mom replied. "Take the pressure off that you so obviously had on your shoulders. I just wanted to give you possibilities."

"I never understood how you could deal with rejection so much," I said by way of some sort of explanation. "Or Dad leaving. Or any of it. To me, I looked at you and thought, she should live more carefully. More boxed in. You kept opening yourself up over and over. How? Love, wanting things, is just . . . painful."

Mom seemed to still, her face scrunched in thought, her hands wringing the steering wheel.

"Charlie, you think you get to choose whether you love or not," Mom said. "You either close yourself off to love or you don't. Those are the only options. There is so much unspent love inside you. It still exists. You just use so much energy trying not to feel it. But where does it go?"

"I just think it's easier to not deal with emotions at all," I replied flatly.

Mom paused again. The radio was set to a low volume and it was the only noise in the car.

She maneuvered into the carpool lane, which was moving marginally faster than the other six lanes of the freeway. She was always cool under pressure. Driving in LA could turn anyone into a maniac, yet she remained calm. I had seen Mom fall apart many times before, but it was less of a rage and more of a withdrawal from life. I had always watched those moments and thought—this was what happened when you opened yourself up, you end up flat out on the bed, comatose and disengaged. God, I had hated seeing her cry.

Mom took in a deep inhale, and when she spoke, her voice was shaky. It made me sit up straighter. "It's easier to give up," she said. "Live behind walls and be guarded. I think about giving up a lot. Of course I do. But I just have this stubborn belief that life is meant to be *lived*. We're not meant to be perfect or even happy all the time. The reason joy can feel so incredible is because we know the absence of it. Everything exists in contrast. If I stop being open to pain, I stop being open to all the other things I love about life. I hate being rejected. I wish my career had taken off already. But I refuse to not *try*. I refuse to close myself off to life. It's not because I'm stronger or anything. I just make a choice over and over to endure it."

I sat back in my seat like I'd had the breath knocked out of me. It was not the answer I had expected. She had been relentlessly positive when I was growing up. But this . . . this was wisdom. This was learned wisdom, and I had no idea how to respond to it.

There wasn't anything left to say. Mom knew what she had dropped in this car.

She turned up the radio. I knew the conversation was done. She knew it was, too. We'd begin again when we got to Manhattan Beach.

I pulled out my phone and texted Alex the first thing that popped into my mind. No overthinking or withdrawing.

> hi, so i can't wait for monday. can't wait to see you. just wanted you to know that. hope your day is going well, perry.

Surprisingly, the typing bubble appeared immediately.

> you can't see me, but i have the stupidest smile on my face. is it monday yet? maybe you should come to the restaurant after we close on sunday night. give it a good send off? i'll make you a late dinner.

Something fizzy erupted inside my body like glittery fireworks going off.

> now i'm the one smiling like an idiot. i'll be there.

He texted me back with a time and I locked my phone and put it in the cup holder.

"I'm seeing Alex tomorrow night," I said. "I guess we couldn't wait until Monday. He's cooking me dinner at the restaurant."

"That is so sexy," Benny said. "I am living vicariously."

"Don't worry," I said. "We will be getting into your love life at brunch. Be ready."

She laughed and sat back, but I knew she was pleased.

When I looked over at Mom, she had a peaceful smile on her face.

"Good," she said to me. "You have but one short wild ride on this earth, Charlotte. All I want is to see you give it all you've got."

I didn't immediately shut her down, and when "Alone" by Heart started playing, all three of us theatrically sang every single word at the top of our lungs as if we were a Heart tribute band performing at a sold-out club.

22

At brunch, I shined the flashlight from my phone right in Benny's eyes. "Your turn to be under investigation," I said. "Love life updates?"

We had just put our order in and were sipping on iced lattes with cinnamon dusted on top. We'd all wanted exactly the same thing—eggs Benedict, iced lattes, and an order of pancakes for the table. Life is nothing but one relentless change after another, but not this. Not Triple Quinn at brunch. We were eggs Benedict and pancake connoisseurs. We'd always been in search of the best of the best and in LA, that wasn't hard to find. We hunted for the best burger, best pizza, best plate of authentic pasta, best plate of modern pasta, best pancakes, best eggs Benedict, best ice cream. Our weekend plans had always been: eat.

No wonder enjoying food was the first thing I cut out seven years ago.

"The thing about me, Charlie," Benny began with a flourish. "I'm just not a commitment person, you know? I don't think there's just one person out there for me. Every time I think I'm in love, I turn around and find someone else I want to be in love with."

"The girl loves love," Mom added, shrugging.

"I like the bohemian, free life that Mom lives," Benny said. She was sipping on her paper straw with her head dipped to the table like a little kid. She looked young and beautiful and her golden eyes shone.

"Hey now, if I found someone worthy of my lifelong commitment," Mom said, "I'd go all in."

"I don't think I would," Benny said. "I like all the choices. I can't be tied down."

"Have you broken Juliana's heart, then?" Mom asked.

"Juliana?" I said. "Do tell."

"We were dating for a few months," Benny said, waving her hand in the air. "She wanted more. But then I met Emery. And if you met Emery, you'd see I couldn't resist. I'm very honest. I never make promises. I keep it casual. Don't worry. I'm not breaking hearts on *purpose*."

"You're young, Ben," I said. "Maybe one day you'll commit. Maybe one day you won't. I say do whatever feels right to you."

Mom and Benny exchanged a look.

"Do whatever feels right?" Benny asked. "Who are you? Have you come around to the Universe? It was running into Alex, wasn't it? Hey, if you ever want to go to a sound bath, just let me know."

"If you're on the Universe's side," Mom said, "I've got a tarot reader, astrologist, and a handful of psychics. Take your pick."

"Alright, slow down, you two," I said, smiling. "Me and the Universe are maybe, sort of, kinda establishing a truce. But this brunch isn't about me. Benny, tell me about work."

"I'm getting my name out there," she said. "I trust that my perfect clients will always show up. I post on Instagram all the time and have a decent following. Mostly, I'm just getting portrait work right now. I did some family photos and even a wedding a couple months ago. It's trickling in."

"What do you really want to do with your photography?" I asked.

"Biggest dream? I want to go on tour with a band or musician and photograph them on stage. But getting the contacts, an agency, all of that—it just hasn't come together."

"Yet," I said.

"YET? Is that . . . optimism I hear?" Benny cried. "Okay, Mom, we need to take Charlie to the emergency room. She's acting weird."

Mom laughed. "Let her be, Benny. Our Charlie has always done things her way and in her own time. Let's just see what she does from here."

Mom glanced at me and gave me an encouraging smile. She squeezed my leg under the table and the gesture said, *I'm trying.* Mom had never been hard on me, but she'd been dismissive in her own way—and even though I knew now she was attempting to encourage me, it had felt like criticism back then. Like I wasn't good enough. Like I wasn't the daughter she wanted. And maybe Benny was.

The three plates of eggs Benedict were dropped in front of each of us, along with a fat stack of pancakes in the middle of the table, a heaping scoop of butter, and a glass bottle of maple syrup.

All three of us dug into the food immediately, groaning at how delicious it was almost in sync. After we were about halfway through our food, Mom cleared her throat.

"I don't want to jinx it," she said. "So don't freak out or get too excited or even ask me any follow-up questions, but I'm bursting and need my two girls to know this. I repeat, no follow-up questions. We are going to just continue eating pancakes. Nobody's hopes get too high up. Got it?" She stopped and looked at us both until we nodded our assent.

"I've met someone special," she said, lifting her hand up to stop any inquiry. "I don't know where it's going yet, but it might be going somewhere. And I've got a screen test for the lead of a TV show. That's it. That's my news. Now, back to your pancakes."

Benny and I both raised our eyebrows at each other across the table.

"Please provide any updates to these two situations as you see fit," Benny said, face stoic and serious.

I gave Benny a little knowing grin. This was a display of vulnerability from Mom that hardly ever happened. She was afraid. Afraid to get her hopes too high and suffer another disappointment. I felt myself physically soften and put my arm around her.

"We're here for whatever happens," I said.

Benny looked at me like I had five heads.

"Mom, seriously, Charlie needs to see a doctor."

Mom just gave Benny that same little grin again and shook her head. "No, our Charlie is *exactly* where she needs to be."

23

Chairs were flipped on top of tables when I walked into the darkened interior of Wavy. There wasn't anyone milling about, no errant employee sweeping or wiping down tables. It was so quiet I could practically hear my heart beating inside my chest. I followed a stream of amber light from under a swinging door and when I arrived inside the kitchen, Alex's back was to me.

He was at a stove with just the light on above it, stirring a wooden spoon inside a tall stainless steel stockpot. It smelled like garlic, onions, and a touch of thyme. He was fully immersed in the task, the sleeves of his black shirt rolled up revealing muscular forearms, a white apron tied around his waist, his shoulders stooping just a little bit because of his height. I felt this tiny ridiculous smile creep up on my face. He was gorgeous. He always had been.

His hesitancy the night of that party popped into my mind. He'd leaned in several times, excused himself to get another drink, bit his lip, kept coming in only to lean back. And I was so uncertain myself that I wondered if it wasn't shyness keeping him from taking the leap, but if he was, in fact, trying to find a way to get out of the situation. For so long, I wondered if I'd imagined the whole thing, saw what I wanted to see. Now I knew that hadn't been true. He'd been waiting for his moment.

I had forgotten what it felt like to be drawn to someone, to want to reach under their shirt and glide across the skin of their back, roam your hands across their chest, anticipate their lips on yours. To want their arms around you so much that you could just sink into them with relief and heat mixed into one. To want to be touched by them so badly it aches like a thirst that cannot ever be quenched until you get the real thing over and over and over. To want to touch them back just as badly. To be starved and desperate for it.

I had never felt like that with Josh. Only Noah. And before Noah, it had been Alex.

"Hi," I said.

Alex whipped around, startled, wooden spoon in hand, but when he saw it was me, his expression softened into a lovesick type of smile that made me want to close my eyes and commit it to memory forever.

My heart practically drummed its own beat.

Shit.

If I didn't put boundaries on this whole thing immediately, I was going to end up hurt. He was leaving in a month. I was going back to my life in San Francisco eventually. This needed to be temporary.

"Hi," he said back, voice low. He deposited the spoon onto a dish next to the stove and came around the large metal prep area to where I was standing.

Lifting up the basket in my hand, I declared, "I made fresh bread." I'd spent the whole day working on it. Benny had sat on a stool in the corner being no help at all, but she kept me company and played lots of music and sang off-key the entire time.

Alex peeked under the towel. "You made fresh bread?" he asked, those green eyes hooded under long dark eyelashes. "Since when do you make bread?"

"It's been years," I told him. "But I've picked it back up."

"Because of this whole say-yes-to-life thing?"

"Yep."

"You know," he said, "my imagination has been running wild about that."

"About my saying yes?"

"To anything? Yeah. I have a lot of ideas."

"I'm sure," I said, and felt my cheeks heat.

I placed the basket on the counter and tried to step back from the intensity, but the moment my hands were free, Alex spread his arms and said, "It's so good to see you," and I stepped forward, feeling him envelop me, my wrists grasped at his waist. He smelled like a collection of spices and good body wash and the tiniest hint of something entirely Alex that could not be identified.

"I hear you smelling me, Quinn," he murmured into my ear. Goose bumps popped up onto my arms.

"Caught me, Perry," I whispered.

"What's the verdict? Good smell?"

"The best."

"Hmmm," he said, and I could feel the vibration of his throat. I never wanted the hug to end. His voice dropped to a whisper right into the most sensitive part of my ear, beard scratching lusciously against the side of my face. "You smell sweet, like summer fruit."

It took every bit of my willpower to wrest myself free of him and put a bit of space between us, but in my mind I had thrown him onto the prep table, climbed on top, and done delicious things to him until whatever he was cooking on the stove burned to a crisp. When he looked at me, it was like he'd read my mind and was, maybe, picturing the very same thing.

I cleared my throat.

The problem with unrequited teenage feelings is that when they become requited, suddenly all that small talk and awkwardness of first dates melts away. We already knew each other.

That familiar intimacy wasn't building—it was *built*. And that made me sweat and shiver at exactly the same time.

"So," I asked, strolling over to the pot on the stove, attempting to get out from his orbit. "What are you making?"

"This has been simmering since lunch," he replied, following behind. "It's my version of French onion soup. Wait." He turned to me, alarmed. "Do you like onions? Oh, God, I should have asked. This is extremely onion-heavy, so if you don't like onions, I'll need to regroup."

"Don't worry," I said, chuckling, stilling him with a hand on his bicep. He glanced over at the touch like it surprised him. "I'm not very picky. And I love French onion soup. As long as it has cheese bubbling on the top. And like, an insane amount of cheese. So much cheese I get a stomachache. When you think you've got enough cheese, add more."

He laughed. "That is the only acceptable level of cheese."

"Thank you."

"Actually, I was going to use some bread from our supplier for on top of the soup, but what flavor is yours?"

I leaned across the prep counter and slid my basket to where we were standing.

"It's thyme, rosemary, apple, and Gruyère," I said. "Here, taste."

I ripped off two pieces from the loaf. It was a perfect crunchy outer layer with a soft, springy interior.

Alex took a bite and moaned a little, which shot straight through to my skin like a thousand tiny bubbles bursting at once.

"I'm not even saying this because I have the biggest crush on you ever," he said. "But this is honestly the best bread I've ever had."

"I thought the crush was past tense," I joked. "Teenage you and all that."

"Present tense," he said, sliding toward me until we were almost touching hips. "*Very* present tense."

I shook my head to try to gather myself. "The bread's that good?" I asked, changing the subject.

"You have a gift," he said. "Perfect seasoning. The saltiness brings out the sweetness of the apple. Honeycrisp?"

"Honeycrisp, yes," I said. "But one Granny Smith, as well. Just to give it a bite."

"Inventive," he praised. "Are you doing this for a living? Are you a baker? I need to stop flirting with you so we can talk and catch up properly."

"I definitely want to catch up," I said. "But let's not take flirting off the table, either."

He gave me a wide smile, and the sage of his eyes nearly twinkled in the golden light above the stove. "You're fun."

I guffawed. "Only very recently."

"Well, I'll tell you what, I like this Say Yes to Anything Charlie. I'm very happy she's here."

"I'm very happy to be here."

"Okay," he said decisively with a firm nod of his head. He pointed to the other side of the kitchen. "You go sit over there on the stool so I can put these soups into a ramekin and load them up with enough cheese to make you sick. Then, we talk. I want to hear how you've been, but you keep drifting closer and closer to me, and I can't stop thinking about kissing you. We have some unfinished business, you know."

"Was I drifting?" I asked, innocently, because I hadn't even noticed I was suddenly right next to him again.

"I'm not complaining," he said. "I just can't focus."

I felt this fluttery tingle move its way from my cheeks to below my belly button. Oh, he'd *grown up*. He'd become a lot more sure of himself.

"Okay," I said, and, just to tease him a little, I grasped his bicep and trailed my hand ever so softly down to his forearm, which elicited a very sexy sharp inhale from him.

"Now, that's just mean," he whispered, breathy and deep.

"Alex, we're going to talk," I said. "But you know where this leads. Unfinished business needs to be attended to."

"Is this part of your month of yes? Seducing me?"

"It wasn't initially, but now it is."

"I'm very glad we ran into each other," he said, smiling almost bashfully.

"Me, too," I agreed and then I swished off toward the waiting stool on the other side of the kitchen. I was wearing black sweats and a baggy sweatshirt, but the way I felt his eyes on me, I may as well have been wearing nothing at all.

24

"I want to hear Alex Perry's life story from the moment you left LA until now," I said, trying to wrestle with a long string of gooey cheese dangling from my soup spoon. "This is beyond delicious, by the way. I'm going to say yes to seconds."

We were sitting across from each other at one of the dining room tables with a soft dim light illuminating the heaping bowls of soup and extra bread between us.

"It's especially good thanks to your bread," he said. "And after I tell you my life story, I need yours, too."

"Okay," I said. I would leave out details, but I'd give him the broad strokes.

"First," Alex declared, lifting his pointer finger. "I need to make us Shirley Temples before we get into it."

"How whimsical," I said, and he stood up and went to the compact bar area, where I heard the rush of soda from the tap and then the plop of cherries into liquid. He handed me the pink concoction and it tasted like pretending to be a grown-up when you were a kid.

"I don't drink, by the way," he said. "It's not a whole thing. I just drank too much to escape when I was younger and so now I don't. I'm skipping ahead, but yeah. Cheers!" He lifted his pint glass toward mine and we clinked. "I don't care if you drink, by the way. If you want some wine . . ."

"I'm good with this," I said. "I'm not really drinking right now, either. Impromptu. I think I need to have a clear head for a bit." I took another sip; it was a perfect blend of grenadine and something else. Something not quite Sprite. "Ginger ale?" I asked, lips still wrapped around the straw. He caught my mouth in his eyes and seemed to forget I'd asked him a question. "Alex? Ginger ale?"

He shook his head and cleared his throat. "Yes, sorry. It's ginger ale and soda water. An upscale spin on the classic."

"I love it," I said, and he smiled like he was so pleased he could please me. "Now, tell me everything." I cupped my face in my hands with my elbows resting on the table, waiting.

"Well," he began. "As you know, my mom passed. It was devastating. That word hardly covers the scope of what it was. My dad was catatonic. My grandparents on his side demanded we move back to Michigan and into their house so they could help. Amber and I tried to fight it, but Dad was incapable of taking care of himself, let alone us. At the time, I was heartbroken, missing my mom and angry with my dad, but looking back, it's like, wow, what a love, you know? To grieve someone that much is a gift.

"My grandmother was a phenomenal cook. Amber went through her rebellious phase, which was probably going to happen whether Mom died or not, but it was worse because of it. She's good now, but it was tough for a while. I went through my own turbulent phase, which explains the Shirley Temple. I started cooking with my grandmother when I stopped drinking. She taught me everything she knew. I had a knack for it. She told me I had a good nose and palate. It gave me purpose."

"Oh, Alex," I said. I reached across the table and grabbed his hand, left it there, feeling the velvety warmth of his touch. "I'm so sorry. I never got to say that about your mom. But I'm so sorry."

"Thank you," he said. He squeezed my hand, and entwined our fingers, keeping me there.

"You don't have to keep going if it's too hard to talk about."

"No, it's okay. It was a long time ago."

"Okay."

"I floated around for a while," he said. "Dad checked out for five years or so and then, finally, checked back in but not all the way. Mom's death changed him forever. I don't blame him. Amber, me, him, we were all drifting balloons without Mom. She was our anchor. We had to completely figure out how to be a new kind of family without her. When I finally got it together, I went to culinary school. Amber became a doctor, of all things." He chuckled.

"She's living in Portland now. Dad started working as a contractor back in Michigan, and that's what he's still doing. My grandfather even helps him, which is cool. I talk to my grandmother almost every other day. She's my favorite person." He stopped for a moment, and his eyes were glassy. "I'm glad Dad has purpose now, because it all fell apart after Mom. Not just because we lost her, but because their production company was running at a deficit. I thought they were super successful, but everything was loaned out and stretched thin. He had to declare bankruptcy. It was a mess for a long time. The messes just kept coming."

"Damn," I said. "That must have been so hard to deal with."

"I know this sounds like a sob story," he said. "But we've all turned out okay now."

"It's not a sob story," I said, caressing my thumb across his hand. "It's your past and I wanted to hear it."

"I don't usually talk about it. Definitely not on a first date." He laughed a little uncomfortably. "But we already know each other. I feel like we can skip the small talk."

"We can," I told him.

He smiled and continued. "So then, after culinary school, I got recruited to work for a big chef in New York prepping fine dining dishes. I moved up quickly because I was older than most of the kids in culinary school and more focused. I knew what I wanted to do and I just put my head down until I landed somewhere solid. I learned a lot. The chef I worked for is now a judge on Food Network competitions. She was an amazing mentor. It took a few more years of working to finally get this executive chef position. I moved here from New York, but it was only for a year. The owner of Wavy wanted to revamp the menu and so I did that, implemented the recipes, and now have a job in Chicago at a new place opening up. It is what it is."

"You don't sound that excited about this new job?"

He gave me a defeated type of smile and then shrugged. "I've always wanted my own place, to do things my own way, cook my food the way I want to cook it."

"Why can't you?"

"Well, I was going to," he said, fingers through his hair, head bowed. "It was ready. Investors were in. Every dollar I'd saved for years was put into it. My grandparents even took out a second mortgage to help me. Our opening date? April 6, 2020."

"Oh, shit."

"Yeah," he said. "Timing wasn't on my side that's for damn sure."

"It fell through?"

"More like, it went up in flames," he said, laughing. "If I don't laugh about it, I'll cry. It was a spectacular comedy of errors. All my investors pulled out and I had to pay the lease until they finally let me out of it in April 2021. My savings were wiped out and I lost the money my grandparents loaned me. I am paying them back, but it has been a very slow repayment. And I couldn't get a new job, because no restaurants were hiring. It was . . . bleak."

"I'm genuinely very sorry to hear that," I said. My heart felt like it was being squeezed in my chest. Now that I looked more closely and had more context, he seemed like he needed a win, badly. I moved my chair so I was sitting right next to him and I laced my fingers through the waves of his dark hair. He closed his eyes and leaned into it, gave me a sound of pleasure that prompted me to continue. Our faces were close now. When he opened his eyes, I could see the watery emotion swimming in them.

"Has life been kinder to you since our almost-kiss?" he asked, voice low, tender. I could smell the grenadine on his breath and wondered if he'd taste like cherries.

"Afraid not," I told him. "I'm in LA because I lost my job, my boyfriend broke up with me, and I'll spare you the gory details, but I had my head stuck in a toilet on my thirtieth birthday, and not for a fun reason."

Alex's eyebrows pinched together. "I am deeply sorry about two out of three of those things." He grinned. "Is it bad to say I'm happy to hear you're single?"

That made me smile.

I shook my head. "Not to me."

The look he gave me made me feel almost dizzy.

"Maybe we both need this whole say-yes-to-life thing," he murmured.

"You're welcome to join me."

"Could I?"

He leaned in even closer, and his eyes dropped to my lips. I took in shallow breaths, anticipating all that was about to happen, and whether kissing Alex Perry could live up to the fantasies I'd harbored for so many years of teenage longing.

"With one rule," I whispered.

"Rule?" he asked playfully.

"Alex, I can only get involved if this is over when you go

to Chicago. I need to know when and how this ends. We both have lives to get to. Let's not get swept away."

"Why is that your rule?"

I couldn't explain it to him. Not here. Not now. Not ever.

"It just is," I told him.

"This is poetic. I'm usually the one not making any promises. I'm usually the one keeping it casual."

"Why?" I asked.

"Can't stand the idea of losing any more than I've already lost."

His words hit me like a punch.

"Yeah," I revealed. "I get that."

"So, if I agree. Are you mine for the month?"

I closed my eyes, savoring his words, feeling like I was dropping off the edge of a cliff.

"Yes," I told him, so low I could hardly hear myself say it.

"So, the rules are: this ends when I leave for Chicago, but until then . . ."

"Yes."

"Yes, what?"

"To all of it."

It was reckless of me, even with the rule in place, but how much damage could really happen if I knew exactly when this would be over? It was a fail-safe, the escape hatch I never had before.

"Have I mentioned I'm really glad I ran into you?" he said, smiling.

He stroked down the length of my nose with the tip of his finger, finding my lips, and brushing across them in featherlight touches with the pad of his finger.

"Not as glad as I am," I said, when I could talk again.

"Debatable."

"So, are you in?"

"Are you serious, Charlie?" he asked. "You know I'm in.

If you actually think I can resist you, you haven't been paying attention. If all I get is what's left of this month, I'm taking it."

I smiled and he poked his fingertip into the curve of my right dimple.

"You're so beautiful," he said.

"You are, too," I replied and I cupped my palm across his cheek. He closed his eyes and slanted into it.

Suddenly, I was hit by a force of inspiration that I never would have listened to had I not been in this month-of-yes situation.

"I have a question," I asked, breathy. His eyes were hooded. I knew he was thinking about kissing me, the same way I was thinking about kissing him. But I wanted to luxuriate in this time before—the delicious anticipation. I'd waited over a decade to kiss Alex Perry. No way was I going to rush it.

"Okay," he said, waiting.

I gave him a grin. "Will you go to Disneyland with me this week?"

He let out a loud laugh that seemed to echo in the converted house.

"I haven't been to Disneyland since I was a kid," he said.

"Me, either," I replied. "But I mean, doesn't it sound delightful and silly and exactly the kind of thing you'd do during a month of yes?"

"It does," he said. "I'm in."

"Benny is not going to let me go without her."

"Invite her," he said. "Your mom, too. The more the merrier. We'll ride Space Mountain until we puke up churros."

I laughed.

"Let's go get seconds in the kitchen," he said. "And now I want to hear Charlie Quinn's life story. You thought I'd forgotten. But I haven't."

"Alright," I said. "But it's not that interesting. I've been a boring workaholic for like the past seven years."

"What have *you* been running from?" he teased, almost like the question was rhetorical.

I didn't answer that, only stood up and began clearing the table. It was late. Much later than I ever stayed up. But I wasn't tired.

No part of me wanted to leave or for this night to end.

25

We'd eaten the entire pot of soup, the whole loaf of bread I'd made, nibbles of various food left over from dinner service earlier, and a butterscotch pudding so perfect I licked the bowl and demanded another helping. The kitchen was dim and sparkling clean now. We were sitting on stools and only a few inches apart. I had my leg between his legs, my foot resting on the bar of his stool.

"Food is so good," I declared, lifting my fork to make the point. "I had forgotten how good food was."

"That's a weird thing to say, Quinn," he said, laughing. His knee brushed mine, causing a zing to electrify its way through my body. "Don't you eat every day? Or are you one of those people who can subsist off air alone?"

"I'm ashamed to admit this to an actual chef, but I've been eating practically the same thing every single day for like seven years."

"Why?" he demanded, lifting his hands up to the sky. "Why would you do that to yourself, Quinn?" His eyebrow cocked. When his hands came back down, one of them landed on my thigh and I held my breath, waiting to see if he'd move it higher.

"I'm realizing I haven't enjoyed my life in a long time," I told him. "I really tuned out. Lived the same day over and over, maybe because it was just safer that way." For some reason, I felt like I could spill my secrets to Alex, say the things I couldn't yet admit to Benny or my mom. In a month, Alex and I would be on separate sides of the country. I wouldn't need to live with the things I revealed to him.

"Survival mode," Alex said. "I know it well. I sometimes still have my moments. When my restaurant fell through, I completely disassociated from life. I even wanted the owners of Wavy to extend me a month so I wouldn't have to be without a job before I start in Chicago." He pointed to his temple. "My mind is not always a good place for me to be."

"Well, aren't we a pair," I said, and even though we were exchanging our pain, all I felt was relief. Sometimes Benny's relentless positivity grated on me. The same way Mom's used to as well. Like nothing ever gets to them. Like I'm the weird one for being deeply affected by life and not able to maintain this steadfast belief that everything works out in the end.

"They told me to take a vacation," he said. "I know I'm weird, but I hate having time off."

I laughed.

"You're not weird, at least that's not weird to me. I hate time off, too. That's what my boss said when I was laid off. Go travel. Enjoy yourself. Enjoy myself? No thanks."

"It's strange, though," he said, leaning even closer. "I don't hate the idea of taking time off and spending it with you. I don't know why. It doesn't make me panicked. I haven't spent a month not working since I started culinary school."

"I haven't taken even a weekend off since I graduated college."

"You must love your work."

I laughed sharply. "No," I said. "I could not have cared less about the actual work I did. It was a job. It paid very well. It kept my mind busy. I definitely didn't love it the way you seem to love cooking."

"What do you love, then?" he asked, low, gaze caught on mine while his thumb brushed across my thigh.

I swallowed hard. He leaned in closer, his eyes intent on mine.

"I don't know," I started, words rough.

His gaze dipped down to my lips. "Not falling for you is going to take all my willpower." He whispered it, like maybe he was uncertain about whether he should say it. When he looked back up at me, his face was too open, too vulnerable.

"I don't do that anymore," I said back forcefully.

"Do what?"

"Fall in love."

"How do you stop yourself?"

I didn't know how to answer that. My heart was racing.

"I don't get involved," I said. "You don't want anything more than that from me. Trust me."

"Why not?"

"I'm not capable of it."

"Of love?"

"Of the kind of love you deserve, Alex."

I wrenched my eyes from his and removed my leg from between him, scooted back the stool so quickly the screeching sound echoed in the kitchen.

"Where are you going?" he asked.

"I need to know," I said urgently. "I need to know that this ends in a month. I don't want to talk about love or anything beyond that. Or this has to stop now. I'll leave and we can go on with our lives."

"What happened, Charlie?" he asked. He stood up, closed the gap between us that I'd created. He brushed a lock of hair from my face and put it so gently behind my ear I almost whimpered. "Who hurt you?"

"Nothing," I lied. "Nobody. If you can't handle this rule, I get it." I stood up to leave. I didn't want to, but I *had* to. There was no way I could have my heart on the line. Especially not after I promised myself I would never lose control again. "You don't have to go along with this. I know it's ridiculous." I began to walk away, but he followed, grabbed me tenderly by the wrist, pulled me in so we were facing each other.

"A month," he said resolutely. "Okay."

"Alex," I whispered. "Only if you're sure. I don't want to force you into anything. I don't want to hurt you."

"You think I can let you leave now?" He shook his head like I was a riddle he couldn't solve. "I don't totally understand this rule, but I respect it."

"Thank you."

My eyes landed on his lips. He was so close to me. I could see each individual bristle of hair on his beard, smell that peppery scent of his, feel heat emanating from him, hear his labored breathing.

"Are you going to kiss me now, Perry?" I asked boldly.

He stepped closer, swept his hand under my hair, and caressed the side of my neck. "Do you want me to?"

"Yes, Chef."

His eyes rolled to the back of his head. "Oh, shit," he muttered, "I like you saying *that* a little too much."

I couldn't help giving him a daring, wicked look.

He brushed the hair off my neck, cupped his hands on my face, stroked his thumb across the plane of my cheek, and practically gazed through to my soul.

"Give me a second," he said roughly. "I've only been waiting a decade to do this properly."

"Hope you haven't built it up too much."

"Not a chance."

He swiveled me and backed me up against a wall that was a few feet away, his hands still seemingly everywhere at once. He placed a deliciously soft kiss at the space below my ear and dragged his lips down my neck.

"I dreamed about what you'd taste like," he whispered.

I grabbed his beard and turned his face, kissed the same space he'd kissed on my neck, and licked so, so softly. His sharp intake of breath emboldened me. "I did, too," I whispered back, breathing into his ear and pulling his body so close to mine there wasn't any space between us.

His hands found their way under my sweatshirt, so his fingertips were trailing across the skin at the low of my back. It was so featherlight and sensitive that I arched and when he flattened me across the wall again, one of his hands was under the hair at my neck and the other was steadying on the bare skin of my hip.

"Come here," he growled and pulled me by the wrist until I was sitting on top of the prep area, my legs wrapped around him as he stood between me.

He guided me toward his mouth and our lips met tenderly at first, like the beginning of an exploration. It was warm velvet, and it felt like my whole body came alive at the contact. I had spent so much time not being kissed like this that I found myself hungry for it, just like the taste of food had ignited the same insatiable nature within me. Shifting my head, I slotted myself onto his mouth, captured his tongue against mine, and moaned.

My hold on Alex tightened and I heard him make a sound that could only be described as a cry. His hands were all over my body, under my sweatshirt, finding purchase wherever they could, and when I finally got my hands under his shirt and felt across his stomach, then onto his chest, he let out a groan that made me feel powerful in a way I'd never felt before.

He stopped kissing me and tilted my head so he could take in my neck with his lips and I softly groaned. My mind went entirely blank. I wanted him so badly there was no turning back. Space and time no longer existed—it was only this moment, only Alex's lips on my collarbone, only his hands curved around my breast.

I let my torso fall to the table, lifted my sweatshirt to reveal I wasn't wearing a bra, and waited for him to touch me, entranced by the look on his face, wanting to never ever forget it, his eyes glassy, his arousal so readily apparent. His hand palmed the middle space between my chest and roved down my stomach, his fingers dancing along the waistband of my sweats.

As I watched him, he was gorgeous and flushed, consumed with the task at hand, the task of touching me, kissing me, devouring me. A chef's attention to detail, to savoring, to meticulously taking his time.

He tore his hands away from my body and let out a frustrated sound.

"I can't do *that* here," he said, pointing to the core of me. "I can't believe I'm saying this, but we have to stop. I can't be as methodical with you if you're splayed out on a metal table. I need to take my time, explore every inch. What I've imagined doing to you cannot be rushed, Quinn."

This *man*. My eyes rolled to the back of my head. My skin was buzzing, adrenaline coursing through me. I was spread open, ready for him, sweatshirt up to my neck, trying to form sentences.

"You look so fucking sexy right now," he said, voice raspy. His hands grasped my thighs, thumbs in a precarious position for someone that couldn't have sex with me right now.

I had gone so long not caring about sex that it was wild to me that I suddenly felt like if I didn't have Alex soon, I was going to be in physical anguish. The hunger was ravenous, watching him above me, feeling his strong hands on my thighs, wishing we were in some hotel room with nowhere to go for three days straight.

I decided to not keep the hotel idea to myself and said, "What about a hotel, three days, room service, and nowhere to go? Thoughts?" It was exactly the kind of thing I would never suggest. A Charlize move, for sure.

"Yes," he replied quickly. "I know the chef over at this incredible hotel in Montecito that's right on the beach. I bet I could get us a room. He owes me a favor."

"I'll pack very little," I teased.

"I love this whole month-of-yes situation," he said, smiling.

"Me, too," I agreed.

Shooting my arms out, I grabbed his hands and he lifted me from the table so I could sit up. He patted my hair down and kissed me on the cheek, then the lips, then drew me into a long hug that I didn't want to end. When he pulled away, he looked into my eyes, shook his head like he couldn't resist, and captured my mouth on his again, his tongue softly grazing across mine, a kiss so intense I felt all the exquisite pressure building inside me, desperate for release.

My cheeks were flushed and my lips were swollen by the time we untangled again.

"Fuck," Alex whispered into my ear, and I knew we were both experiencing the same kind of luscious torture. "I want to take you back to my place right this minute, Quinn, and kiss every single inch of your skin until you couldn't take it any longer."

My eyes rolled to the back of my head, and I crumpled just the slightest bit.

His words were so heated I nearly lost myself to them—and I had a sudden thought that falling for Alex Perry would be way too easy, and I remembered what it had been like with Noah, how I was guarded one minute and the next I was desperate with need for him. It was startling how quickly love could scale even the tallest walls. Never could I allow myself to be so vulnerable and defenseless like that again. Never.

Still, part of me wanted to say yes, to let this heady moment continue for hours on end, but the smarter, more practical part of me disentangled us, knowing I needed to go home and cool down. If he took me back to his place right now, I may not ever leave. This was escalating at a frightening pace.

I could already feel walls I spent years constructing breaking down, bricks flying off without my consent. It was time to go back to Quinn Canyon and rebuild, make a fortress before I saw him again.

My hands involuntarily pushed on his chest to give me space.

"We have time," I said to him, even though, really, we didn't.

He still didn't move, unfazed by my rejection, his fingers dancing along the back of my neck.

"By the way, it lived up," I said. "Actually, it was better."

"What was?"

"The kiss," I told him. "I spent so much time imagining it, and I was worried it wouldn't live up to my fantasies. But it did. You did. You do."

He gave me a wide grin and said, "So far, you're better than the fantasy."

Then, he pulled me close to him, kissed me longer, harder, deeper than before, until I hardly knew where I was, until my head was swimming. It took every ounce of willpower available to me to walk away from him.

It was past four in the morning when I finally drove back to Quinn Canyon and tucked myself into bed, energy reverberating off my body, trying to fall asleep, but wound up and turned on so much that it took me another two hours until I could finally relax.

Even then, my dreams were vivid, explicit, wild.

Hunger, desire, pleasure were funny things—you could suppress them for only so long until they came back with a vengeance.

26

When I woke up the next morning, it wasn't morning anymore. Fuzzy tree-shaded light was streaming in through the gauzy curtains. I was used to waking up before the sunrise and downing coffee to keep me awake, but I found that I was so well rested and boneless that I could stay in bed all day.

When I grabbed my phone I saw it was 12:32 in the afternoon and I had texts from Mom, Benny, Alex, and Georgia, my headhunter.

> ARE YOU STILL SLEEPING? Wow. Good for you, Charlie baby!

> WAKE UP AND COME PLAY!!!!

> can't stop thinking about you. it's a problem.

> Call me. Got you an interview!

In a group text, I texted Mom and Benny that I was coming down soon, then replied to Alex and said I was having the same exact problem. After that, I called Georgia. She answered quickly and got right to it without any pleasantries.

"Hi, Charlie, so there's a corporate consulting firm based in Cupertino that is looking for someone to analyze their clients' HR and marketing policies and give them risk assessment. I told them about your experience and how diligent and hardworking you are. They want to do an interview in person at their offices as soon as possible. Tomorrow would be ideal. They need the role filled immediately and this one is yours for the taking. You would get a significant salary bump, too. This is a really stable position with lots of room for upward growth."

"Oh, wow," I said. It was the type of job that, even just a week ago, I would have taken, no questions asked. Stable, predictable work and a new ladder to climb.

So, when I had the urge to scream *NO!!* my pulse immediately quickened at the impulse.

The idea of even driving back to San Francisco and putting on my tight pencil skirts and itchy blazers made me feel lightheaded with resistance. Interviewing with a bunch of people in cookie-cutter suits, trying to impress upon them my unbeatable work ethic, it all felt so unappealing.

It was a shocking and sudden disgust.

A long drawn-out pause hung between Georgia and me as I waited for my logic to make the right decision. Even my brain was saying, *No, no, no,* while thundering white noise and static.

"When can you do an interview?" Georgia asked into the silence with a touch of irritation. "I want to get back to them as soon as possible."

Still more silence stretched as I willed myself to say I'll leave immediately, get back on track, get back to my life. But I couldn't. Not even *forcing* those words out was possible, never mind actually packing and getting in my car to make the drive.

I don't want to live the same day over and over and call it a life.

Josh's words reverberated in my mind, bounced off far-flung corners, echoing until I couldn't do anything but really hear them for the first time since he spoke them.

"Charlie?" Georgia asked into the long, now exceedingly awkward pause. "Did I lose you?"

"No," I stammered, clearing my throat. "I'm here." My chest expanded with air and I steadied myself to speak. "I'm in Los Angeles visiting my family right now." Another pause, not quite believing the words coming out of my mouth. "I'm so sorry, but I don't think this position will work for me. Can you hold off on the search? I can let you know if I want to start looking again. I think I'm going to take some time off actually."

A tense beat passed, then Georgia said, "Really?" The judgment was unmistakable, like she was raising an eyebrow at me. "I wouldn't advise anyone right now to turn a good job down."

A deep anxiety pulsed through me, but something else did as well.

Exhilaration.

"I know," I said to Georgia. "I appreciate that. But I need to see something through here. I'll let you know when I want to start looking again."

"This is the *one* interview I managed to get for you, Charlie. Do you understand that? You are accomplished and if this were pre-pandemic, I would have had several interviews lined up for you already. Are you sure about this?"

"It'll all work out," I heard myself say.

She made a sound that could have been a scoff. It surprised me. "Well, I hope so, for your sake," she said, wryly. "Let me know when you want to start looking again and make sure you're serious about it. I really sold you to this company and they were excited about you."

"I apologize, Georgia. My circumstances changed."

"You get out of the rat race for too long you don't want to jump back in," she warned. "The best thing is to keep working. But let me know. I'll be here when you're serious again."

She hung up before I said anything else, and I was a bit taken aback from her forceful tone. Had she always been this cutthroat? It grated on me, that sense of desperate grasping, like if you stopped working even for a month, you'd lose *everything*. Mom would call that a "scarcity mindset." I saw it for what it was—fear.

No wonder hardly anyone I knew took vacations, even when their company offered unlimited time off. No wonder everyone worked until they were sick to their very bones. It was a badge of honor to never take a day off. A badge of honor to reply to emails at midnight, and to start answering them again at four or five in the morning. It was all completely normal, expected, seemingly the only way to get ahead these days. I lived to work for so long I didn't even know any other way of operating. But now, strangely, that life felt like it belonged to an entirely different person.

I heard a door open and close downstairs, muffled voices, and all I wanted to do was get dressed and see what Mom and Benny were up to. To tell them about Disneyland, to text Alex, make bread, eat pizza, see the beach again, and actually live in the day I was in.

I had no idea what these desires meant for my future.

But for the first time, I wasn't thinking of the future at all.

27

"Question," I said, about to take a bite out of a chopped salad so good I was trying to parse out the ingredients in the dressing in my head. "How do you feel about going to Disneyland with Alex and me this week?"

Mom, Benny, and I were sitting at a long family-style table at a well-known café in Studio City, all three of us eating the chopped salad they were known for. There were also three desserts in front of us. We'd ordered carrot cake, an apricot bar, and a brownie, declaring that we'd split them. It was so typical Triple Quinn that I felt nostalgic about it. Ordering the exact same meal and then wanting three different desserts. Everything had to be the same, or equal.

"Disneyland?" Benny gasped. "Your idea or his?"

"Mine," I said, smiling.

"Mom, seriously, what happened to Charlie? She's borderline whimsical!"

"Let her be, Benny," Mom said, lightly chastising. "We knew she'd come around eventually."

That irked me. I was getting pretty tired of them both acting like they had it all together and I was the only messed up one.

"Can you not say stuff like that, Mom?" I asked. "It's very 'I told you so' and condescending."

"Charlie," Benny warned.

"No, Benny, let me say this," I told her calmly. "I know I can change some things about myself. I get it. But you don't have to act like you've been sitting around talking about and pitying me. It doesn't feel good, actually. I could talk about both of your flaws, too. This is how it felt growing up with you two, like I was the odd one out. I don't like it. There are a lot of great things about me, too, that if given the chance, I wouldn't change."

It was as though I were realizing this as I said it and it felt good to express myself, to tell them both exactly how I felt without getting worked up or running away from the conversation.

Benny looked like she was about to launch into something, but Mom cut in first.

"Charlie, you're right," Mom said. "You're absolutely right. I am so proud of you. Have I told you that lately? You went to an incredible college, paid your way, and graduated with honors. You can be absolutely whoever you want to be and it wouldn't change how much I love you. Do I want to see you smile? Laugh? Experience some joy alongside all those accomplishments? Of course I do. I love seeing you happy, Charlie. But there's nothing wrong with you. Ever. You got that? We love you exactly how you are." Mom wiped away a tear and smiled hesitantly.

"I'm sorry, Charlie," Benny said, head and voice low. "I don't mean anything by it. I'm just having fun. I miss you, you know? You were my whole world growing up. You were magic. You were the best big sister ever. All my friends were jealous of Triple Quinn. And then you went to college and when you came back . . ."

"You didn't really come back," Mom said gently. "Our Charlie left for college and never came back. Of course, we sit around and talk about you. We love you so much it hurts."

Mom was right, but I couldn't tell her that. I couldn't even fully identify why I didn't want to tell her about Noah, why I couldn't discuss it with Benny, or anyone. Maybe I felt ashamed for how deeply and quickly I fell. Embarrassed. And how could I explain spending years *not* telling her, about him, about what happened, about everything? She loved me; I felt that. I knew she did.

Maybe there was a part of me that understood once you open that box, there's no putting it back.

There was so much wrapped up in Noah and that time of my life that to unravel it now . . . Well, I felt like I'd entirely unravel myself if I went there.

"Thank you for understanding," I said, because there was so much to give in the way of an explanation, but all I could do was withhold it from her. There was no telling how she'd react or what she'd say.

"*Soooooo*, anyway," Benny cooed. "Disneyland? Yeah, I'm in. I haven't been since we were kids and I threw up and cried on Big Thunder Mountain Railroad."

"I remember that," Mom said. "Petra and I were exhausted."

"Benny got scared on the Jungle Cruise, too," I said, chuckling. "She thought the crocodile was real."

"The only kid that hated Disneyland," Mom said. "I never took you girls again because of it."

"Excuse me," Benny said, indignant. "I was six years old, and that crocodile violently *chomped* at me. How was I to know that it was animatronic?"

"You screamed so loud the other kids started crying, too," I said, laughing.

"Seriously traumatic event for all involved," Mom said, laughing now, too.

"What can I say?" Benny replied, in a flourish. "I was born to be the drama."

Mom and I caught eyes and rolled them together, then laughed again.

We resumed eating and then finished our chopped salads at the same time, setting them aside. Mom started divvying up the desserts, so eventually all of us had a plate with the same combination of threes.

"Mom, do you want to come?" I asked her.

She looked at me and blinked, like maybe she hadn't expected the invitation to include her. It made my chest constrict.

"You don't mind?" she asked. "Maybe you kids want to enjoy it alone."

"It would be really fun if you came," I said. "Hopefully Benny will be less of a scaredy-cat this time." I eyed Benny and she sent me an exaggerated angry face.

"I was six," she said, deadpan. "I think I can handle an animatronic crocodile now."

"Can you, Ben?" I quipped. "Can you?"

"I'll try to be brave," she said sarcastically.

"Come on, Mom," I said. "Invite Petra. We'll have a do-over."

"Okay," she said, looking pleased. "I'd love to come. Thank you for inviting me."

"Yay," Benny and I cried out at the same time.

I took a bite from the brownie and pointed to it, making an mmm-hmm sound.

"Damn, that's the best brownie I've ever had," I said.

"It is," Benny said. "But we need details about Alex. Immediately. We just skipped right over it."

"Yeah," Mom said, through a mouthful of carrot cake. "Spill."

I blushed so hard I had to cover my face with my hands. When I peered at them both across from me through my slotted fingers, they were smiling broadly, waiting.

"Oh, my God," Benny said. "You're smitten. You're swooning!"

"He's . . ." I started, not even knowing how to describe it. "He's better than the crush. He's . . ." I sighed like I was in a Jane Austen novel ". . . lovely."

"I'm not sure I've ever seen you smile quite like this before," Mom said.

"Is it something real?" Benny asked. "What will happen when you both leave LA?"

"It ends," I told her. "It's not real. We have a rule. It ends in a month. No strings."

"What?" Benny cried out, aghast. "Why?"

"Because I'm not falling in love," I said.

"Again, I ask, why?" Benny demanded.

"He's going to Chicago. I'm going back to San Francisco. I don't want any complications."

"That's very pragmatic of you," Mom said, but I could tell she was holding back. Mom wasn't one to *appreciate* pragmatism.

"I know you think I should just say fuck it and risk everything for him," I said to her.

"Actually," Mom replied, "I don't. Love is fickle and I think you need to be careful who you give your heart to. Not everybody needs to end up with someone. Men are . . . tricky. And relationships are hard. You can't just follow your heart when it comes to love. That's a great way to break and spend years piecing yourself back together."

My eyes went wide, and when I looked to Benny, her mouth was open in shock. It was perhaps the most unlikely thing that Jackie Quinn could say.

"Did something happen, Mom?" I asked.

"Of course," she said. "What hasn't happened with me and love? I'm alone, aren't I? I expected I'd find someone by this time. But no. I get close and then I get left. It would be better for me if I had some of that pragmatism. My hopeless romantic self has gotten burned so many times."

"Mom," I said. "I had no idea. Does this have to do with the man you told us about the other day?"

"Him," she said, shrugging. "And all the others."

She sounded like the kind of person I wanted her to be for years—cautious, realistic, practical—and yet hearing her sound so defeated made my stomach sink with dread.

"I'll be fine," she said, sitting up straighter. "Don't worry about me. I'm an actress. Sometimes I get dramatic. I pour all that pain into my auditions. But you just do what you think is best, Charlie. Don't give your heart away too easily. And I think this rule of yours is very smart. You have no idea if Alex and you would ever work out and given *my* track record, I'm guessing it probably won't."

Benny and I exchanged another wide-eyed look of disbelief.

"What happened, Mom?" I asked.

"He went back to his ex-wife," she said. "Always the bridesmaid, right?"

"You'll find—" Benny began, but Mom stopped her.

"Maybe I won't," she said. "And that's fine. The Universe works in mysterious ways. I'm being overemotional." She laughed dryly. "I know how much you hate that, Charlie. Let's change the subject, girls. Where to, next? Should we go to LACMA and see what new art they have? I need to look at some beautiful things."

"Okay," I said, wanting to say more, but so caught off guard I didn't even know what to do.

"Let's do it," Benny said, in a faux-enthusiastic voice. It was too high-pitched and forced. I could tell her world had just been rocked as well.

Even at Mom's lowest points when I was younger, she'd always believed that it was all going to work out for her, that eventually she'd get every last thing she wanted. I'd never in my life heard her question that or applaud being realistic or risk-averse. Even through tears, she'd maintained faith. It used to inspire me, before it started to infuriate me.

The idea that I had somehow rubbed off on her made me sick with nausea. Unexpectedly, I wanted my positive, upbeat mom back with such a vengeance that it shook me to my very core.

We finished our desserts, got in the car, and drove in relative silence to LACMA, where we looked at art and spoke in hushed whispers about all the beautiful pieces.

I tried to get her mind off her disappointment, because if my mom was anything like me—and it seemed like maybe she was, more than I ever thought—a distraction was exactly what she needed.

28

The first thing we did when we arrived on Main Street was buy some over-the-top Mickey ears. We all looked silly and cheesy and yet Alex, Benny, Mom, Petra, and I were smiling from Mickey ear to ear when we placed them on our heads and took a group picture.

"I request Indiana Jones first," I said to the four of them as we finally procured some coffee and started walking toward Sleeping Beauty's castle. "I did research." I lifted up my phone and had a rough itinerary written in the Notes app. "The top things we need to do are Indiana Jones, Space Mountain if it's not closed for maintenance, Jungle Cruise if little Benny can handle it."

"Rude," Benny said, shaking her head.

"Benny and Disneyland really did not mix," Petra said, chuckling. People kept stealing glances at her and it took me a minute to remember that she used to be a supermodel. An older woman surreptitiously took a picture of Petra, but she didn't notice. She practically floated through the park, impervious to all the heads turning in her direction.

It made me think about the last time we were here when she was at the very height of her fame and people stopped her constantly. I also remember my mom biting back tears, watching her best friend flourish while she was still auditioning for roles that went to other blond-haired starlets. I'd felt all of it—took on Mom's pain as my own, helped with Benny so she wouldn't be overwhelmed, tried to soothe her.

"We carried Benny out of the park and the only one of us that wasn't sobbing was Charlie," Mom said. "Charlie asked if she could stay without us. At Disneyland! Such a precocious eleven-year-old."

"I thought I'd just hop on the monorail and meet up with you guys later," I said, shrugging.

"You were fearless," Mom said.

Fearless? I didn't tell Mom or Petra that part of the reason I wanted to stay at the park alone was because I was overwhelmed by how much emotion I'd been picking up on between the two of them. Petra's annoyance at not being able to walk through Disneyland like a "normal person" and Mom's frustration that she was still a "normal person." Benny, feeling ignored and scared, and me feeling like I had to be her mom even though our own mom was right there, caught in the tangle of being happy for her best friend but also sick with envy. Petra, having found out that she would be incapable of having children, trying to be our second mom. Unsaid words, but intense energy for an eleven-year-old girl to pick up on. Precocious? No, I remember feeling drained and anxious, needing time alone in a way no eleven-year-old should need it.

"Can I make a request?" Alex piped in. He was trailing behind us, and then caught up.

"Of course," I said. He pulled up next to me, boldly grabbed my hand, and I felt myself take a surprised inhale. His hand was warm and soft in mine and the contact shot through my body like a firecracker. When I looked up at him, he had a secret little smile, like he knew he'd caught me off guard.

"We have to do the Jungle Cruise first," he said. "We need to give Benny a chance to face her fears about this crocodile."

His tone had this solemn sarcasm and the four of us, all in a line, burst out laughing.

"Not you, too, Alex," Benny said, groaning. "Leave me alone."

"Oh, my God, she's still scared of it," I cried.

"I'm not," Benny screamed.

"We'll have to get on the Jungle Cruise to find out," Alex said.

"I hate all of you," Benny said, sticking her bottom lip out.

"We'll go now and do Indiana Jones after," I said. "It's all in Frontierland. Follow me."

"I'm glad someone is organized," Mom said. "And has a map."

"I don't think we've ever planned a single thing in our lives, Jack," Petra said, laughing.

"I know," I told them, veering us all to the left of the massive courtyard in front of Sleeping Beauty's castle and into Frontierland. "It used to stress me out."

"And you being a stressed-out kid stressed *me* out," Mom said. "You had so many lists!"

I held up my phone with a list of all the places we needed to hit. "What can I say? I love a list."

"Me, too," Alex whispered, just for me, and that camaraderie—having one person on my side—warmed me from the inside out. When I was eleven and here in Disneyland with Benny, Mom, and Petra, I'd had a list then, too, written on a piece of lined paper ripped from a spiral-bound notebook. I'd only checked off a couple things before we had to leave. They had all wanted to "wing it" in the park, but there I was, wanting to experience everything. It had been something so small, but that list made me feel apart from them, like I wasn't the easygoing girl they expected or wanted. It's so funny how those seemingly inconsequential moments of little rejections stick with you for years.

"Can you come with me into the bazaar real quick?" Alex asked, pointing to the left. We were almost to the Jungle Cruise, but there was a little marketplace next to us.

"Sure," I told him. And to everyone else I said, "We'll be right back."

He pulled me into this little alcove and pushed me up against one of the red clay walls.

"Sorry," he whispered. "I needed to get you alone for a minute."

I smiled and joked, "Wow, you're obsessed with me."

His lips were grazing across my neck in tantalizing slowness.

"Oh, I totally am."

"I'm not complaining."

"I can't wait till I have you all to myself for three days."

His eyes were locked on mine. I could feel his breath on my lips.

"Kiss me before they come looking for us," I commanded and his smile in response was so radiant that my body felt like a shaken can of Diet Coke, just ready to pop.

"I like when you tell me exactly what you want," he whispered, and before I could say anything, his hands were framing my face and his mouth was on mine, and it was so delicious I moaned, right in broad daylight in Frontierland, of all places.

He took his time with this kiss, lingered on my lips, skimmed his tongue across mine, put his hands in my hair, pushed himself against me. He was such a chef—he savored me like he wanted to lick the plate, get every last drop. He kissed the corners of my lips, the tops of my cheeks, the center of my forehead, and I repeated the pattern on his face, hearing him softly groan at each bit of contact.

We were lost in each other, and it wasn't until I heard the cry of a small child having a loud tantrum that I returned to my body and said, "Oh, shit, they're waiting for us."

He stared at me, dazed, and took a while before he answered and said, "I just went to another dimension I think."

"Me, too," I said, laughing. "If you told me the park was closing and we missed everything, I'd believe you."

He smiled. "I used to hate being in the moment, but you make me want to be present, so I don't miss a single minute."

I had to shake off the emotion that bolted through my body. "Say more things like that, please."

"I really do like you telling me exactly what you want," he replied, placing a kiss on my forehead as I closed my eyes and fully appreciated it, like that spot was now anointed and precious.

"I'll keep doing that, then."

"Good."

"Good."

"Alright, let's get back before Benny sends a squadron of Disney security after us."

We walked out of the bazaar to find Benny, Mom, and Petra with their arms crossed across their chests, smiling, like they knew exactly what we'd done back there.

"Let's get in line," I said. "What are we waiting for?"

They all rolled their eyes and I laughed. Benny, Alex, and Petra walked ahead, while Mom and I hung back. The park was too crowded for all five of us to walk in a line together.

"It's good to see you like this," Mom said, hooking her arm into mine the same way Benny always did.

"How are you feeling?" I asked. "Since the other day?" I hadn't wanted to bring it up again in front of everyone, but now that I had her alone, I wanted to check in.

"I'm good," she said. I shot her a look. "No, really, I am. Everything works out the way it's meant to."

"You really believe that?" I asked.

"Of course I do."

"But, how? Don't you want things to work out differently?"

"If I spend all my time wishing things had worked out differently, I miss the life I'm having right here, right now. Why would I torture myself like that? If I resist what's meant for me, I end up unhappy. But if I see all that is working for me, I'm left with peace. If I can just trust that a rejection is a redirection and everything works out in perfect, divine timing, then the moment I am having right here becomes precious and perfect. I am exactly where I'm supposed to be and nothing is wrong."

"But isn't that passive and complacent? Can't you work hard to change your circumstances?"

"Maybe," she said, shrugging. "I just don't think we have as much control as we want to believe. I trust that what's meant to be, will be. And what's meant to go, needs to go. And all of it is working for my highest good."

"I believe in hard work," I said. "And being in control of everything."

She laughed. "I know you do," she replied. "And if that makes you happy, I love that for you."

"It definitely does not make me happy," I confessed.

"Then why do you do it?"

Because I didn't want to turn out like you, or get hurt ever again.

"It's the only way I know how to be," I said.

"I think you deserve to be happy, Charlie," she said. "You can't wait for the other shoe to drop your whole life. You wait long enough, and before you know it, your life will be over."

"You're right."

"I am?" she asked, turning to me in surprise. "Since when?" She chuckled.

"I've been living in fear for a long time, Mom. I think I might be open to another way, but let me do it on my own terms. In my own time. Okay?"

"Always," she said. "I'm here for the journey, Charlie baby. I go where you go."

She pulled me into a hug.

The rest of the day passed in perfect succession. We hit up all the rides we wanted. Benny made peace with the crocodile. Space Mountain was miraculously open, and we all screamed at each twist and turn. We got the good Star Wars adventure and laughed like kids. We ate corn dogs and popcorn and something gourmet near Toontown for dinner. We stayed for the fireworks, our feet aching.

On the way home, Mom drove us back and I fell asleep on Alex's shoulder.

It was the happiest I'd felt in as long as I could remember. Maybe ever.

It might have been one of the happiest days of my life.

29

Benny must be stopped. She was wielding her power over me too much. She'd wrangled me into going to a farm, while wearing overalls and a flannel shirt, brushing my hair into pigtails as she giggled at the ridiculousness.

"Pigtails, Benny?" I asked, giving her a pointed look in the mirror of the upstairs bathroom. "Were the overalls not punishment enough?"

"Be careful or I'll demand you keep a stick of hay in your mouth all day like Old MacDonald," Benny said, cackling. "Ee i ee i ohhhhh."

I deadpanned, "You really need to grow up."

"Growing up is a scam."

I didn't know what to say to that, considering I'd been an adult since I was twelve.

"Life is very serious," Benny continued. "But you can't take it *that* seriously."

"So the answer is to go pick autumnal vegetables at a farm?"

"Charlie, when you can go pick squash out of the ground while wearing overalls and pigtails, you do it. If you don't invest in your joy, you lose it."

"Joy," I whispered. It was a simple three-letter word that I probably hadn't thought about or even considered since before I left for college. Mom and Benny were, of course, joy enthusiasts. But I thought joy was silly and flimsy in the face of the horrors of the world. What was the point of it when everything was so terrible? We had just lived through a pandemic and if you watched the news, you'd find a lot more things that inspire horror rather than joy. If I had spent any time thinking about joy over the last few years, I would have found it lacking and callous.

I'd concede to some happy moments during this whole experiment, but joy was something else entirely. Joy was a line in the sand I couldn't cross.

Benny tapped the top of my parted hair and declared me finished. We descended the stairs in tandem, put on ratty sneakers that could stand to get dirty from the farm, and got in the car. We had a bit of a drive out to Moorpark and Alex was meeting us.

"I take it you don't care about joy?" Benny picked the conversation back up while we were driving.

"It's not a priority for me, no," I said to her. "I feel like when you're a kid, you have all this fun, but then you have to grow up. You have to get serious about your life. You have to be responsible. And life is hard, Ben. Mom sheltered us from just how hard it really is. Joy doesn't put food on the table. It doesn't do anything."

"I know you worried our entire life would fall apart, but Charlie, you're thirty now. Mom *did* put food on the table. Nothing catastrophic happened during our childhood. Mom's methods were unconventional, but you never did have to save us, did you?"

I paused, not wanting to give Benny the satisfaction that she was right. That all the energy I spent convinced I knew better was . . . wasted.

"So you're saying I worried for nothing, right?" My words had an edge to them I couldn't shake.

"No. I mean, Charlie, you were an anxious kid. It hurt my heart to see it, because it seemed like everything Mom did upset you or made you more stressed out. But we're all good now. You can relax. Let go of that fear."

"Relax?" I scoffed. "I can *never* relax, Benny."

"What did you think would happen? What worried you so much?"

"Ben, you thought Mom was fun and so did I, but she was unpredictable. We never had a stable home."

"See, I liked that about our life."

"Well, I didn't."

"Okay, I understand that. We're different people. All I'm saying is that you had a bunch of fears and they didn't all come true, so maybe letting them go once and for all could do you some good."

"Maybe."

"But, yeah, about joy, you're right," Benny said. "It doesn't *do* anything . . ." she paused ". . . except make life worth living. Without joy, what is the freaking point, Charlie? When you're a kid, all you care about is getting to the joy. People who focus on how horrible the world is are not any better than people who decide to feel joy despite all the reasons not to. You have a choice. You can see all this pain in the world and decide to bring light to it. Or you can harden because of it. But, it's a *choice*."

"I don't have time for joy," I replied.

"Well, this month you do." She scooted into the carpool lane and shot up to eighty-five miles per hour. "Do me a favor, and this is a request—clear your mind today. Just be in the moment. Don't think about whether this is worth your time or if it's stupid or if you should be doing something more productive. Just fall into it. Let go for an afternoon. Be a kid again. Will you do that for me?"

"It's a request," I told her. "So, yeah, I'll try."

I didn't tell her that joy also felt dangerous to me. It reminded me of those first euphoric months with Noah, the letting go, the giving in. Or times with our dad when he'd sweep into town and the world felt glittery and magical again. Because, the depth of your joy can also match the depth of your despair. If you feel it all, you have to feel the bad things, too. That was the part I couldn't shake. It seemed to me that giving up joy was a fair trade for never having to be irreparably broken ever again.

Benny turned up the music and I listened to her singing under her breath as she drove the rest of the way to the farm with such high speeds that I found myself trying to push my foot onto an imaginary brake.

We arrived at the farm with my jaw clenched, but when Alex got out of his car in sweatpants and a black Henley, his face bright, I looked at Benny and swallowed hard.

"He looks hot," I said, eyebrows raised.

"Yeah, he does," she said. "Let's go objectify him while he picks romaine for us."

I laughed.

"You're horrible."

"Hey, being just a little bad can be joyous, Charlize."

I shook my head at her. "I've said it before and I'll say it again, you're a bad influence."

"And I'll say it again: *thank you*. I take it as the highest compliment. Plus, I got you to laugh and really, that's all I've ever tried to do. Your clown concierge, at your service." She did a little curtsy.

"Alright, let's go, Chuckles," I said to her, opening the car door, and without looking back, I heard her bust out a howl of laughter.

Benny and I both walked up to Alex and he gave her a hug, then pulled me into his arms and kissed me hard, leaving me a little breathless.

"You look the part," he said, twirling one of my pigtails around on his finger.

"I look absurd," I said.

"I think you look adorable."

"You know what, you two?" Benny cried. "Don't third-wheel me. This whole thing was *my* idea."

Alex and I both made a show of turning toward her, bestowing all our attention on Benny, giving each other a little side smile as we did so. She nodded in triumph and then clasped arms with us both, walking us to the line of people waiting to pay for their tickets.

"Alex," Benny said. "The plan is to have silly fun. Are you in?" She pointed her thumb over at me. "This one over here doesn't believe in joy."

"I'm in," Alex said. "Me and joy have a bit of a complicated relationship, too."

"Both of you," Benny said, tsking. "You're made for each other."

I bumped Benny with my elbow and didn't look over at Alex. She couldn't go around saying things like that.

Within twenty minutes, we were at an open field of late September strawberries with a high hot sun above us, a paper bag in each of our hands, watching a flurry of children run around wildly.

"Here's the deal," Benny said, eyes alight with mischief. "I'm going to set my stopwatch for five minutes and we're each going to gather as many strawberries as we can in that time. Whoever has the least at the end has to buy lunch for everyone. Whoever has the most gets to choose the place."

I rolled my eyes. "Fine," I said.

"Alex?" Benny asked.

"Let's do this." He smiled and made a show of cracking his knuckles.

Benny pulled out her phone, set the timer, and then cried, "Ready, set, GO."

And then we were off, scattering in different directions. It was muddy from the rain from two days ago and you had to get up and under the bushes to find the fruit, but soon I was on my knees in the dirt, pulling deep red strawberries off bushes and throwing them into the bag, fully immersed in this task of taking Benny down.

The area was picked-through, so I ran to the farther end and on my way there bumped into Benny, who was screeching with laughter and delight, and it was so contagious we did a little spin together until we became strawberry-picking rivals again.

"THREE MINUTES LEFT," Benny screamed, and even the kids around us stopped to look at her.

Alex was at the front of the crop, now watching us, taller than anyone within his immediate radius, laughing and shaking his head like this was all silly, but also lovely and fun and sort of perfect. He shrugged and got back to work, dipping down.

At a particularly abundant supply, I started pulling strawberries as fast as I could, branches clipping at my hands, sweat starting to pool on my forehead. I was so immersed in picking the berries that I only stopped when Benny clapped me on the shoulder, laughing hard when I screamed.

"Having fun yet?" she asked, grinning, helping me up with an outstretched hand.

"No," I said, just to mess with her.

"Liar. You were smiling like a kid picking all those strawberries."

"I just want to beat you."

"We'll see about that," she replied, holding up her haul.

Alex joined us, the top of his cheeks crimson from exertion.

"Okay," Benny said. "Count it up and don't say your number until we're done." She was like a camp counselor with boundless energy.

We all counted under our breath until Benny told us to reveal our number on three, two, one.

"Eighty-seven!" Alex declared.

"Ninety-two!" Benny squealed.

"Ninety-four!" I shrieked.

"YES," I screamed, skipping around Benny and celebrating. "VICTORY!"

"Damn it," Benny said, kicking at the dirt. "I thought I had this in the bag." She cackled. "Get it?" She held up the paper bag. "Bag?"

Alex and I glanced at each other and rolled our eyes, laughing.

"Alright, Princess Strawberry," Benny said, looking at me and bowing. "Lunch is on Alex. Where are we going to make him take us?"

"Did we really lose, Benny?" Alex asked, leaning casually on Benny's shoulder. "Look at Charlie. Watching her do a victory lap was the real win here. Who knew she was so competitive?"

"Me," Benny said. "She used to clear the board with a swipe of her arm when I was winning in Candy Land. Charlie is *such* a sore loser."

Alex gave me a look of resigned respect. "Wait, now I remember. Didn't you win a spelling bee or something?"

"Excuse me," I said, tipping my chin up. "I won *five*."

Benny and Alex burst out laughing.

"P-S-E-U-D-O-N-Y-M, pseudonym," I declared like I was on stage. "That won me the regional championship, thank you very much."

Alex and Benny laughed more as I bowed.

"I know you're supposed to pick our lunch spot because you're the winner," Benny said, as we walked across the fields back toward orange trees and several vegetable patches filled with zucchini, broccoli, and cucumber. "But I think we should do sushi. There's a Sugarfish in Calabasas that we have to pass by on our way home."

"Oh," Alex said. "I will *happily* buy us all Nozawa Trust Me's from Sugarfish."

"And we can get gelato," Benny said, excited. "And look at all the turtles in the ponds."

"Turtles?" I asked.

"The Commons at Calabasas are so extra," Benny said. "They have these two man-made ponds where like hundreds of turtles live. It's so ridiculous and also fun."

"That has been the theme of the day," I told her. "Let's do it."

We washed off and paid for our haul at the cashier.

When Alex left to use the restroom, Benny sidled up next to me and handed me her phone. On it was a picture of me in the strawberry fields, head tipped back, generous smile on my face.

"Look at this," she said. "This is you, looking at Alex, celebrating your win."

"I was victorious," I said.

"No," she said. She hit her phone with her fingertip. "Look, Charlie. Look how happy you are. You can't deny this. You're beaming." She pinched the picture and zoomed in on my face. "*This* is joy."

"I just won a free lunch," I said. "Of course I'm happy."

"Stop it," she ordered. "Stop doing that. Stop being sarcastic and cutting. Enough. This is the real you. And you deserve to feel like this every single day, damn it."

She didn't even wait for me to answer. She knew what she'd said. When Alex popped out of the restrooms, she pulled him ahead by the arm and they walked off together.

Eating fresh strawberries from the bag, I strolled behind them while mulling over Benny's words. I was sweaty and gross; I still had dirt under my fingernails and my knees hurt a little from all the bending down; Alex and Benny were laughing about something I couldn't hear; and we were about to eat sushi and hang out with turtles apparently and get gelato. Alex looked back at me, beaming, like he couldn't have me out of his sight for a moment, and I just smiled and thought, *This joy thing may not be so bad.*

As much as it *killed* me to admit it, maybe Benny was just the *tiniest* bit right.

30

The force of Benny staring at me woke me up. She was in my bed, propped up on her elbow like she didn't even know the concept of boundaries existed.

"I thought you were an early bird," she said. "It's past nine."

"I thought I was, too," I replied, groggy, rubbing the sleep from my eyes. Ever since I'd arrived in LA, I'd been waking up later and later. It almost felt like I was catching up on years of missed sleep. I was starting to worry if I didn't get back on my schedule, I never would, and I'd become lazy, but then Benny would make her requests and I'd be up until midnight or 2:00 a.m., with Jasper, or Willow, or Petra, or some other interesting person that dropped by Quinn Canyon, and I just kept sleeping in.

"I have a request," Benny said.

"Wow, big surprise," I told her, smiling. She knocked me on the shoulder.

"We're going to do a throwback Triple Quinn Ultimate Movie Day," she said. "Mom is in."

My stomach dropped. Those memories of our iconic movie days spent eating junk food, ordering pizza, and watching five movies in a row had turned so bittersweet over the years. Or, maybe, to justify staying away for so long, I'd allowed them to turn sour, so I'd never miss it too much.

"Benny, I need a day off," I said.

"Then you owe me ten grand," she said, smile dropping from her face. "This is important, Charlie."

"I'm not a kid anymore, Benny."

"You know, Mom and I still have our movie days and there hasn't been one in all these years you haven't come home that we haven't looked at each other with tears in our eyes and wished you were with us. Sometimes you only see what *you* need and not what *we* might need from you."

Well, that made me feel awful.

"Okay, okay," I said, and she brightened immediately.

"Stay in your pajamas," she commanded. "I'm going to go get us all the junk food we can handle and be back in an hour, then we start." She got up off the bed and almost made it to the doorway before she doubled back. "Remember we used to go to Blockbuster the night before and pick out all the movies we wanted to see and the next day it felt like Christmas morning, waking up to stay in all day?"

I felt my eyes prickle at the memory. When I was younger, Mom would critique the performances, dream out loud about the roles she couldn't wait to play. All Benny and I could do was dream with her.

"I remember," I said. "Now we have every movie at our fingertips. I kinda miss waiting for things, the anticipation of seeing if the movie you wanted to rent was available."

"The best feeling was *not* seeing the movie you wanted out on the shelves and then going up to the counter to see if any copies had come in."

"We died that one time when they told us someone had just returned *Clueless*."

"Oh, my God, we need to watch that today."

"YES," I cried.

"Kids these days will never understand the joy of Blockbuster on a Friday night," Benny lamented like she wasn't twenty-five.

She then nodded, like she'd completed something she had

set out to do. What that was, I didn't know, but then she was gone and I didn't venture downstairs until I heard her come back in the house. When I did, there was a full French press and a whole breakfast spread on the coffee table in the living room and Mom came out of the kitchen holding a jug of orange juice, triumphantly declaring, "I made breakfast!"

There was a big plate of eggs, bacon, and several pieces of toast. Some part of my heart seemed to thaw at the sight of it and I sat down on the couch next to my mom and said, "This looks amazing."

"I *can* cook," she said. "I just like to do it sporadically so when I do, I impress you."

"I am impressed," I told her, chuckling.

"And I'm starving," Benny said, squeezing herself right into the middle of us so we both had to scoot over to make space for her. "This is going to be the best day."

All three of us started on our plates of food, adding the exact same amount of cream and sugar to our coffees. I felt myself too easily falling back into the familiarity of belonging to these two women.

"We have so many movies to catch up on," Mom said, between a forkful of eggs with ketchup on them (the way we all always ate our eggs). I forgot how much I used to like being a part of Triple Quinn. Family was so complicated, threads of good and bad and hurtful and incredible memories all tangled together. One minute you love them, the next you can't wait to get away.

We spent the rest of the breakfast deciding our list of movies, ranging from classics like *Clueless* and *Grease* (our personal favorite, of which we knew every word and lyric) to new releases we hadn't seen yet. By the time we'd cleared the dishes, it was almost eleven o'clock. We turned on the first movie, while I threw a blanket over our three laps, then Benny's head landed on my shoulder, and Mom's outstretched arm held us both.

We ate pizza. We didn't talk about anything serious. They didn't ask me any questions and I didn't ask any of them. We just existed in each other's company and I remembered a time before life swooped in and it got complicated.

Somehow I was able to access the good memories of these movie days, when I didn't want to be somewhere else, when I wasn't trying to rebel against the Triple Quinn force and be my own person.

Like when we'd watch *Grease* at least once a month, and sing every song at full volume. One year when I was fifteen, I even got us special Pink Ladies jackets to wear for Halloween. Petra was "bad" Sandy in all black. Mom threw a *Grease*-themed party on October 31 and I performed a near-perfect rendition of "Summer Nights" with some aspiring actor that had a voice just like John Travolta's.

Those were good times. Really good times. So many of them, stacked up like boxes I'd stashed in storage somewhere, gathering dust, forgotten.

The thing is, when you repeatedly deny yourself something, you can almost convince yourself you don't miss it. But family can see through you. They know who you've been. They can chart the course of who you used to be and who you are now.

And sometimes, you don't *want* them to see you. When you stay away, you can't be reminded by how much you've changed, what you've given up.

If you never confront the past, never let it catch up, you can *almost* convince yourself you've outrun it entirely.

Almost.

31

The next week played out in movie montage moments.

Willow got us tickets to see a reunion tour for one of my favorite bands from when I was younger, and so Alex, Benny, Mom, Willow, Petra, and I went to the Hollywood Bowl, singing until our throats burned, our ears ringing as we walked back to our cars parked on Hollywood Boulevard.

Alex, Benny, and I went to the farmers market in Malibu one Saturday and taste-tested sweet clementines, thick olive oil, and Ojai-grown honey. We laughed until we cried, then stayed all day at the beach until a vibrant pink, purple, and orange sunset burst through the sky like a painting just for us.

Mom and I went to the movies at Universal CityWalk, ears blown out from the IMAX, sharing Raisinets and a large popcorn doused in butter.

Alex and I hiked in Griffith Park and then went up to the Observatory, learning all about space while lying down in the domed theater, Alex's warm hand in mine throughout the entire film, him peppering me with little kisses every couple minutes or so, my heart beating wildly in my chest.

Benny and I drove out to Ojai, went to their iconic used bookstore, ate a delicious lunch of all fresh and local ingredients, then got expensive massages at a spa.

Near Pacific Palisades, I went on a hike by myself and stood at the summit, overlooking a sweeping expanse of the ocean while sticky, sweaty, and thirsty. I threw my arms out at the view and smiled into the sunshine and took a bunch of deep breaths, and my body hummed with the sweet feeling of accomplishment and being in nature and giving myself a fucking break for once. Afterward, I devoured fries and a Double-Double and a crisp Diet Coke from In-N-Out.

One late night, Jasper came over and asked if Benny, Mom, and I wanted to go to Willow's show at Hotel Café. We went and she was wonderful and I wondered if her career was going to take off the way she'd dreamed. She certainly deserved it; I found myself holding a rare instance of hope for her.

Alex, Benny, Mom, and I went to Venice Beach, rented bikes, and rode them all the way to Santa Monica for fish tacos, and then back to Venice, an early October heat wave tanning our skin, salty sweat caked on our flushed faces.

Sitting on the sand in Venice, Alex leaned over to me and asked, "So, about that beach getaway we talked about before? I got the room. Still want to go?"

The answer was the only word I'd been saying since I'd been in LA: *Yes.*

32

"What the hell," I cried, staring out at the most beautiful view of bright blue ocean water from the terrace of the suite that Alex had booked in Montecito. "This is way too decadent. Take me to a normal hotel immediately."

He burst out laughing.

"Relax," he said, coming up behind me and placing his hands on my shoulders. He kissed the top of my head. "It was comped by my friend."

I whipped around. "Are you hiding dead bodies for him or something? How is this room comped?"

"He did owe me a favor," Alex explained. "But only because I catered a last-minute dinner party for him a few months back when he was in a tight spot and he demanded I let him know a way he could repay me."

"Okay."

"And I also hid a dead body for him," Alex said, straight-faced.

I hit him on the shoulder, then turned back around to the view—gradients of blue with only a few white streaks of clouds in the sky. It was warm, the water was sparkling, and I had three days alone with Alex. How had I ended up here? The power of yes, indeed.

"This is perfect," I said.

He came up behind me again, kissed the soft spot below my ear, and wrapped his arms around my middle.

"You like it?" he asked. "Because I could book us a motel if it's too fancy for you . . ."

I watched him over my shoulder and saw his wry smile. "Honestly, I'd spend three days with you anywhere."

"Just three?"

"How many do you want?"

"All of them," he said. "But I'll take the ten or so that we have left."

I turned back toward the horizon trying to get the *all of them* out of my head and the melancholic way he said it. He worked as hard as I did, had a life to return to, and he was meeting a version of me that wasn't real. If anything, he wanted to spend all his days with Charlize, not Charlie.

"So," he said, sitting down on the outdoor couch and patting the space next to him. I sat down close, and he pulled me in, arm outstretched across my shoulders. "Are we going to be reclusive? Or should we hit the pool? The ocean? The restaurant?"

"Well, I am not against getting some salt water on my skin," I said.

"So, we're going to the beach."

I smiled. "Do you mind?"

"Mind? Why would I mind?"

"Because, maybe you wanted to just . . . stay in bed."

"We have plenty of time for that. I've spent so much time in the restaurant over the last year I've hardly enjoyed being back in LA at all."

"So, we're going to the beach," I said, mimicking him.

"Let's order some lunch first and then go."

He brought out menus and we decided on a feast. He called the order in, and when he returned, he sat next to me, pulled me in again, and kissed me until everything faded away.

I was breathless when we stopped. My hand was under his shirt and at the cusp of his waistband.

"I'm going to need to do a lot of things to you tonight in that bed," I said, nodding toward the open balcony doors. "Nobody around to disturb us for three days? I have a lot of ideas."

"You say things like that," he said, tracing across my collarbone, "and I lose my mind a little in a way I never have before."

"That doesn't sound good?"

"No, it is," he said. "Very good. But it makes me nervous. *You* make me nervous."

"Me? What? Why?"

"I am never a fool for anyone," he said quietly. "But I am a fool for you, which I know sounds so cheesy. It's sick."

"You're just swept up in the moment," I said, pointing to the view. "Who wouldn't be?"

He shook his head, like that wasn't it, like it was something more.

"I never let my guard down, Charlie," he revealed. "Ever. Not even for a day."

"Neither do I."

"All I've done for years is work. That's all I've cared about. My last girlfriend broke up with me because I never had time for her. The one before that, too. I didn't *want* to make time for them."

"I get it," I said. "If anyone truly gets it, it's me."

"That's what makes me nervous, though. I want to make time for you. This feels too easy to fall into."

"Alex, it's only easy because we know it ends."

"What if we find out it's real?"

"It's not. It won't be. I don't think I'm capable of real."

"All these years, I thought I wasn't, either," he said. "But it's different with you."

"Only because there's no pressure," I told him, not sure who

I was trying to convince more, him or myself. "I said it before and I'll say it again—if this arrangement ever stops working for you, just tell me and I'm gone."

He exhaled tightly. "You'd be able to end this just like that?"

No. "Yes," I said, shaky.

There was a ding at the door for our room service, and he jumped up to answer it. I was determined to steer us into other conversation topics when he returned, but then a scene started playing. I thought this had stopped, thought I was done reliving this part of my life, thought maybe it was finally behind me. But I guess the truth was, getting close to Alex, having fun, letting loose, it was making these memories more vivid, more present, more urgent like an incessant knocking in my mind, always calling me forth, always pulling me in. And I couldn't stop this scene from coming.

"I told my parents about traveling, you, our plans," Noah said to her, in a hushed whisper, like he was trying not to be overheard.

"And?" she asked, a lump caught in her throat.

"They won't budge," he said. "It's traveling or them. You or my inheritance. I stupidly thought I could talk to them and get them to see my side. I don't know what to do."

She could no longer hold herself up and fell back on the bed, the phone lost in the sheets for a moment as she tried to grab it. His indecision was enough for her. She knew he didn't want to alienate himself from his family, or let go of the money that was owed to him. Somehow, she knew this was coming. That's why she'd been secretly making plans of her own. Plans that hadn't included him.

"Noah, it's okay," she said. "We haven't been together that long. Don't risk everything for me." She wanted to give him permission to make the choice she knew he wanted to make. She wanted him to do it guilt-free, to let her go. "I can get a job. You don't have to choose."

She'd been applying, just in case. Her mom had never had a plan B, but Charlie wasn't her mom. She had contingency plans for her contingency plans, even when she was desperately in love. Actually, that's when she needed the plans the most. She'd be catatonic right now, knowing he wasn't going to choose her, if she didn't have backups.

She always had to control the fallout.

"Is that what you really want? To get a job?" Noah asked. "We had a plan."

She didn't want to force him. The last thing she could live with was Noah detaching from his family all because he felt guilty for making a promise to her when everything felt possible. She knew what she was saying. She knew what she was implying. She knew she was going to lose him. But what was the alternative? Beg him to choose her when she knew he'd end up resenting her for it?

Noah did not want to be disowned from his family. In their most intimate moments, he had revealed his hope that he could turn his relationship with his parents around. He wanted that. She couldn't ask him to leave them behind forever, even if his parents would be the ones making that choice.

"I want you to do what's best for you," she said.

"I don't know what's best for me," he admitted.

"That's your answer," she said. "I love you, but I'm setting you free. Let's go our separate ways, Noah. It's okay. It's really okay. You don't owe me anything."

"Charlie, stop—"

She hung up before she lost her nerve or before he could say anything more and it was the last time she ever spoke to him.

Taking a deep breath, I clenched my fists and shook my head like maybe it could shake the memories away. I wish the story of Noah and me *had* ended there. Fade to black, credits rolling, Charlie Quinn triumphant and safe. If I had left on my own terms, if it was just a bad breakup with a disappointing guy who made promises he couldn't keep—I may have survived it all better. That is the kind of man I could have hated, could have left behind.

But that's not how we ended.

Alex returned with a room service attendant and I pretended like nothing had just seized me while he was gone.

The attendant set up our lunch on the terrace and I plastered a smile on my face and tried to come back to the moment. We'd ordered a plethora of sushi so fresh it melted on my tongue. The sensation of the sweet ponzu with seared albacore belly brought me back straight into the present.

I had a little more than a week left until I could descend back to who I used to be, impenetrable. This month of yes had been a much-needed vacation, but that's all it was. A departure. Soon enough, there would need to be an arrival, a return.

But today, there was this delicious salmon nigiri and there was Alex.

"You okay?" Alex asked, perhaps sensing my distance. I'd chosen to sit across from him, on a chair, while we ate.

I nodded. "Yeah, I'm good."

"Sometimes, you go somewhere else," he said. "Do you know that? Sometimes you just leave the moment."

"I know."

"It happened at Disneyland," he said.

It had. I'd been assaulted by memories. I'd remembered a perfect day at Disneyland when I was only four years old. I couldn't believe those scenes returned to me, but when I walked past the Dumbo ride, I could see Mom and me inside it, waving down to my dad, who was watching us with a big smile on his face. That was his cliché pattern—when he came into town, it was time to have fun. He wanted to leave me with memories. But what he didn't know was that when he left forever, those memories, no matter how golden, turned to ash.

Dad had weaponized fun against me for the first ten years of my life. I always let him back in, always lowered my walls, got swept up in his energy, in the whirlwind he'd create when he deemed me important enough to return to for a weekend. He thought if he distracted me, plied me with sugar, and gave me anything I could ever want for those few days, all sins would be forgiven. And they were, over and over. I always believed I could be enough to make him stay. Fun enough, good enough, exciting enough. But he always left.

"I know," I said again. "I know I do that, Alex."

"I recognize it," he said. "Because I used to do it, too."

I nodded, not wanting to say more. Not wanting to reveal more.

"Do they have beach chairs down there or do we need towels?" I asked. It was a blatant need to change the subject, but Alex didn't flinch.

"They have everything," he said.

"Then let's go," I told him, shaking off my disassociation.

I changed into my swimsuit in the bathroom and when I came out, he was sitting on the edge of the bed, shirtless, with a pair of navy blue bathing suit shorts on. They were cut above the knee and he looked ridiculously sexy.

When I climbed on top of him, his back fell to the bed. I palmed my way across his torso, grabbed his face, and kissed him while my hips dipped. The kiss didn't last nearly as long as I wanted it to, because Alex stopped me and stood me upright.

"We need to get some salt water on that skin," he said, biting my shoulder. "If we don't leave now, I fear I will not be able to let you leave."

I laughed. "Okay."

He put on a T-shirt and we exited the room, flip-flops smacking on the wood walkway, Alex's arm slung around me like it was meant to be there.

33

We ordered fruity mocktails from a server while spread out on blue-and-white-striped beach loungers, shaded from the high hot sun by a matching umbrella. When the drinks were delivered, we clinked a celebratory "cheers."

"How come you never asked me out, Perry?" I asked. "Back in high school."

"Asked you out? Quinn, I was the shyest person ever and you were this beautiful girl who seemed completely above high school. You think I had the confidence to walk up to you?"

"I wouldn't have rejected you."

"I had no idea."

"You think I was above high school?"

"You seemed like it. You weren't trying to be popular. You were just . . . yourself. It was intimidating. You were like the smartest person in our class. I didn't even think I could keep up with you, never mind ask you out on a date."

I liked that. For some reason, I really liked that, but I hadn't been above high school at all. Securing my future and receiving anything but stellar grades and a perfect SAT score was all I thought about. I had friends, but being part of Triple Quinn took up most of my free time.

"And now?" I asked. "I'm not intimidating?"

"Oh, you are," he said. "But I'm not nearly as shy as I used to be."

"What changed?"

He glanced toward the horizon at the waves crashing hard against the sand.

"I guess losing my mom," he finally said, voice low and cracking. "It puts things into perspective." He shrugged, turned back to me. "At least, it does eventually."

"First, it's the most horrible thing imaginable."

"Right."

"And, then what?" Then *what*? I was still stuck in the first part.

"Then," he began, "if you can process it and stop being afraid that life is really that uncertain, it can make you brave. More honest. More willing to go after anything you want. More determined to live to the fullest. Grief can somehow make you more courageous, more willing to not waste any time. I haven't always seen it that way, but I'm beginning to, more and more."

"I think you're incredible," I told him, looking down at my hands, trying not to face him directly. "Losing your mom like that could have hardened you. Could have made you afraid of life. Could have made you resentful, bitter, angry. Could have made you want to retreat from everything. But you're not. You didn't."

He laughed sharply. "I did," he said. "I really, really did. You're meeting me on better days. You wouldn't have wanted to know me when I was in the worst of it."

"I would have," I said quickly. "I would have wanted to know you on all the days."

He lifted his sunglasses into his hair and grabbed my wrist softly.

"Charlie, I need you to maybe stop saying things like that," he whispered.

"Okay."

"It's just that, you say things like that, and I start thinking this is real."

"I'll stop," I said, and he looked disappointed for a moment, like maybe he didn't want me to agree with him. Once again, I changed the subject. "By the way, I wasn't too cool for high school. At least, I don't think I was. I couldn't wait for it to be over so I could start my real life."

"I never knew that," he said, placing his sunglasses back on his face. I turned and took a sip from my drink and pulled my feet in closer. The sun had moved slightly and my feet were starting to burn. "I always thought you, Benny, and your mom were so close. Why did you want to move away?"

"We *were* close. But that can be complicated. Codependent even. Living with my mom was stressful for me. She was always up and down with her moods. Got an audition, she was taking us out for dinner. Didn't get a part, she was in bed for two days. She always bounced back, but as a kid, watching that, I felt like I had no control over my life. I found myself worrying about the electric bill or the day Mom's luck would run out and who would take care of her? Benny? It would all fall on me."

"That's a lot for one kid to handle."

"Yeah, so if I was acting too cool for high school, it was probably because I was too busy to care about popularity or gossip or whatnot, because I was studying, or working an after-school job, or trying to be responsible enough to overcompensate for the two parents I didn't have."

"When did your dad leave?" Alex asked. This was more than I'd ever told Josh about myself in two years. I started to understand why he'd left me. I'd given him nothing, kept him not just an arm's length away, but entirely apart from me. At first, it was because he hadn't asked. We were both consumed with work. But during lockdown, he'd asked. He'd pried. He'd wanted to know.

"The day before my tenth birthday," I told Alex. "He wasn't around all the time, but he'd show up a few times a year. I'd stupidly wait for him. I loved him, despite it all. And then, he was gone. Benny was only five. She doesn't even remember him. I think he spent time with her only a handful of times before he left for good. After that, Mom got her shit together a lot more. Benny got a more solid Jackie Quinn. But by the time he was gone, I was already too stressed out for a ten-year-old."

"You haven't talked to him at all? Or looked for him?"

"Nope. Never."

"Did you ask your mom if he was coming back? Or where he was?"

"She said he was gone for good," I told him. "She never said where."

"Weren't you devastated? Didn't you want to know?"

"No," I said. "I mean, yeah, sure, at first. I was pretty catatonic, honestly. Worst birthday ever. Hate birthdays to this day. But then my heart sort of . . . closed? That gave me the control back. If he didn't want me, I didn't want him. I wasn't going to beg."

Alex let out a long exhale and fell back on his chair, looking up at the umbrella.

"Damn," he said. I couldn't tell if he was feeling sorry for me, shocked, impressed, or a mixture of all. "So that's why you never want to get close." He flattened his palm across the exposed skin on my stomach.

"Maybe," was all I said, even though there was more to reveal.

"Let's go swimming," I said and leaped off the chair. I was knee-deep in the bracingly cold water before he even caught up to me. When he did, I splashed at him.

"Fuck," he cried. "It's freezing!"

"I know." I liked it. It shocked me out of the memories as I dove under a cresting wave and swam out the other side, where

I bobbed in calmer water, letting my body get used to the chill. When Alex did the same, I swam over to him, wrapped my legs around his hips, and kissed him hard until there was nothing else to remember except this moment.

He tasted salty and we stayed just like that until the water felt warm and our fingertips were pruned.

34

By the time I looked up from my book, the sun had started setting in the most stunning streaks of orange and golden yellow. I earmarked the new Poppy Banks thriller I'd gotten halfway through and set it aside. My skin had that perfect sensation of hours in the sun, all baked and warm, and I couldn't stop thinking of the shower I was going to take, the feeling of dropping into that bed with Alex.

He was watching the sunset as well and had absentmindedly grabbed my hand, placed it on his chest and covered his other hand with it. My phone dinged.

"Sorry," I said to him, pulling my hand out from under the clasp of his and holding it up. "I need that back for a second."

"Only for a second," he said, smiling. He had color on the tops of his cheeks that made him look youthful and happy.

Benny had texted me ten times in a row.

> DINNER WHEN YOU'RE BACK!?!!!

> i miss you and i miss alex

> you guys down?

> well, you have to say yes

> it's a request

> invite alex

> that's also a request

> i'll third wheel it as always

> hope you're doing lots of naughty things, charlize

> charliiiiiiizzzzze

I burst out laughing. Alex looked at me quizzically and I just said, "Benny," in response. He nodded like that explained everything, which to be fair, it did.

> dearest sister—i accept your request. i will check in with alex re: dinner.

> charlize is having a very good time, by the way.

> why are you texting me like you're corresponding with a gentleman of the high court?

> don't know. felt right in the moment.

Placing my phone face down on the side table, I turned to Alex.

"Benny wants to do dinner when we're back," I said. "If you're up for it."

"I am," he said. "Or I could cook for you all? Maybe Friday night? I could cook at your house?"

My smile started slowly and then took over my face. "I think my mom and Benny would absolutely love that."

"And you?" he asked, low, intimate. "Would *you* like that?"

"Yes, Chef."

He made a display of shivering.

"Please never stop saying that." His eyes darkened. "I may have had enough of the beach. And being with you in public. And not doing all the things to you I've been dreaming about doing to you."

"Same," I said, and we were both on our feet, packing up quickly.

On the walk to the room, I texted Benny back.

> alex is in for dinner, but he wants to be the one to cook it. friday night? that cool?

COOL!?!!!!

of course it's cool

how are you not in love with him?????

if you don't fall in love with him, i may have to

I rolled my eyes at the phone.

> i'm rolling my eyes at you right now. see you when i get back. don't get up to any trouble.

I WILL

I laughed and then I put my phone in my bag, caught up to Alex and slid my hand into his.

"Benny is ecstatic you're going to be cooking for us," I told him.

"I personally can't wait to see Quinn Canyon in the flesh."

"You know the name?"

"You do know that your house was, and is, famous, right?"

"No . . . ?"

"Didn't your mom have like actors, models, and musicians over all the time? Usually right before they broke out and made it big? Last I heard, she still did."

I laughed. "Yes," I said. "That was basically my childhood."

"People used to say that your house was magical," he said. We were at the door to our suite and he tapped the keycard. Once inside, I dropped my heavy tote bag on the carpet by the door and flung my flip-flops off. "That anyone who stepped inside would finally get the call that would change their life."

"Who said that?" I'd never heard of this.

"It was sort of an urban legend," he said. "The Magic House."

"Fascinating. If that's even true, it's a heartbreaking story, because the one person who never got the call that changed their life was my mom."

"You never know," he said, shrugging. "It could still happen."

"Right," I scoffed. "That's what she seems to believe, too."

"And you don't?"

"I don't know," I said. "Maybe she could have found something else that she loved if she had quit. It was hard watching her get rejected all the time, year after year."

"The pleasure is sometimes in the pursuit, though," he said. "The journey and all that. Does she regret it?"

"Not at all," I said. "She still believes she's due her big break."

"It doesn't hurt to have hope."

"It doesn't?"

"What's the point of anything, if you don't have hope?"

I fiddled with the tassel on the swimsuit cover-up I'd borrowed from Benny. Me and hope had a fraught relationship.

Who was I kidding? Me and anything but certainty, predictability, and control had a fraught relationship.

"You're a good man," I said to Alex. "I'm going to shower."

"I'd ask if I could join, but I have to call the owners of the restaurant in Chicago for a minute. They have some questions about the menu I developed for them." He kissed me on the shoulder and then walked toward the terrace.

I got in the shower, letting the lukewarm water crest across my burnt skin, pointedly avoiding questions like why did it bother me so much that my mom still had hope for her big break and why couldn't I just support her.

Fruitless questions to which I had no answers, or, perhaps, they did have answers, but I just didn't want to face them, didn't want to let go of all this resentment I'd been carrying like body armor, desperate to not be obliterated ever again.

35

The shower was a luxury, rainfall cascading across my skin, soap that smelled like peppermint and tingled on my sunburnt limbs. I took my time in there, basking in what it felt like to be wanted, to want someone so much just the anticipation sent floods of pleasure all through my body.

It was Wednesday, late afternoon, and back in San Francisco—back in the life I used to have—I'd be working, mindless and insatiable, not letting myself stop for even a coffee.

It wasn't strange there, because back in that world, everyone was like me. Everyone was trying to outpace each other. Everyone was waiting for work to be the thing that saves them. It wasn't forty-hour weeks. It was sixty. Eighty. Burning the midnight oil. If you weren't grinding, you weren't getting anywhere. And if you ever stopped, someone else was going to take your place.

I was like a bullet train that hit the emergency brake.

My body felt heavy and slow and inert, but I didn't mind it.

Maybe my boss had been right—I'd needed a break. Didn't people always say that? "Take your vacations!" But what nobody ever really said was that the people who took vacations didn't get the promotions. They lost momentum. You were looked down on if you took too much time off, or any at all. It was like a hamster wheel, and you knew it, but then you'd think—if I get off this wheel, what's left? Who will I be? What will I do?

Work becomes an all-consuming obsession in that way. Work doesn't want you home for dinner. Work doesn't leave you. Work doesn't break your heart. All work wants is your time, and if you have a lot to avoid—work is a savior. Work is the perfect distraction. There is always another achievement to feed the insatiable beast within that says you aren't good enough or lovable. You can prove that feeling wrong with another promotion, another external hit of value. *See?* I'm worth *something*. Work and productivity can be addicting, because you never ever have to stop. You can keep filling yourself up with titles, money, accolades until, one day, maybe, you'll be full.

Funny, though, that when I stopped, all I felt was hunger.

I was off the wheel. Out of the train. And frankly, I didn't know where I was going to go or what I was going to do now, but I felt like I was seeing the world for the first time, blinking against the blinding sun.

After I wrapped myself in a pillowy robe, I found Alex on the terrace. Clouds had moved in and the breeze had a bite to it. He was staring at his phone, bewildered. He didn't notice me until I sat down next to him and he jumped a bit.

"Everything okay?" I asked.

He looked over at me, eyes glassy. "Yeah," he murmured. "I think so. Yeah."

"What's going on? Something with the restaurant?"

"They want me to come earlier. Like now. There's some event in Chicago and they want to move up the soft opening."

It felt like my stomach rushed to my throat.

"Oh," I managed to say.

"Should I say yes?" he asked, voice quiet and muffled since he'd covered his face with his hands, elbows on his knees. He looked tortured. Like maybe he thought I was going to tell him to go, like he was bracing for something bad.

I felt like I was on the precipice of a vital and important

moment, my heart racing. The old me would have said, *Yes, say yes, go, bye.* But I wanted the next ten days with him. It was impractical and ridiculous and maybe even selfish, but I didn't want him to go yet. By the end of October, he'd be across the country, but for now, if I could have him until then, I was going to ask for it.

"I want you to stay," I whispered. "If you can. If they'll allow it."

He looked up at me through those thick lashes. He looked somehow vulnerable, like this mattered so much to him.

"You do?" he asked.

"Yeah," I said, low. "I do."

"Me, too," he said, exhaling. "I'll tell them I'm not coming until the agreed-upon date. They'll have to make it work."

He sat back, typed on his phone, and then placed it next to him. When he looked over at me this time, his face was bright. His eyes seemed to drink me in from top to bottom.

With the side of his finger, he brushed my smooth sun-kissed cheek.

"You're so beautiful it kind of hurts my heart to look at you," he said.

My skin broke out in sensitive goose bumps.

I stood up and straddled his lap, let the robe cascade open, and his warm hands plunged inside, cupping my skin, his palm on my breastbone, moving down my stomach. Arching toward him and closing my eyes, the feel of his hands roving across my skin made the past and the future seem irrelevant.

There was only right now, with Alex Perry, touching my body, breathing hard, telling me his heart hurts when he looks at me.

His eyes were blazing when I finally caught them in mine. I softly grasped the side of his neck, and then lifted my hands into his hair. His head fell back, his mouth supple and open. When I kissed the tender skin of his neck, he gasped.

Finding his ear, I practically purred into it, "Let's go to bed and never leave."

There was only a murmur of assent and then he hitched his arms under my legs and heaved me up. Now it was my turn to gasp and when I did, he shot me a sinful smile. He threw me on the bed on my back and the robe fell to my sides, the belt limp across my stomach.

He kneeled on the edge of the bed and said, "Just lie back, Quinn. I need to get my mouth on you."

"Yes, Chef," I whispered and heard him groan.

I was shivering with anticipation, felt the heat of his hands on my thighs as if they were branded into me.

There was nothing else in the world I wanted to do but spread my legs and give in.

So, that's what I did.

For the next two days, there was no beach, no books, no anything. There was no leaving the hotel room. There was only the bed with its immaculate white sheets and pliant duvet, imprinted with our bodies. The shower, Alex's fingertips running across my scalp to get the shampoo out, the feel of him hard against me. The room service, us both scrambling to get fully clothed, knowing the room smelled of sex and insatiability, neither of us ashamed of it. The incessant giggling, a sort of heightened hysteria from the complete departure from both our normal lives. Movies running on TV that we hadn't seen in years, kisses during commercials, forgetting to watch until the end because we were busy exploring each other's bodies again. The sheer amount of orgasms I had no idea I was capable of, proof that Alex had earned my body's trust.

By the time we checked out, I was confident I had traversed every inch of his skin, that he'd done the same.

If I were a hopeless romantic, I'd believe this was the beginning of an incredible love story.

Thankfully, I wasn't.

Knowing I could control myself—it was the only reason I didn't run.

36

Someone was playing the guitar when I walked into Quinn Canyon after Alex dropped me off. It was a melodically sad song at odds with the cloudless sky and stiflingly hot October afternoon outside. You could never imagine there was an autumnal heat wave happening when you were cocooned here. It was both a physical and metaphorical refuge to so many people during my childhood. But, of course, the only person who seemed incapable of taking shelter in it was me.

Maybe because I had witnessed the underbelly of a house like this, where dreams were fanned to flames and turned to ashes. When the party was over, the fire extinguished, I was always the one that picked Mom up from the bathroom floor after her quiet sobs had woken me up in the middle of the night. She tried so hard. She wanted to make it so bad. But she had to watch everyone else's dreams blossom, while she became a footnote in their story. She was always the one left behind. By my dad. By her friends. By her own hopes.

She was enough hopeless romantic for all of us. She had enough belief to take over an entire room. And she was still doing it.

I watched her in the teal velvet armchair, on the edge of her seat, swaying to the music, eyes closed, hands grasped together. The man playing the guitar seemed to be around Benny's age, of Indian descent, with a closely trimmed beard and long, slightly curled, black hair.

His voice was hauntingly beautiful and I couldn't take my eyes off him. He was an alluring performer, gorgeous and charismatic. Willow and Jasper were there. And so was Ali's daughter, Aya, two large boxes of pizzas open on the coffee table that I assumed she brought from her dad's shop.

Scattered around the living room were a few other people I didn't recognize. It was like stepping into the past, a remnant of how life used to be. Mom, surrounded by virtuosos, believing in their talent so much that within a year they'd be at the Grammys or the Academy Awards, or playing opposite some A-list star on an indie movie, about to be discovered. The artwork that lined nearly every bit of open wall space were from people Mom knew, who'd passed through Quinn Canyon on their rise to fame.

I had never known people called it the Magic House, but now it seemed obvious.

I couldn't believe Mom could sit there peacefully immersed in the music, soft smile on her face, and not be overwhelmed by bitterness and resentment. It occurred to me that it's exactly how I'd feel if our positions were switched. If I had spent my whole life chasing a dream that didn't want to be caught, I'd hate anyone who'd made it. It was such an ungenerous look at life.

The man stopped playing and I removed my hands from over my heart where they'd somehow moved to, and clapped loudly. The song was beautiful and I had never heard it before. He must have written it. Mom caught me watching and her eyes went wide like she hadn't expected to see me there. She waved me over and patted the low broad arm of the armchair. When I sat down, her arm fit snugly around my waist.

"That's Ravi," she whispered. "He's just flown in from London to meet with some American labels. He's amazing, isn't he?" I gave a sound of agreement, transfixed on Ravi. He was tuning his guitar and his horde of admirers were all quiet, waiting for him to begin again. Silently, I waved to Willow, Jasper, and Aya. It felt like we all knew we were in the presence of greatness, like we were aware that we'd lose Ravi to the mechanisms of fame and success eventually but right now, right here, he belonged only to us.

He was about to begin his next song, his long tapered fingers grasping the neck of his guitar, sliding them down the strings the way one might slide down a body. I shook my head, laughing, aware that I'd had a lot of sex recently and everything was becoming erotic because of it.

Just as Ravi strummed his first chord, the door flew open and Benny, in her chaotic glory, whooshed in with a camera swinging around her neck, her phone in her hand, and two tote bags overflowing with various detritus. She stopped short when she saw everyone looking at her.

"Oh, shit," she said. "Sorry."

"I thought you had a job," Mom said. "You said you wouldn't be home until dinner."

"I didn't get it," she replied, eyes darting around to the audience watching her. The wince was barely perceptible, but I didn't miss it. "Ignore me," she added. "Keep playing, stranger." She nodded toward Ravi and we all turned around to look at him.

But he was looking at my little sister as if he, himself, had been the one starstruck.

"Hello? I'm Ravi," he said, an introduction very clearly directed at my sister. His voice was a precise English accent that suddenly made his appeal ten times more potent. Benny was oblivious. She had her back turned to us all and was rummaging through her tote, cursing under her breath.

Mom was watching this all intently and said, "Benny," loudly until she turned back around. "Come sit."

Benny gave us a weird look, but then put all her belongings down and sat on the ground with her back up against Mom's chair. It was unmistakable that Ravi could not tear his eyes away from her. One woman who was quite young and had been silently watching this all from near the fireplace let out a little mewl of a cry, and ran out the front door.

"That's just Jolene," Mom said. "She lives down the street. She's in love with any guy who can play a guitar. Poor girl. God knows I've been there."

I looked over at Aya and we both stifled the kind of laughter that said, *Is anyone else seeing the absurdity unfolding before us?*

Ravi was still incapable of playing the guitar, bewitched by Benny, who was scrolling her phone. Mom kicked her. "Benny, the phone. Let's listen. This is Ravi. This is Benny, my daughter."

"Benny," he whispered under his breath.

Her head finally snapped up.

"Hey," she said. "Sorry. I'm listening. Go ahead."

Aya and I caught eyes again. The tension was so palpable I felt like I might giggle uncontrollably because of it. Aya looked like she was having the same problem.

"This is a love song," Ravi said, only looking at Benny. "A heartbreak song," he added, composure breaking. "Not like a current love. I'm single. It's a past love."

Again, Aya and I caught eyes and had to look away, lest we ruin this perfect moment.

Ravi started playing, his voice casting out around the incredible acoustics of Quinn Canyon's living room. It took about five seconds of him playing for Benny to still and regard him in an entirely different way. I watched it happen, watched Ravi play every note in her direction, watched as she hardly blinked for three full minutes.

I had a ludicrous thought that nearly made me fall off the arm of the chair. It dropped into my head like a dream. *I hope they fall in love.* The idea of it made me feel like golden glitter was dancing around in the air, which I found incredibly odd and suspicious, given I didn't believe in love, or romance, or destiny, or soulmates. Why did I even care?

I decided to swiftly ignore it.

When Ravi's beautiful song was over, I stood up and headed to the kitchen, wanting to get very far away from whatever chemical reaction was happening between Ravi and Benny, and whatever it was inspiring within me. I placed my hands on the kitchen island, taking in deep breaths, not realizing how shaken up I was until I had a moment alone. It was panic, creeping up like a freight train, gathering speed.

Mom popped her head into the doorway.

"You okay?" she asked as I quickly regained my composure.

"Of course," I said.

"You sure?"

"Yes, I'm sure."

"Okay, well, quick question," she asked. "Alex is making dinner, right? You think he'd mind a few more people to feed?"

"Let me ask," I said, still a little shaken up.

"If not, I can kick all these people out," she said, smiling.

"Or he can cook another night."

"Don't you want him to cook tonight?"

"Sure. But maybe he's tired and doesn't want to do it."

"What happened?"

"Nothing."

"Oh, I get it," Mom said. "You're pulling away."

"I'm not pulling away."

"Yeah," she said. "You are. That's what you do. You pull away."

"I'll text him, okay?" I told her, annoyed.

"Don't you dare tell him not to come. I'd rather kick everyone out than give you an excuse to cancel on that man."

"Fine," I said. "But you do know he's leaving soon, right? Like he's moving away? Does it really matter whether I pull away now or later?"

"Yes," she replied, definitively. "It matters."

"Why? Why does it matter?"

"Because you promised him, you promised me, and you

promised your sister you'd give it a month and the month isn't over yet and you already want to run. You need to see where this all goes."

"I know where it goes," I mumbled.

"You think you do," she said. "You always think you have it all figured out."

I shook my head, crossed my arms across my chest.

"I'm going to politely ask Ravi's admirers to leave. He'll stay for dinner with Jasper, Willow, and Aya. Unless Alex really has a problem with more people."

"I'll ask him."

"Good."

She flitted out of the kitchen and I was reminded of another reason this place had never been a refuge for me: because my mom could see right through me, always.

Sometimes you just want to make your bad decisions in peace.

I texted Alex, asking if he minded feeding four extra people.

> of course i don't mind

> i always make plenty

> also, i miss you

> can i say that?

> i miss you

> it's only been an hour

> i keep getting flashes of you under me, on top of me, my head between your legs hearing all your sounds and i can't function

> you are so fucking beautiful
>
> and sexy
>
> and smart
>
> and funny
>
> just needed you to know that
>
> see you soon

I did not appreciate the swoop my heart made at reading these texts. My stupid heart, betraying me, yet again.

> when will you be here?
>
> i miss you, too
>
> too much actually

> be there in an hour
>
> meet me outside so i can take my time saying hello before i have to meet people
>
> i can't say hello to you the right way if people are around

I literally had to force the corners of my lips to go back to neutral, so blazing was my preposterous smile.

37

My traitorous heart was still yammering away when I went upstairs to change. Having walked into a concert in full bloom, I hadn't even had a chance to unpack my duffel. When I went upstairs and placed the bag in my room, I heard my mom muttering to herself from her bedroom.

"Knock, knock," I said to the ajar door and swung it open. She was on her colorful bed, propped up by a mountain of pillows, holding open a script, her glasses on the tip of her nose. It was so familiar it was like time travel.

I could remember the hundreds of times I walked in on her like this over the years, her patting the empty side of the bed, me lying down, my head in her lap, one hand playing with my hair, the other flipping pages, her muttering under her breath, memorizing lines for an audition, hoping, reaching for her dream. I lost hope in her dreams so much quicker than she did.

By the time I was a senior in high school, I stopped coming in here when I heard that telltale murmur. I didn't want to see the excitement on her face. Didn't want to, eventually, deal with the crash of rejection, when she'd be in bed for an entirely different reason. One week, she was jubilant, the next, unreachable. Why would anyone choose that kind of life?

She patted the space next to her and I lay on the bed. She put the script down and faced me. I'd been wanting to ask her about this magical house business since Alex brought it up.

"Mom, did you know people have been calling this the Magic House since I was in high school?"

She shushed me. "It doesn't work if you talk about it."

"What?" I exclaimed. "You know about it?"

"I do," she said. "People say that if you act as though you already have what you most want while in this house, it will happen."

"And it's true?"

She shrugged. "It's a lot of coincidences. One might call it a pattern by now."

"But, Mom, you haven't gotten what you most wanted."

She laughed. "Yes, I have actually."

"But you're not an actr—"

She lifted her hand and interrupted me. "Listen. When James first gave me this house, it was a blank slate. I hated it. Have I ever told you that? I had a lonely childhood. I didn't want a lonely life. All I ever wanted was to have a family. James didn't even know I was pregnant when he died. He left me the house and there I was, with my biggest wish in my belly. You."

"Me?"

"Yes. I wanted a family. I wanted to never be alone. I wanted to be surrounded by people who didn't reject me—daughters, especially. Daughters I could raise my way, give them what I never had. And then, all this year, I wanted you back home. I thought of this exact moment, you and me in this room, connecting like old times. And here you are." She cupped my cheek with her palm, her eyes glassy.

"I didn't know that," I said.

"You and Benny *are* my magic," she said. And it was so honest and raw that I felt like the most horrible daughter for all the ways I'd been resenting her. All the ways I'd withheld from her. She hadn't wanted to be rejected, but all I'd done for years was reject her. My eyes stung. But, how do you stop a pattern?

How do you get out of the well-worn groove of your own anger and hurt?

"You're afraid to let go," Mom said into the silence. She had picked up her script again, but she was talking to me like she was reading my mind. Maybe she actually was. "That's why you can't pull away, Charlie baby. You've got some more work to do."

Giving her a nod, not knowing what else there was to say, I got up from the bed, and went back to my room, shell-shocked. I unpacked my clothes robotically, my mind staticky. An hour or so later, the moment I heard the chime of a text from Alex letting me know he was here, I was suddenly alive again, racing down the stairs.

A nearly dizzying feeling of yearning gripped me, and I headed outside at a fast clip. His back was to me when I arrived at his car and when he turned around and saw me, he dropped the two paper bags in his hands and hungrily pulled me to him, as if we'd been apart for years, as opposed to mere hours.

Within milliseconds, he had me up against the side of his SUV, hands roaming through my hair, fingertips brushed against my neck, lips hungry as they landed urgently on mine, him eliciting a moan of relief so acute I pulled his body even closer to mine until I was flat against the car. I had always used Noah as the metric of passion, but even this was more intense and electric than what he and I had. Maybe because Alex and I shared a history of unfinished business with each other, and maybe the finality of it was a turn-on, too.

Somehow I was both a teenage version of myself, all hormonal need, and also the version of me now, who hadn't been kissed with this type of hunger in a very long time. It was frighteningly easy to get used to a passionless life. How could we ever sustain this long-term? This was the kind of thing that burned too bright, got too close to the sun, exploded into fractured pieces.

I wouldn't survive the end of this if I didn't know it was coming.

When Alex came up for breath, he stroked the pads of his fingers across my swollen bottom lip and whispered, "Hello."

"Ohhh," I replied. "So, when you said you wanted to say hello, what you meant was make out like teenagers before my mom sees us?"

He smiled. "Exactly. Once we go in there . . ." he nodded toward the house ". . . I'll have to be on my best behavior."

"Well, that doesn't sound like any fun."

"Feel free to pull me into an empty room at your earliest convenience, then."

"And in this empty room you speak of," I purred. "What will we do in there?"

"Anything you want," he said. "You should know that by now. Anything you want, take it."

Warmth flooded my body like basking in direct sunlight.

Alex stroked the plane of my cheek. "This flush of your cheeks right here drives me crazy."

"Yeah?"

"*You* drive me crazy," he whispered, eyes blazing with intensity.

The way he was looking at me, it didn't feel like just lust. It was something more, something too soft and forbidden at the same time. Too intimate. Too real. Like he couldn't hide his emotions even if he tried.

"Let's go inside," I said, voice high-pitched as I grabbed one of the paper bags and headed up to the house. When Alex caught up, he seemed unaware that I was trying to avoid seeing that look on his face again.

"Benny and my mom are here," I told him, smoothly changing the subject. "Then there's Willow and Ravi, both musicians. Jasper, a young actor. And Aya. Her dad owns our favorite pizza place and she's taking it over. We've known the family for years."

"An eclectic group," Alex said. "What else would I expect from the Magic House?"

"Watch, next year Ravi'll win a Grammy," I said. "He's halfway in love with Benny, by the way."

"Godspeed to the people who fall for the Quinn women," Alex replied. His tone was light, but there was a bit of an edge to it.

"What are you making?" I asked. We reached the doorway and went inside. I knew his words contained subtext, but I had to ignore it.

"The best macaroni and cheese you've ever had in your entire life," he said. "Also, fried chicken. Also, corn bread. Also, my secret coleslaw recipe."

When I turned around, his eyes were locked on me like nothing else in the entire world was worth looking at.

"Is that it?" I quipped, laughing. "Doesn't seem like nearly enough."

He swatted me on the ass. "I also made an apple pie."

"Show-off," I said, sticking my tongue out at him. "Everyone will be very impressed."

He dropped his bag in the hallway and I did the same, then he lifted my arms and crossed them behind his neck, got real close to me. Everyone was talking in the kitchen, but there was a door between us and them.

"Will *you* be impressed?" he asked, soft, right into my ear. "Because you're the only one I'm trying to impress."

"I'll have to taste everything and let you know." I licked the side of his neck and his knees buckled. I laughed.

"Making me earn it," he whispered. "I like that, Quinn."

He kissed me, slowly, his hand sliding up my T-shirt to the skin of my back. I arched toward him until I heard the kitchen door fly open. We immediately jumped away from each other like we'd been caught doing something we shouldn't.

"Oh, don't stop on my account," Benny said, laughing. "I approve completely of clandestine meetings in darkened hallways with family in the other room. But, we're starving. Any chance you all want to stop making out for a second and cook this dinner?"

She picked up both paper bags that Alex and I couldn't seem to get from the car to the kitchen without dropping, then looked over her shoulder and smiled with a goddamn twinkle in her eye, like nothing could get by her, especially not this.

38

Watching Alex prep the ingredients and delegate roles to every single person in the kitchen was a study in my own self-control.

He was in his element, orchestrating as if he were at the helm of a symphony. With his organization and precision, his passion for food was readily apparent. When Willow was slicing cabbage for the coleslaw, he gently instructed her to make the ribbons thinner without being chastising. I could practically see the hearts in her eyes when she gazed up at him. When Aya was given the grater to shred massive piles of sharp cheddar for the macaroni and cheese, Alex passed through just to tell her good job and she beamed like his approval meant everything to her. Jasper was put to work on the homemade breadcrumbs, and Ravi was playing DJ, singing along to his choices, trying to take his eyes off Benny, who was cutting corn from the cob into a large bowl while giggling with Mom.

Alex had us all in the palm of his hand and he knew it. Every time I caught his eyes, they were shining with genuine joy. I forced myself to focus on peeling carrots so I wouldn't just sit there on a stool and worship him.

Eventually, I had to use every bit of self-control to stop imagining a life where this was a weekly event, a group of artistic characters being put to work by an effusively beautiful chef named Alex Perry and a woman, on a stool, peeling carrots, adoring him.

We'd all adopted a "yes, Chef" approach and each time we said it, Alex would guffaw with charming laughter, little hints of pink on his cheeks from the slight embarrassment, looking over at me because he knew the sexual undertones of those two words within our own private world. When he passed by me to check on my carrot peeling, I purred, "Yes, Chef" into his ear and he told me to stop or he'd need to clear the kitchen and have his way with me. I told him I wasn't against that idea and he told me I was "a bad influence," and I have to say, when it came out of his mouth, I didn't hate the sound of it.

Friday nights in my old life were so stale and lifeless. Some bland dinner, asleep by 9:00 p.m., waking up on Saturday morning just to work more. *I can't live the same day over and over and call it a life.* I understood it now, the vast emptiness of a life like that.

Benny found me when the mac and cheese was in the oven with the corn bread, Alex at the stove with the chicken, oil popping loudly over the soundtrack of Ravi's varied and vast selection of songs ranging from Redbone's "Come and Get Your Love" to Tracy Chapman's "Fast Car."

Benny nodded toward Alex's back. "Have you seen the way this man looks at you?" she whispered. She was holding a wineglass full of sparkling water. "It's in the eyes, Charlie. He's gone. Nobody else in this house matters except you."

I brushed her off with a pfff. "We just spent three days in bed together, Ben. That's all it is."

Benny let out a sharp laugh. "No, it's not. It's decidedly not all it is, not even a little bit. That man is one open invitation away from risking it all for you."

"You don't know what you're talking about," I told her. "He has a job to get to."

"I know this might come as a shock to you, Char, but some people are willing to turn down a job for love. Crazy, I know.

But it's been known to happen." She leveled me with a wry grin.

"I wouldn't ask him to do that," I said resolutely.

"You'll regret not knowing where this could go," she said back, just as firmly.

"And what about Ravi, then? He's been watching you all night. I think it's love at first sight."

"A masterful change of subject," she said appraisingly. "Fine, I'll allow it. I'm into him, but it's actually not going anywhere."

"So you can tell *me* all about risk, but will never take any of your own, is that it?" I meant to say this jokingly, but it came out with a bite.

"First," she began, "Ravi and I just met. We didn't love each other secretly as teenagers, so there's that. Second, he's at the cusp of his career and so am I. The difference between you and me is that I'm not *afraid* of love, Charlie. I just don't *want* to be tied down right now. But if I met someone I could really love, I wouldn't turn away from them."

"What happened with the shoot?" I asked softly. Some online brand had hired Benny to do pictures for their website. She hadn't been thrilled about it, but she'd said yes.

"They fired me," she said. "On day one."

"What? Why?"

I expected Benny to quip about how what's meant for her will always find her, bring some levity to it all like she usually did, but instead her smile fell, tears shining in her eyes, and she ran out of the kitchen. It stunned me. When I followed after her, I found her quietly crying on the stairwell, head in her hands.

"Benny," I said, squeezing in next to her and placing my arm around her shoulder. "Whoa. What happened?"

She didn't speak for a while, just vibrated and let out little hiccups of sobs. It nearly broke my heart in half. I was about to ask again, but then she lifted her head up, cheeks streaked with tears, and she said, "I did some test shots. They hated them.

Fired me right there. It was horrible. I'm horrible. I don't know what I'm doing. I'm not good enough for this industry. LA is too cutthroat. I'm an imposter. I feel like an idiot. What was I even thinking trying to become a photographer? A pipe dream. I need to find something realistic. You're right. You've been right all along and I just didn't want to see it. I'm twenty-five. I'm not a kid anymore."

She threw her face back into her hands and I heard her sniffling.

I had no idea what to do.

She sounded . . . like me.

The distress I felt nearly made me choke.

I hated hearing my own protestations coming out of her mouth.

"Benny, listen to me," I said, not sure where I was even going with this, trusting I had some wisdom I could impart. "You're an incredibly talented photographer. You love doing it. It's your calling. Truthfully, I wish I had something like that. I wish I had your courage and determination, and your optimism. It's not a pipe dream. Don't give up." I almost didn't say the next thing, but I wanted to use her words back on her. "What's meant for you will be for you, remember? Maybe this is making space for something better."

She finally looked at me, wiped her eyes.

"You really think so?" she asked, hopeful. "And here I thought you were going to judge me."

"I've done that for a long time, haven't I? Judged you?"

Benny shrugged. "You haven't always approved of the way Mom and I approach life."

"Understatement of the year," I said, laughing. "Have I apologized for that yet? Because I'm sorry. What the hell do I know, Benny? Seriously?" I lifted my hands up. "What do I know?"

"I thought you knew everything."

"Well, I don't. I think I'm finding out that I know nothing."

She laughed. "Join the club!"

I hugged her and whispered, "Sorry. For everything."

We stayed grasping each other for a long while, until Benny pulled back.

"You okay?" I asked her, knocking her on the shoulder.

"I am now," she replied. "You know, we need you, Charlie. You make us better."

"I do?"

"You really do."

I extended a hand out to help her up, and we then made our way into the kitchen. When we did, it was time to eat.

Benny had set the table with tapered candles and the fancy burnt orange napkins we never used, along with ceramic plates with various flowers on them, each one different than the other. Handmade, apparently, by a ceramicist that Benny and Mom had met a couple years back. Of course they were. The candles were soy, from a candlemaker down the road. The vase was from the ceramicist, the flowers from the farmers market—every single thing had been selected with love and cherishment. Back home, I ate off paper plates to avoid doing the dishes. I couldn't remember if I'd ever set a table.

We all sat down amid the soft glow of candlelight, a foreign sense of belonging suddenly washing over me. Fear came alongside it, as if any good thing was a matched set to my terror.

How do you love people without knowing when you'll lose them? How do you bear it? Isn't it easier to just not love at all?

And why did it seem like it was so much easier for everyone else to go through life unguarded? Every single day, people made vows. Every single day, they had children and promised to love them. Every single day, they brought each other closer even though they knew that one day, they could be gone.

It was unfathomable to me, the pain of it.

The heartbreak.

And, somehow, the beauty.

39

For the first five to seven minutes of the meal, no words were spoken. All you could hear was faint music, the scraping of forks and knives across handmade ceramic, and the occasional sigh of pure delight from how good the food was.

We all had seconds, then thirds, until every platter on the wide table was empty. Perfect creamy mac and cheese. Soft, pillowy corn bread with real bits of sweet corn and honey butter that Aya had made, per Alex's instructions. Coleslaw so light and tangy and acidic that we all ate piles of it, exclaiming that coleslaw had never tasted so good. And then the fried chicken—my God, the fried chicken. Juicy in the middle, a crunch that echoed throughout the dining room, and a spicy ketchup dipping sauce that Alex had made from scratch.

It was a feast, and Alex had put it together as if it were nothing.

"I'll be the first to say it," Jasper declared once his fork was finally down. "That was the best meal I've ever had in my life."

"Couldn't agree more," Mom said. "Alex, you are a culinary genius."

"I might need to lick the plate," Willow said. "I need you all to look away."

"Thank you," Alex said, lifting his hands up and dipping his head down. "You're all way too kind." When he looked over at me, it was intimate, a look of bashfulness, like the attention was too much. My chest swooped. In that moment, it felt like Alex belonged to me, like everybody wanted this version of him, and I was the one that got it.

"Alex promised the best mac and cheese of my life," I said. "And he delivered. A perfect meal. I'm impressed."

Alex's smile beamed like sunlight through clouds. "My job here is done," he said, rubbing his hands together. "No offense to you guys, but Charlie is the only one I came here to impress."

I shook my head, cheeks flushed, and laughed.

"Yeah, we know," Benny shouted.

I couldn't stop myself and framed my hands with Alex's face and kissed him, right there, right in front of everyone. When it was over, his eyes were wide with surprise.

He whispered, "You keep doing that, I'm going to get the wrong idea about where this is going."

I was starting to give *myself* the wrong idea about where this was going. Given I had been buttoned-up for so long, I had no idea why I couldn't control myself around Alex. It was as if my heart had a mind of its own, which actually didn't make any sense.

"Is this the kind of food you'll be cooking at that restaurant you're opening in Chicago?" Ravi asked.

"Unfortunately, no," Alex said. "The place in Chicago will be a super high-end fine dining tasting menu. Like the kind you plate with tweezers. What I made tonight is the food I learned from my grandmother."

"Do you want to open your own restaurant one day?" Aya asked. She'd been peppering Alex with questions all night. It was apparently her dream to turn her dad's pizza counter into a more diversified restaurant experience, with a fast casual concept along with a sit-down restaurant.

Alex gave a dry laugh. "Of course," he said, sighing heavily. It was the first time all night I'd seen him look tired. "I was about to open my own place, but it was the beginning of 2020. Bad luck. Worse timing. The menu was all comfort food like this.

Dishes crafted around creating the most perfect bite of food, the salt, the fat, the acid, the crunch, the texture. All of it. It's why you put crunchy breadcrumbs on soft mac and cheese, why you vary the cheese in the béchamel to give it layers of surprising tastes and combinations. Why we love fried chicken, the crunch with the juiciness. Even the reason you love that coleslaw—it's got just enough acid to make it insanely craveable. It's incredible to me that you can take the same ingredients, and each chef will interpret them differently. I want my own restaurant so I can share my interpretation of food, my way, but it feels like an impossible dream now." He looked down at his fidgeting hands. "Sorry, long answer to a short question." He shrugged.

"It sounds like you love food the way I love music," Ravi said.

"Yeah, it does," Willow said. "Like the idea that Ravi and I have the exact same chords to work with, but the way we arrange them is what creates our artistic expression—that's fascinating to me."

"That's why I love acting," Jasper added. "No actor will take on a role the same way, no matter what. The interpretation is where the art comes from."

"Yep," Mom said. "That's why I hold on to my dream. That moment when you drop into a character, when you're not saying the lines, but the lines are coming through you. You can tell in your food, Alex, that you are passionate about the way *you* create art with your ingredients. The dishes come *through* you."

"That's why I love photography," Benny said. "It's crazy to me that twenty photographers can take a picture of the exact same thing and it's going to look twenty different ways. Like, that is actually magic."

Everyone turned to Aya, because it was clear that this table had become a sharing circle.

"I mean, I feel the same way Alex does about cooking," she said, smiling. "My dad was always fascinated that there are a million pizza joints using practically the same base ingredients, and each one tastes different. How is that possible? On paper, it doesn't make sense. But the fact that every little factor can change the cooking process is endlessly interesting to me. All we're ever doing with creativity is making different combinations of the same base ingredients. Writers, with the same collection of letters. Actors, interpreting those written words based on their own experiences. Photographers, showing us how they see the world. I love that about art."

I was staring down at my empty plate and instantly felt everyone's eyes on me. There was a whirring in my head, a panic, breathing short and staccato, my cheeks hot with shame.

What could I say?

That I loved nothing?

That I had no passion?

That I'm dead inside, broken?

That I think I might be incapable of love?

That I couldn't relate to a single word any of them were saying?

Instead of speaking, I threw the chair back with a loud scrape and started clearing plates frenetically.

Thankfully, this group of good people took mercy on me and helped, busying themselves with their own conversations, and letting me wash dishes in peace. My short breathing evened out. The whirring in my head lessened.

And when Alex took the apple pie out of the oven and then pulled up next to me at the sink, my hands sudsy with soap and warm water, I leaned in when he kissed my hair instead of pushing him away.

To my relief, when we returned to the table to have dessert, the conversation had floated into easier topics and I could breathe again.

40

By midnight, we were all writhing in pain and pleasure from how much food we'd consumed when Willow procured a pack of large tarot cards from her tote bag and asked, "Who wants a reading?"

"Charlie does," Benny chimed in, pointing at me across the table. She mouthed, "Request," to me and I halfheartedly nodded.

"Sure," I said to Willow, who was conveniently sitting across from me, her eyes bright and inquisitive. I knew tarot cards were a bunch of bullshit, so I didn't see the harm in allowing Willow to pretend. Tarots were like anything else spiritual or astrological, vague enough that the gullible would feel understood. Mom had been tracking moon cycles and planet retrogrades since I was young and, even then, I was skeptical.

"Willow is amazing," Mom said. She was sitting at the head of the table with Ravi and Jasper at her sides. "She did a reading for me the other day and confirmed that I'm a late bloomer in my career, the same I've been seeing in my astrology chart and from another tarot reader who used to live down the way and moved to Sedona. Crazy how I've been hearing the same thing for so many years."

Yeah, I thought, *super crazy that someone could see exactly what you want to hear and tell it to you*. I didn't say that out loud, but I wanted to. Benny was watching me, like she knew what was going through my mind.

Willow didn't know anything about me, so I couldn't wait to hear the formless conclusions she'd try to sell back to me. I liked her, but I didn't like people who used vulnerabilities against others, told them things they wanted to hear, gave them false hope.

Willow started shuffling her cards.

"Okay, Charlie," she said. "Think of what you want the most while I do this."

I want this to be over, I thought, but only nodded.

"I'm going to do a three-card spread of past, present, and future," Willow told me. "This isn't fortune-telling. It's a portal for self-discovery." Willow's voice was rhythmic and calming, but I suddenly felt warm and panicked again.

I reminded myself that tarot cards were a joke and Willow was just having a bit of fun.

She had me cut the deck three times. While she was doing a rapid shuffle, a card flung from the deck and landed face down in front of us.

"That one really wanted to get out," she said and straightened it in front of me face down. "That's your Present card."

After some more shuffling, she placed two more cards from the deck on either side of the one that flung out. Gently, she flipped each one. The middle card, the one that flew out, gave me a start. It was called The Tower and it was pure calamity on the tarot card, a man and a woman literally jumping from a tower on fire.

"Interesting," Willow said, studying the three cards in between us. Her eyes met mine eagerly and she said, "What happened, Charlie? Something horrible happened. It's been following you around, binding you. You can see it here in the Past card." She pointed to the card on my right, which showed someone bound in rope.

Everyone's eyes were on me. My cheeks flamed again.

"I don't know what you're talking about," I lied, voice wobbling. I kept my gaze trained on the cards, and didn't dare look at Benny, Mom, or Alex. This was the problem with having people care about you—they wanted to *know* things. They wanted to *talk* about things.

"Well, here's what I see in the cards," Willow said, seemingly ignoring my apprehension, or not even noticing it at all. "You suffered a terrible heartbreak of some kind. Maybe romantic. It has made you scared of the world. You are currently in a massive transformation—that's what The Tower card here represents. It looks like calamity, but it's actually a purification process. Let the old you crumble so the new you can emerge. And then, this Future card is interesting. It's a choice, actually.

"You can stay comfortable and live a predictable life, like you have been doing, from what I can see in this Past card. Or you can step into the unknown, take chances, take risks, and heal from that past heartbreak by letting the light back in. It all depends on what you choose in this Tower moment you're in right now. Will you let go of the past and step into the new you? Or will you go back to the old you and stay safe and protected from life?"

I was stunned into speechlessness, letting out a breath I didn't know I was holding.

Willow shrugged, collected the cards, and said, "Not sure if that resonates. If it doesn't, ignore everything I just said." She laughed. "Anyone else want one?"

Ravi jumped in and Willow switched seats with Jasper so she could do Ravi's cards.

My heart was pounding in my chest. I wish she had been wrong. Wished she had been vague and off the mark, but that was too specific. My breathing came out short and stunted again.

My mind was blaring, buzzing, flashbacks flickering in and out. Ravi was being told that his dreams were about to come true and he needed to keep a sensible head about him. He beamed, like letting good things happen to you was the easiest thing in the world.

When I looked over at Mom, she wasn't looking at Ravi and Willow—she was watching me. She was watching me like she knew everything. I could almost hear her pleading, *What happened?*

Benny's eyes were on me, too, but I didn't meet them. She knew it all too well. I could imagine how much she wanted to tell Mom, to tell everyone, to make me reveal it all. She'd say that was the purification process I needed, but it wasn't. The past had to stay buried.

God, what was *wrong* with me?

I would rather live within the confines of a safe and predictable life than ever take a risk again. I would rather never speak to my mom again before I would let myself be vulnerable. I would rather let Alex go than ever take a chance and open myself up to something real.

I wanted to be impenetrable, to figure out how life couldn't hurt me anymore.

Everybody seemed capable of love with such startling ease.

And all I ever wanted was to stop my heart from wanting it.

41

Mom insisted that Alex stay over, since everyone else lived closer and Alex's sublet apartment was in Malibu. The house was dead quiet, but I spent over an hour tossing in bed next to him as he slept, my mind trying to force me to relive the one part of my past I refused to ever think about. I wished I could detach entirely from my thinking, from this incessant chatter. The only thing I could never escape was myself. If I didn't have my work, what would be left? *This?* This constant, endless loop of battering thoughts?

Clearly needing a good distraction, I gently woke Alex up. When his eyes opened, I crawled on top of him. Reaching down into his boxer briefs, I watched as his eyes rolled to the back of his head and took the opportunity to kiss him, hard, doing two things at once, getting him ready for me.

"Wait," he mumbled against my lips. "Wait a second, Charlie."

He gathered my hands in front of him and I stopped.

"Not that I'm not enjoying this, but your mom and sister are right next door."

"Trust me, Benny would approve."

"And your mom?"

"Honestly? She'd probably approve, too."

He laughed. "I did have many fantasies about doing this exact thing with you when I was sixteen. In fact, you straddling me like this featured heavily in the rotation."

That made me lightheaded with lust.

"All my fantasies included sneaking you into this house and having my way with you."

"Far be it from me to kill the moment," he said, cupping my face with his free hand. "But you seemed . . . introspective tonight. Can we talk?"

"I don't want to talk."

"I've noticed that."

"Sorry I'm not willing to spill all my feelings all the time," I snapped, edgier than I wanted it to sound.

"Talking about things is good, though," he said gently. "Your mom told me tonight you haven't been home in a long time. Did something happen? Was Willow's tarot reading right? You kind of went quiet after it."

Sighing loudly, I said, "So you and my mom were talking about me? And no, Willow's tarot reading wasn't right. Do you hear yourself? They are *tarot cards*. Wow, big swing of her to assume someone had a heartbreak in their past. Yeah, like nobody has ever been hurt. Come on."

"Whoa," Alex said, lifting his palms up. I moved off him and sat on the edge of the bed, my back to him, crossing my arms across my chest. "I'm just trying to get to know you, Charlie. I want to know you."

"What's there to know?" I burst out. "I'm a terrible daughter and a worse sister. I don't come home for years. I work until my eyes burn and I'm too tired to keep my head up. I had a breakup recently and don't even miss him, don't even care. Why would you want to know a person like that, Alex? Let's just call this what it is—sex until you go to Chicago and start your new life. We don't need to make it anything more. I know you're a good guy. You don't have to prove anything to me by asking questions. We can just hook up and say goodbye."

Alex let out a long breath and I couldn't even look at him. Instead, I stared at my feet on the shaggy area rug.

"Charlie," he said quietly. "I'm not trying to prove to you I'm a good guy. I think you're interesting and complex and fascinating and smart and beautiful and I want to know who you are, who you've been. Tonight was the happiest I've been in a long time. If you wanted me to stay—"

"Don't," I cried. "Don't finish that sentence. You don't know what you're saying."

"I do," he said. I felt his hand on the back of my neck and closed my eyes to it. "I'd stay for you. For this. For a life like this. For a chance to see if this is real between us."

"I would never ask you to do that."

"I would do it even if you didn't ask. Even if I thought there was a chance."

"Why, Alex? Why? I'll only hurt you. Or you'll hurt me. Or you'll leave. Or I will."

"That's the risk you take."

"I can't take that risk."

"Even for love?"

"*Especially* for love."

He sighed and I felt him shift in the bed.

"I don't know what happened," he said softly. "Something or someone hurt you. And I'm so sorry for that. But you're letting it close you off. Trust me, I've *been* closed off. I've had one heartbreak after another. Losing the chance with you back in high school broke my heart. I thought about it constantly, even when my heart was shattered from losing my mom. I know loss. I have *lived* loss. And I wanted to close off from everyone and everything. I wanted to so badly. If it weren't for my grandmother, I probably would have. So, I know how you feel. You think I don't. But I do. I know what it's like to want to retreat from the world. But that isn't a life. It isn't living. There are people here, right here, right now, that want to love you so badly. Present tense, Charlie. You don't see it. But tonight, I saw it. And if you don't let them love you, what's the point?"

"You don't know me, Alex," I snapped.

"You're right," he said calmly. "And that's what I'm saying. I want to know you. I want to be there for you. I want to figure it out with you. I know it hasn't been long, but sometimes a connection comes along that you know is special. We got a second chance. This is rare. I'm not the kind of person that can just let that go without a fight. I don't make declarations like this. I don't want to stay for people. I am always the one leaving. But I don't want to leave you."

"I know most women would love to hear this," I said. "But I'm not that kind of woman."

He sighed deeply behind me. I couldn't look at him. I *couldn't*. A long silence stretched between us.

"Okay," Alex finally said, defeated. "Even if it's not me, I wish you'd let *someone* in, Charlie."

"I don't make mistakes like that anymore."

"I get it."

"I don't think you do."

"No, I do. I was closed off from most people. Never wanted to risk. Worked like crazy. It wasn't until I met you that I thought—well, this could be worth opening up for. But you don't feel the same and I understand. Maybe meeting you was just showing me I was ready to meet someone for real." He took a long inhale and let it out slowly. "Maybe it was never meant to be you."

I stifled a whimper that was about to take me over. What could I say? I couldn't promise a single thing, didn't think I was even capable of what Alex was asking of me. But even the thought of him going to Chicago, ready to meet someone else, and falling in love with them—it made me feel crushed under a claustrophobic weight. How selfish was that? To not want someone, but not want them to be with anyone else? A sick feeling of self-hatred slithered across my skin like a snake, coiling around me.

This was why I kept myself sequestered away. Because I hurt people. Because I forced people to do things that went against their better judgment. Love wasn't worth this.

"Maybe," I whispered.

I heard him rustling.

"I'm gonna go actually," he said. "Staying here was a mistake."

I didn't turn around to look at him.

"Is this over, then?" I asked quietly.

"No," he said. "I don't know. I'll call you later today. We can still see each other until I leave. I'm not strong enough to resist you for as long as I can have you. But I need to get my head together. I keep looking at you from across the room and not wanting to be in rooms without you. I can't help it."

"Okay," I said. I know what I should have told him, what the rom-coms dictate in this moment. She runs to him. Opens her heart. They live happily ever after. They make it seem so easy when it's not.

It's just never that easy.

Love doesn't conquer all. Love destroys.

When he left, I stared at the ceiling, eyes glazing over.

Okay, I thought to myself. *Fine. Let's do this.*

Reliving the worst day of my life was the least I could do. This time, the punishment was deserved.

The last scene in the film rolled on and I forced myself to bear it.

42

Her breath hitched when she saw the text from Noah. She hadn't expected him to text her. Or to ever talk to her again. She'd given him the out she thought he wanted. Told him to forget about her, let her go. She wasn't going to be the reason he lost his family.

She had spent the last few hours secretly relieved that he'd chosen them over her. That she didn't have to risk for him any longer. But the moment his text came through—and she read what it said—she was back in, dreaming up her future with him, heart swooping.

> i'm leaving. the hell with this family. taking the first flight out. i miss you. i love you.

He'd chosen her. Her.

> did they agree?

> no. it's their loss. i'll make my own money. you and i will be a family. let's go see your mom and benny. i want to meet them before our trip.

She couldn't believe it.

He told her the flight he intended to take. She promised she'd meet him at the airport. The way she missed him, now knowing he was coming back, was all-consuming like she hadn't let herself feel it until she was safe in the knowledge that he was hers. She'd always wanted him to make this decision on his own, not because she forced him or gave him an ultimatum. If she had done that, she was no better than his heartless parents.

The hours ticked by endlessly. He was taking a red-eye flight and would arrive at SFO in the morning. She tried to sleep, but kept waking up, staring at her phone, wondering if it was time yet.

She felt as if she were on the precipice of the rest of her life. She couldn't wait to introduce Noah to Mom and Benny, to show them she was out there, living, risking, being a little like them in their audacious belief that the world might actually be a positive place. She wanted to surprise her mom, bring Noah like a gift, forgive, let go, and usher in a new version of herself as someone open to love and life. She thought maybe she'd try to find her dad, give him a chance to explain himself. It had been long enough. She could forgive him if he was willing to try.

She was uncomplicated in her happiness. She felt that life was beckoning her forward with its arms wide open, waiting for her to just walk into them.

Finally, it was morning. She drove to the airport, parked her car. She needed to see him arrive, see his wide smile as he bounded toward her, before wrapping her in that world-stopping hug of his. She had flowers with her. It was ridiculous. Cheesy. But she was so in love everything seemed like a perfect idea. Cheesy was the only approach.

She drank a hot mocha latte in the arrivals area, watching flights go from in-air to landed on the TV screens.

When his flight popped up, her chest rose. She thought about the day ahead of her. Now that she knew Noah was hers to keep, that nothing stood between them, she could throw herself at him with complete abandon. She'd been so hesitant. Now she wanted to give him everything, give him all of her, tell him every story, every pain, every single thing. She wanted the romance, the vulnerability, the life spent side by side. She'd had no idea how much she wanted it until she knew she was about to have it. He was coming home to her. Nothing could hold her back now.

They would travel and she'd never be alone and they'd stay at Quinn Canyon for weeks on end and maybe they'd move to LA eventually and maybe she'd get that culinary degree, go to pastry school, start a little bakery, choose an entirely different, but wildly beautiful, life. It all felt possible in that moment. All of it.

His flight landed on time. She hadn't heard from him but figured the night before he had a narrow window to return his rental car and sprint to his flight. She didn't even think to be nervous. She'd remember that forever.

She stood at baggage claim, with her hand-printed sign that said WELCOME HOME NOAH with red-glitter-painted hearts all around it, and a mixed bouquet that was so heavy she had to keep switching hands.

When an hour passed, she called him, but it just rang until it hit his voicemail. That was strange. Where was he?

She went to a customer service kiosk and asked the attendant if a Noah Hawthorne had gotten off the flight yet. Or if there was a delay in the deboarding process. Maybe his luggage was lost and he was at baggage claim still. But why hadn't he texted her?

This was the first moment she worried.

The lady did not want to give out any information, but Charlie begged and begged.

Finally, she divulged that Noah Hawthorne had never taken the flight. All the passengers had collected their bags.

"He didn't get on the flight?" she asked.

"No," the attendant told her. "He never checked in."

She called him again. It rang and rang and rang and Charlie left multiple voicemails. She didn't know if it was time to panic. He changed his mind? Lost his nerve? Couldn't risk losing the money? Could he have done that without telling her? Was he really that cruel?

She ripped the sign in half and stuffed it in a trash can with the massive bouquet of flowers.

She circled the arrivals area trying to figure out what to do, her breathing shallow.

For some strange reason, she started calling rental car agencies. She reached several companies; all of them said Noah Hawthorne had never rented a car with them.

She called the last company on the list, simply because she had to finish what she started. If he never turned the car in, then he'd stayed and changed his mind. That could be closure. She needed to know. The loop was open.

She'd deal with processing later. For now, she needed answers.

She was pacing in the airport arrivals area. It was like purgatory. She couldn't leave yet. Her emotions hadn't caught up to her. She was in business mode.

When she reached a customer service representative, she asked if they had rented a car to a Noah Hawthorne and once the name was said, the woman on the other end gasped.

"What?" Charlie asked. "What is it?"

"Are you his wife?" the woman asked.

Yes, she wanted to say. *Yes, I am his wife.* The ferocity of her desire to claim this role was so intense it startled her. Instead, she said, "I'm his girlfriend."

"We've been trying to reach someone all day. He didn't leave an emergency contact."

"An emergency contact? What happened? Is he okay?" Charlie was lightheaded all of a sudden. There was a pause on the other end and heavy breathing.

"I'm sorry," the woman said. "I'm so sorry."

"WHAT HAPPENED?" Charlie screamed the words out, and several people around her turned to look. She didn't care.

There was another long pause. It sounded like the woman was crying, or, at least, stifling a sob.

"I was told the driver of the car didn't make it," the woman said quietly.

The arrivals area went blurry.

"Didn't make it?" Charlie asked. "Didn't return the car, you mean?" Charlie's ears were ringing, her body swaying. She sat down roughly on a chair next to a young man with headphones on.

"I'm so sorry, miss, but what I mean is that the driver passed. He got into an accident and died on impact."

The world was spinning. She felt like she was plummeting off a cliff.

"Noah Hawthorne? My Noah? Are you sure? Are you absolutely sure?"

"Yes, miss, I'm sure."

The phone clattered to the ground, startling the young man beside Charlie. He retrieved it and handed it to her but Charlie's vision had fogged over.

"Are you okay?" she heard the young man ask.

"No," she said, garbled, as if she were underwater, drowning.

"Do you need a doctor?"

"No," she managed to reply. "No."

She took the phone from him and staggered back to her car. She should have told Noah not to come. She should have let him go, not encouraged him. He wouldn't have been on the road, upset, late at night, if it weren't for her. She had done this. She had caused this. She had wanted something she knew she wasn't meant to have. When she got into the driver's seat and closed the door she let out a piercing howl and kept murmuring, "No, no, no, no, no," over and over and over.

Her heart was ripped open.

She said, "No," a hundred times, at least, sobbing like maybe she would never stop, like she'd still be sobbing fifty years from now, like she'd never ever leave this car, not even when she physically left this car, she'd still be in this car forever.

Three agonizing hours passed, sobs ripped from her throat, her emotions flayed out and stripped bare, and then she halted abruptly, taking a sharp breath in. Finally, she forced herself to stop crying in the parking lot of the San Francisco International Airport.

And then, she made solemn, unbreakable promises to herself. Never again, *she vowed.* Never again will I fall in love. Never again will I do anything the way my mom would do it. Never again will I be so irresponsible. Never again will my heart break like this.

Never. Again.

Charlie decided in that moment she would get a stable job. She would tell Benny about what happened to Noah, but she would swear her to secrecy, make her promise she'd never bring it up, never tell their mom. She never wanted Jackie to know about any of this, about how foolish Charlie had been, about how she had tried to be like her, and it had blown up in Charlie's face.

She took a deep, steadying breath, and started driving. She was numb and it felt better somehow. Noah had never been hers, not really.

She distanced herself from all her friends, especially the ones that knew Noah, because all she wanted to do was never be reminded of this time in her life. She didn't receive a single phone call from Noah's family, and she never attempted to reach out. She moved out of her Stanford apartment and got that stable job in San Francisco, and never looked back.

She could almost convince herself it had all been a movie, like it belonged to someone else.

But, for seven long years, it still felt like she was in that car, stuck and sobbing and irreparably broken.

43

When I came to from the scene, I was somehow outside my mother's bedroom door, fire burning inside me, blind with unspent rage and emotion. Without thinking, I burst in, turned on the light, and screamed, "IT'S ALL YOUR FAULT."

Mom scrambled to sit up in the bed, taken aback. I was at boiling point, ready to blow like a bomb.

"What's going on?" Mom asked. "Is everything okay?"

"No," I said, teeth clenched. "No, nothing is okay."

"Charlie, what happened?"

There was only bellowing alarms in my head. Nothing but the final explosion in a long drawn-out fight to keep my emotions on a simmer.

"It's YOUR fault, Mom! It's your fault that I'm like this! All broken and messed up! I should have been cautious. You never let me be realistic! You never let me protect myself! You gave me hope! I should have *never* let go of control! Hope is the most destructive thing in the whole fucking world, and you convinced me to have it!"

"Whoa. Whoa. Whoa. Back up, Charlie," Mom said, now alert and sitting upright. "I don't understand what you're saying. Let's go have some tea and talk."

"I don't want to have any tea with *you*."

She sat back on the pillow as if I'd slapped her.

"I can't help you if you don't tell me what's going on."

"I don't need your help." I scoffed, laughing bitterly. "I never did."

"I'm going downstairs," was all she said in lieu of a reply. "If you want to talk to me, you can come, too."

She wrapped herself up in a multicolored silk robe and walked past me quickly. My breathing was labored, body vibrating with fury. I waited sixty long seconds before I followed, making some childish and futile point.

The kettle was starting to whistle when I stepped into the kitchen. Mom had two mugs with tea bags hanging out of them on the island, and it enraged me—that she *knew* I'd come down here. I sat on one of the stools and crossed my arms, like a defiant teenager.

"You know what, Charlie?" Mom said after thirty seconds of tense silence. "I gave you a good childhood. I wasn't perfect, but who was? I tried to steer you as best I could. I tried to be there for you while also not sacrificing all of myself like I'd seen from many women before me. You went to college as my Charlie and by the time you came back, you were someone different, someone I couldn't connect to or even recognize sometimes. I've given you a lot of space to tell me why. I've tried to honor your process. I've stayed away when maybe I should have pushed. But it's time. Tell me what happened to my baby."

Suddenly and violently, I didn't want to have this conversation. If I had spent even one second thinking about it before I burst into her room, I would have left LA without looking back. I didn't want to let her into this part of me. Or, maybe I didn't want what happened to be real, like if I kept it locked up like a little movie I avoided, then maybe I could keep the pain locked up, too.

If this part of my past was never witnessed by anyone else, if I could keep Benny from speaking about it to me forever, then maybe I could convince myself it hadn't happened. Maybe I would never have to face it.

But then again, wasn't I facing it all the time? Wasn't it coloring every interaction? Wasn't it acting like a wall keeping me from my life?

I'd been holding my emotions off like tigers in a cage when, actually, I realized, I didn't want to push them back in. Whatever was about to come to blows was maybe too many years too late, but it had to happen.

"I met someone," I whispered. Mom had been patiently waiting, filled the teacups, poured a splash of milk and a bit of honey in mine the way I used to take it. That little act of love made me continue. "A few months before I graduated. His name was—" I stopped, bit back the emotion that was bubbling right on the surface.

"Go on, Charlie," Mom said. "Please." I didn't deserve this much grace, but I took it.

"Noah," I said. "His name was Noah Hawthorne."

"Noah," Mom echoed.

I took a deep breath, knowing this was it. No turning back. Besides telling Benny about it the day I found out and commanding her to never speak of Noah again, this story had been locked up. My voice shook, but I squared my shoulders and pressed on.

"I tried to resist him. But I heard your voice in my head, encouraging me to let go, to experience life, to get out of my comfort zone. He had harsh parents with old family money. His dad wanted him to follow in his footsteps and threatened him, saying if he didn't, then he would be cut out of his own family, disowned, and without his inheritance. But Noah wanted to travel. He was so charismatic and full of life, I felt like I'd follow him anywhere. We fell in love. It happened so fast. One day he was a stranger and the next I wanted to wake up next to him every morning for the rest of my life. I didn't even know I was *capable* of that kind of love.

"We decided to travel together after graduation. I'd delay looking for a job. It sounded like something you'd tell me to do, something that would mean I was truly living my life and not just going through the motions. But I was scared Noah was going to leave me, just like Dad did. That he was going to choose something else that was more important than me. I thought at the last moment he'd go back to his parents and realize he couldn't live without the money."

I paused and took a shaky sip of my tea, trying to gather myself before continuing. Mom sat in stillness, listening.

"He went home to Connecticut to tell his parents about us, to try to convince his dad to relent on his demands. His dad wouldn't. And I gave Noah the out, told him we didn't know each other long enough for him to risk everything. I thought it was over. I was even a little relieved it was over, so that my heart was no longer outside my body. I didn't have to love him anymore. But really, it was just because I loved him so much and I wanted the life we were planning. It was terrifying how much I wanted it."

My hands were trembling, and I inhaled deeply, steadying myself before this next part.

"And then he called me and told me he was coming home, that he'd chosen me, and . . . God, I was *so* happy. I couldn't wait to tell you. I couldn't wait for you to meet him. I thought you'd be so proud of me, risking my heart for love, taking an adventure and traveling. It was maybe the first time I felt alive. Not worried or scared or overly responsible or super realistic, but really, truly *alive*. It felt like Noah had handed me the keys to a life I never thought I could inhabit. Not because of money, which of course we wouldn't have. But a life where I wasn't on the sidelines, afraid of everything."

My voice was shaking and I was talking so fast. Before I lost my nerve, I had to get this all out.

"I waited for him at the airport, Mom," I whimpered. "But he didn't show up. I waited for so long."

Mom was clutching her chest, eyebrows pinched together. "What happened, honey? Did he change his mind?"

"No," I cried. "He was on his way to me. He was coming."

"Oh, no," Mom whispered.

"Car accident," I told her. "Died on impact. He never made it on the plane. Never even returned the rental car. One minute he was alive and vibrant and making plans for our future and the next he was gone."

"Oh, God." Mom's voice felt far away. "I'm so sorry, Charlie. No. Oh, no."

For a flicker of a moment, I thought maybe I could rush toward her, hug her, and everything would be okay. But I didn't, and instead I felt an ugly onslaught of tears that rolled down my cheeks. The grief I never let myself feel gripped me like a vise. My breathing turned shallow and the force of a primal scream nearly ripped through my throat.

Then, in an instant, when I saw what seemed to be a look of pity on Mom's face, I could do nothing but feel the rush of blood between my ears.

"You. Did. This," I bellowed, through brutal sobs. "If you hadn't been telling me my whole life to let go, to believe in love, to believe in good things—I would have *never* let Noah in. I would have never been left at an airport, heart shattered beyond repair!"

"Charlie," she said. There were tears in her eyes and she tried to come to me, but I stood up quickly, crossed my arms across my chest, and got away.

"You were brave," she whispered. "It's better to have loved and lost than not to have loved at all."

"Don't spit stupid clichés at me! Don't fucking do that. *Nothing* happens for a reason. I should have *never* listened to you."

She lifted her arms in the air like she was surrendering in battle. She sighed deeply, and when I finally looked at her, she seemed so tired and worn down.

"Charlie," she said, shaking her head. "I bet holding on to this anger against me for all these years was a lot easier than feeling the grief, facing this trauma. This was a trauma, Charlie." Mom's voice was eerily calm. I wanted to scream. "You've been nursing this grudge for so long I don't think you even know who you'd be without it."

"NO!" I shouted. "You don't get to do that. You don't know me, Mom. You were wrong. You should have taught me to be cautious."

"It's okay if you need to hate me until you're ready to feel the sadness, Charlie. I know I made mistakes with you. I could have done better. Life is messy, though. You get hurt, you get back up again. You find yourself broken only to figure out how to put yourself back together. How could I have shielded you from the very nature of being alive? Why would I have wanted to? You wanted me to confirm your worst fears, tell you to hide from life? You wanted me to make you afraid of all the many ways life could wound you and knock you down? Well, I could never do that. I wouldn't be a good mother if I did. I will never apologize for encouraging you to live your life, heart wide open. That's something I won't do."

The fury seemed to evaporate from my body in an instant and, where I was rigidly standing upright before, I sank.

"But you can get really hurt that way," I said, voice quivering and faint. "Hope hurts."

"You can and it can, honey. But that's life. Without hope, what do you have left? You're hiding all that love you have inside you from the world."

"I don't have love inside me to give."

"Then why do you try to protect yourself so much?" Mom asked. "What are you so afraid of? If you had no love inside you to give, then you wouldn't be trying to keep it all in. You're afraid of how much you *want* to love."

"I tried, Mom. I loved him. I loved him *so* much. And then he was gone. And then everything hit me. I went numb. Dad leaving because of me. Your pain. Your losses. Me growing up too fast. Everything. It was just one thing after another. I couldn't catch my breath. So I shut down."

"Back up." Mom threw up her hand, confusion etched on her face. "Your dad didn't leave because of you. Is that what you thought all these years?"

"Why else would he leave? You guys weren't together anymore. He just stopped being *my* dad."

"Charlie," Mom said, stilling me. "I *made* your father leave and never come back."

"*What?*"

"You never saw your face when he left," Mom replied. "You would be despondent. He wasn't going to come back for your birthday party, Charlie. The party we planned around *his* schedule. I lost it. I told him if he couldn't be a real father, to never come back. I didn't expect him to actually leave, but I guess that was my answer. He was never going to show up for you or Benny or even me and I couldn't take it anymore. I needed him, too, don't you understand that? I needed him to be around, to stay with me, to actually be a partner. But, he couldn't do that. When he left, I could finally raise you two the way I wanted, instead of waiting to see if he'd ever come through for us."

"What?" I stood up, that fury returning. "Why would you send him away like that?"

"I did it to protect you. I didn't want you thinking that's what you deserve from a man, someone who just shows up once in a while, demanding you love him as if he were here all the time."

"That wasn't your choice to make!"

"I am your mother," she said, her voice rising. "Whose choice was it? Who was going to protect you? We just spent this entire conversation with you telling me I should have protected you from the harm of this world and I did just that. Your father was breaking your damn heart all the time. I couldn't keep it up. I had to protect my babies from getting their hopes up. I gave him a chance, Charlie. I told him if he could be a real father, I'd never keep him from you and Benny. But he couldn't. He told me *himself* that he couldn't. I needed to spare you the pain of his inconsistency and now you blame me for that, too?"

"I can't believe you never told me," I cried. "You let me believe he *left* me. You let me feel abandoned."

"How in the world could I have ever known that's how you felt when all you've ever done is close the most vulnerable parts of yourself off from me?"

"You should have known! You should have been honest with me!"

"I tried my hardest to do what I thought was right. Being a mom means making a thousand difficult decisions, not knowing if they're the good ones, or if you're going to irrevocably mess your child up." Tears streamed down her face. "I did my best," she rasped out.

"Well, your best didn't cut it," I leveled at her, and she winced, and I wanted to take the words back the moment I said them.

But just then, the door flew open at that exact moment and Benny—hair wild, eyes unblinking—screamed, "THAT'S ENOUGH!"

44

Mom and I turned, both stunned into silence. Benny was standing in the kitchen in an oversized sweatshirt and sweats, face red, voice booming.

"Yeah, that *is* enough," I said, thinking Benny was on my side.

Instead, she turned to me and got in my face, finger to my chest. "No, that's enough from *you*, Charlie. *Wow*, I am so stupid. I thought this experiment might actually soften you up, bring us all closer. But, everything is still Mom's fault and nothing is ever your fault, is that it?"

"You don't know what you're talking about, Benny."

"Oh, I do," she said. "And then some. I've been listening to your whole conversation. I'm very sorry that you lost Noah, but honestly, Charlie, you are blaming all the wrong people. Mom is not your fucking scapegoat."

"Oh, here she goes," I said, scoffing. "Defending Mom. Of course. I'm always wrong, always the bad guy, always the one who doesn't 'get it' like you two get it. Always on the outside. Sorry I'm not a ray of fucking sunshine like Benny and Jackie Quinn."

"Well, I'd rather be a ray of fucking sunshine than a negative, cold person who's closed off from the world. I should have never agreed to keep what happened with Noah from Mom. It has made you a bitter person. I'm sorry Noah died, but it was seven years ago, Charlie, and Mom didn't cause this. Mom has done nothing but love and support us our whole lives."

"YOU KNEW?" Mom boomed, standing up forcefully, crossing the kitchen to where Benny was standing. "You're telling me you knew?"

"Charlie told me the day it happened, but she swore me to secrecy. Said if I told you, she'd never speak to either of us again!"

"Benny, how could you possibly keep something like this from me?" Mom asked, furious.

"Look what you've done," Benny said, hard stare in my direction, throwing her hands up in the air. "Now you have Mom against me, which I guess was your plan all along. Get us all to hate each other and be miserable like you! Misery sure does love company, huh, Charlie?"

"Benny!" Mom cried. "Stop that. I'm not against you. I just wish you had told me. I could have saved Charlie if I knew. I could have brought her back to life."

"Stop talking about me like I'm not even here," I screamed. "I wasn't some pity project. You didn't need to *save* me then and you don't need to save me now! Both of you think you know better than me about everything. I'm *done*."

"You're done?" Benny spat. "Well, I'm MORE DONE."

"Girls, please," Mom pleaded, trying to step in, but both of us raised our palms to stop her.

"You know what?" Benny said, sighing loudly. "Maybe you're right. Maybe we don't fit. Maybe you should have stayed away. Maybe you *are* incapable of love, I don't know. I'm tired. I'm so tired of trying to get you to open up. To get you to smile. To get us all back to who we used to be together. Maybe you're just lost to the world now. I can't keep trying to love someone that doesn't even want to be loved."

Mom gasped. "Benny, you don't mean that."

"I do, Mom," she said, shaking her head. "If Charlie wants to stay locked in the past forever, then I guess I'm going to let her. If you hate us so much, Charlie, then why are you here? Why don't you just leave and never come back?"

"I don't hate you and Mom."

"Well, it sure feels like you do," Benny said. "You want us to be like you? Closed off from everyone? Working eighty-hour weeks? Turning good men away who just want a chance to love you? Where's Alex? Let me guess. You pushed him away. You push everyone away, Charlie. And soon enough, you're going to end up the way you've always wanted it. *Alone.*"

Being alone was easier. Being alone meant there was no room for heartbreak. No room for beauty or joy or love, either, but maybe it was the price you pay to be safe. It's too much—that in order to understand how beautiful life was, sometimes it needed to break your heart. I couldn't take that chance.

In that moment, I felt I'd rather live a life of numb indifference and brutal apathy than risk having my heart broken. Risk being loved by Benny and Mom and getting hurt and having it be as messy as it was right here, in the middle of the night, in this kitchen. It was too complicated. They wanted me to be someone I wasn't. And I thought it would be easier for everyone if I was just out of the picture.

That's how I felt right then. Like everyone's life would be easier if I weren't the added complication. Like my life would be easier if I was on my own, yet again.

Which was why I said, "I'm leaving."

"Going where?" Mom asked, practically screeching. "Don't leave. You can't leave."

"No," Benny said, lethally calm. "Let her go, Mom. She doesn't even want to be here, anyway. This is her excuse. She's been waiting to make her escape from us. Because we're the source of all her problems, apparently."

"Charlie, don't go," Mom begged, crying. "We can work this out."

"You can only work out something with a person who actually *wants* to work it out," Benny said, letting out a wry, harsh laugh. "If she wants to blame us for everything wrong in her life, let her. Obviously, she has no desire to take responsibility for anything. You think we're too positive, too optimistic, but we do the *work*, Charlie. We work through our issues, heal, open ourselves back up to life over and over again. Can you say the same? Our optimism is hard-won. Your pessimism is just the default. Who has the real work ethic here? Do you even want to change?"

"No," I said quickly.

"There you go," Benny said, outstretching her arms in an exaggerated shrug. "You're lost and you don't even want to find a way back. This has been a huge fucking waste of time."

"I'm leaving, Benny, okay? You can go back to being in your little perfect life where nothing ever goes wrong. Fuck you, alright? Fuck you."

"Bye, Charlie. Don't call me if you need anything."

"Girls, please, stop," Mom begged.

But it was broken. It was irreparable.

And I couldn't get out of there fast enough. I rushed upstairs, packed what little I'd brought, and was in my car within minutes, Mom running after me, imploring me to stay, but there was nothing to fix. Nothing I *wanted* to fix. I didn't need this in my life, didn't need to be constantly reminded of my deficiencies.

I turned the ignition, and as I drove in the dark, I kept repeating to myself like a mantra, "I don't need them."

I don't need them.

I don't need them.

I don't need them.

By the time I hit the Grapevine, I was in a trance, not allowing myself to think of a single thing, locking this all up in the same place I kept Noah.

I would be a fortress now. There was nobody left to open myself up for.

I didn't want to do "the work" like Benny said.

The only way you could stand to live was to protect yourself.

And the only way I could protect myself was to isolate myself.

Through the stubborn, ridiculous tears that would not stop falling, I could hardly see in front of me in the heavy fog. I slowed down, thinking I was going to pull over to the shoulder until it cleared, until I could stop my chest from aching, tears blurring my vision.

But before I could pull over, I heard an ear-piercing crunch of metal on metal and everything faded to black.

25 YEARS LATER

45

Everybody was dressed in black. I was at an outdoor chapel with walls of glass in Malibu that my mom loved. I looked down at my hands and they were speckled with age spots. I wore a black pantsuit.

Up at the front of the chapel, as I made my way through hordes of people, I stopped at the closed casket and gasped. There was a large picture of my radiant mother on a wooden easel right next to it. Someone handed me a program and I took it wordlessly. It said, "In loving memory of Jacqueline Ruby Quinn." My knees buckled. I nearly fell to the pew behind me when I saw the date. Twenty-five years since the last time I saw her.

Where had the time gone?

Looking at the program in my hand, I began to read.

> Jackie Quinn was a loving mother, incredible friend, generous mentor, and a Golden Globe–, Emmy–, and Academy Award–winning actress. Jackie was a self-proclaimed "late bloomer," but when she landed the starring role in the TV show *Starlet* as a washed-up actress trying to restart her career, she became not only a Golden Globe winner, but a bona fide superstar. Her career spanned twenty-five years and in that time, she became an icon . . .

I couldn't read any more. My eyes were blurry with tears—a mix of unbelievable pride that my mom had achieved all her dreams and more and sinking, sour regret that I'd missed it all.

"I didn't think you'd show," a hardened voice behind me said and I flipped around to come face-to-face with Benny. But it wasn't the Benny I left in that kitchen all those years ago. It was Benny at fifty, gray-streaked hair and very fine lines at the corners of her eyes. She wasn't smiling. She was assessing me like I might make some sort of scene.

"Where did the time go?" I asked her in a desperate whisper.

"I haven't seen you in twenty-five years and that's the first thing you say to me?" Benny said, in a ruthlessly dismissive tone. "Life moved on without you. That's what happens when you leave people behind and never come back."

"But I don't remember any of the past two decades."

"Not surprising," Benny said, barely concealing her loathing toward me. "Mom called you every week. You never answered. You left us and probably just worked until you forgot we even existed. I hope it was worth it. You didn't even say goodbye to your own mom. You broke her heart, but we survived. Not that you care."

"You told me to leave," I cried. "That night. You told me to leave."

"I was angry," she said, voice rising. Several people looked over at us. "I never in a million years thought you wouldn't come back."

"I can't believe I didn't come back."

"What?" Benny said. "You made the decision to stay away from us every single day for the past twenty-five years. What are you saying? That was *your* choice. You missed everything."

"Mom had her big break," I managed to say, my voice wobbling.

"Mom had a lot more than just her big break. She had the most incredible career. I did, too, not like you cared. Ravi brought me on as his tour photographer and I got to have the career of my dreams as a photographer. Alex won a James Beard Award for his restaurant, The Perfect Bite. Did you even know any of this? Did you not keep tabs on us at all? You really left and cut us all out? That easily? How *could* you, Charlie?"

If it was twenty-five years later, that meant I was fifty-five. Had I really left that night and thrown myself into work? Had I never come back?

"Oh, wow, he came," Benny said, nodding toward the entrance of the chapel. "Another one of the broken hearts you left in your wake."

I looked behind me and saw an older version of Alex, walking hand in hand with a dark-haired woman and two teenagers that looked exactly like the spitting image of both Alex and the woman. My heart stopped when his eyes landed on mine. We stared at each other across the thrush of people for one, two, three seconds before he shook his head and turned back to his wife and kids. So he'd been ready to meet someone else, and all those years ago, I drove him straight into this woman's arms.

I deserved that.

I deserved all of this.

"I'm sorry, Benny," I told her. "I'm so sorry."

She narrowed her eyes at me with a look I'd never seen her face make. Pure, undisguised hatred.

"Sorry?" she scoffed. "If you think you can come here to Mom's funeral and beg for my forgiveness, you're wrong. I gave you a million chances. Sorry won't cut it. I will never ever forgive you for what you put Mom through. I will never forgive you for abandoning us."

"Please, Benny," I begged. "Please."

"No." She lifted her hand up to stop me and she walked away, leaving me in the aisle, alone. I walked toward the doors, like I was an outsider. Like I didn't even belong here at all.

I deserved Benny's ire, her refusal to even touch me, her lack of warmth. Even seeing her a little broken was my punishment, like she was an orphan without any family, because basically, that was what she was. My mom had called me for years and I hadn't returned her calls, had never talked to my little sister again. I'd driven away the man I could have loved and told him to meet someone else.

My entire life was spent alone. Just the way I supposedly wanted it.

So, why didn't it feel nearly as satisfying as I thought it would?

Regret was a pain worse than heartbreak.

Regret was a sickening drop of your stomach.

Regret was knowing you could have changed it all, but decided, every single day, not to.

Regret was having to live with your failures.

Regret was ceaseless emptiness.

Regret was intolerable, a sickening reminder that the only thing you can never ever get back is . . . time.

And I deserved nobody's forgiveness, especially the one person I wanted it the most from, who was now lying in a casket, without ever reconciling with the daughter that was her biggest wish in the whole world.

It was too much to bear. Leaving Benny and Mom that night, I told myself the pain of heartbreak hadn't been worth the reward of love and beauty and aliveness and light.

How wrong I'd been. I knew that now. All I had left were regrets.

I wished I could go back to that night, make a different choice, stay, work it out.

But it was too late.

This was what I got for running away, for choosing the safety of isolation over the potential for love.

I loved Benny. Loved my mom. Loved Alex. I loved *life*. Loved life so much that sometimes it broke my heart. But that was the point!

Benny and Mom had been right—you need to give life every last bit of you, hold back from nothing, throw yourself at risk. Cautious living was no life at all.

If I could go back, I'd do everything differently. I'd try to repair what I broke. I'd apologize to Mom and Benny until they forgave me. I'd beg Alex to take me back, to give us the chance he wanted to give us.

Standing by the door, I was ready to leave again, tears streaming down my face. Benny was speaking at a podium at the front. She looked so tired. So worn and bruised. I wanted to go to her, hug her.

"I NEED TO GO BACK TWENTY-FIVE YEARS," I screamed fruitlessly, but nobody seemed to hear me. "TAKE ME BACK. I NEED TO DO IT ALL OVER AGAIN. PLEASE. PLEASE. PLEASE."

My vision swam, and my peripheral was shadowed gradients, like the walls were closing in on me.

I banged and banged on the closed door until the sides of my hands ached, cried until my throat burned, screamed, and begged, and pleaded with a God I'd never believed in.

"I NEED TO GO BACK."

More banging.

Nobody heard me.

Nobody cared.

Nobody wondered where I was.

I was invisible.

And I deserved it.

The church started to swirl and blur, the people at the pews fading into blackness, and suddenly I was falling to the ground, and I heard loud voices, footsteps, beeping, sounds of what seemed to be a hospital at work . . .

46

Benny

Her eyes fluttered, and I thought for sure I was imagining it. I could be delirious, seeing what I wanted to see after three long merciless days of waiting, worrying, pacing, praying, and sleeping a desperate, broken sleep on hard chairs. But then I heard her voice, hoarse from disuse, and I was on my feet, calling nurses, grappling for the water jug, cup, and straw, thrusting it in front of her, waiting to see her take a sip, like that was proof she was alive.

"Oh, my God," I said. "Charlie. You're okay."

She was mumbling. I watched her struggle to sit up, her eyes blinking rapidly, adjusting to the light. She was trying to talk, her limbs too heavy to lift the cup. Placing it in front of her, and guiding the straw to her lips, I helped her take a long slow drink of the water.

Finally, her throat cleared and she said, "Benny. Benny. You're here. Benny. My beautiful Benny. I'm so sorry. I love you. I love you so much. Mom is gone. I can't believe Mom is dead. I ruined everything."

"Mom is what?" I asked, confused, not knowing if I heard correctly. I wanted to say more, but then a flurry of activity coalesced at the doorway and two nurses burst in, with Mom following right behind.

"WHERE'S MY BABY?" she screamed and when I looked at Charlie, her eyes were wide, tears streaming down her cheeks.

"MOM?" Charlie cried out, almost catatonic with shock. "Mom. Mom! You're alive? Mom, oh, my God."

Mom and I exchanged a panicked glance, but Charlie's arms were outstretched for her and she moved a nurse out of the way to pull Charlie into a fierce hug. I could see Charlie's face over Mom's shoulder and her eyes were tightly closed, cheeks red and wet with tears streaming down, hanging on like she refused to let go.

It startled me, this marked change. The last time I'd seen Charlie, she was leaving Quinn Canyon in the middle of the night, declaring she'd never see us ever again, and then she was in the hospital, fighting for her life. It didn't seem like enough time for her to have such a change of heart, but here she was, holding her hand out to me so I could hug them both, like she was finally the sister I had always hoped she'd become.

Within a few moments, we were shooed away to the lobby outside so the nurses and doctor could do a full examination.

We heard Charlie desperately crying for us, pleading, "No, don't go. Mom, Benny, no. Come back!"

We looked at each other, too stunned to speak. We'd all been waiting in agony for days to see if she was going to wake up. Not in our wildest dreams did we expect she'd wake up as an entirely different person. It was a miracle she was even alive. Her car had flipped three times on the Grapevine. The first responders found her upside down and unconscious. We were all prepared for the possibility that Charlie might die. It had hung between us for three long excruciating days.

"What's going on?"

Mom and I, still shocked, turned around to see Alex holding three cups of coffee and a paper bag collecting grease already. All three of us had been here, waiting, taking turns between leaving to shower and get food. Petra, Jasper, Willow, Aya, Ali, Ravi, and several of our friends had turned up over the last three days, but nobody had stayed like Mom, Alex, and me. We couldn't leave. We had nowhere else to go.

"She's awake," I told him, and he swayed, nearly dropping everything to the ground before I grabbed it and placed it on a side table.

"Is she okay?" he asked.

"We honestly don't know yet," Mom said. "The doctor is examining her now. We saw her for a brief moment, and she seemed out of it."

"She thought Mom was dead?" I said. "She was so happy to see me? It was not what any of us expected."

"The only thing that matters is she's alive," Alex said. He looked exhausted, eyes bloodshot, skin a bit sallow from lack of sleep. I had thought Alex definitely *liked* Charlie, but I hadn't realized until the last few days that Alex was wildly in love with her. Heart-stricken that she didn't want him back, but still by her side, constantly, loving her from afar. Even if he couldn't have her for himself, he could not rest until he knew she was okay. I had wanted to shake Charlie awake, to tell her that she was throwing everything away, that she was going to regret choosing to run when she could have stayed.

The doctor stepped out of the room, and came to talk to the three of us. Her smile made us all relax, like one big collective exhale.

"She's doing very well," Dr. Culpa told us. "As you know, we have not been able to explain Charlie's coma with anything we saw on her MRI. Sometimes this happens, as the body is trying to heal itself. It's not always understood why people drop into comas, or even how they wake up from them. But she's alert now and I don't see any lasting damage. I'm a woman of science, but sometimes you need to call a miracle when you see one. And this is a miracle."

"She's okay?" Mom asked, voice shaky, her hand to her heart.

"She's okay," Dr. Culpa repeated, nodding. "We're going to keep her here for a couple days to observe and make sure nothing changes. Once that's done, she can go home."

We said our thank-yous and when the doctor left, all three of us hugged each other, the relief palpable, as if all the energy in the hospital suddenly brightened just for us.

"What do we do now?" Alex asked. "Maybe you two should go in. I'll wait out here."

"Alex," I said.

"I don't know if she wants to see me," he replied, cutting me off. "I just wanted to make sure she was okay."

I vacillated between anger at Charlie and stark, unrelenting relief that she was okay. Of course, I hated the way we left things, and I regretted some of what I'd said, but mostly I was so hurt that she could callously leave Mom and me behind. That we meant so little to her that she could cast us away. I never understood what we'd ever done to her. Or, more specifically, why she stayed away, why she blamed Mom all the time. Jackie Quinn wasn't perfect, but she was a mom who loved us, wanted the absolute best for us, and was always there. What else Charlie expected or needed, I didn't know.

Charlie never let anyone help her. Never let anyone in. Never let her guard down.

And I was ashamed to admit when she left that night, I'd been perversely relieved I wouldn't be hurt by her any longer.

Never having my sister's love had wounded me deeply. I could never be enough for her. Neither could Mom.

The thing with Charlie was she was always building walls.

And I was always foolishly climbing them.

I couldn't keep that up, was so tired of being rejected by my own sister.

So when Mom and I entered the room, I stood near the doorway, let Mom get closer to Charlie, let her forgive, because now that I knew she was alive, I was *furious* with her.

And I was prepared for this to be the last time we ever talked.

I was prepared for this moment to be a goodbye.

47

Charlie

What the hell had just happened?

I blinked furiously, unable to trust what I was seeing. Not only was I not at a chapel in Malibu and fifty-five years old, but I was in the hospital. Apparently, I'd been in an accident. Benny wasn't fifty. Actually, twenty-five-year-old Benny was regarding me skeptically from the doorway and my mom—my beautiful, vivacious mom—was alive, right here, looking at me, crying.

"I'm so happy you're okay," Mom kept saying, touching my forearm, holding my hand to her chest like she never wanted to let go of me again.

I was still so groggy. The doctor had told me to expect that, to expect fuzziness around the edges of my memory, but I hadn't told her what I'd experienced, where I'd gone, because I could hardly make any sense of it.

"Are you really here?" I asked Mom and she gave me a look of anguish.

"I'm really here," she said through tears. "We thought we lost you."

"I thought I lost *you*," I told her. "Prop me up, please. I have to tell you both what I just saw."

Mom shoved some pillows behind me and used the remote to put me into more of a sitting position. Benny still wouldn't come close and I didn't blame her. But, I needed to find out first if what I'd experienced had been one long coma-induced dream, or something else.

Something like a *vision*.

My mind felt different, clearer, more alert. I had survived and seen our future. Or, at least a version of it. Now I needed to find out if I had the chance to change it.

"Mom, that role you talked about that you didn't want to talk about for the TV show," I said. "The screen test. Is the show, by any chance, called *Starlet*?"

She doubled back and gasped. "What?" she asked. "How would you know that? I had to sign an NDA. Nobody knows about that."

Chills broke out on my skin.

"Benny," I said. "Have you and Ravi talked about your photography yet? Like maybe you could be his tour photographer?"

Her eyes widened, but she stifled it. "How could you know that? He texted me right before your accident about it. Did he talk to you that night you met?"

"No," I said, those chills intensifying, now moving to a buzzy, sparkly feeling at the top of my head. "So, it *was* a vision."

"What are you saying?" Mom asked. "You seem different."

"I am, Mom," I said. "I just saw what my life would be like twenty-five years from now if I closed off from everyone. I hated it. I thought I was stuck there. I thought I'd lost you, Mom. Like, really lost you. Permanently. All I wanted was to come back and make things right with you and Benny. I am so sorry. You were right, Benny. I regretted everything. I was alone. We never spoke. I had nothing to live for. I never want to end up like that. I will do everything in my power to not end up like that. I love you, Benny. I love you, Mom. Can we start over? Or, can I start over? Can you both forgive me?"

"Of course I forgive you," Mom said, hugging me. "Do you forgive me? I'm so sorry for all I did wrong and all I didn't even know I was doing wrong."

"Mom," I said. "It's in the past. It's forgotten. You were perfect. You are perfect."

My tears dropped softly onto Mom's shoulder.

"Also," I told her. "Take the *Starlet* job when they offer it. Trust me." I didn't want to give it all away for her, but I knew it was the catalyst for the acting career she'd been dreaming of, and I was so happy in that moment I was about to be around to witness it all unfold.

The dread of regret in my stomach from the funeral vision was still lingering. She'd won all those awards without me cheering her on every step of the way. I couldn't believe I'd been given another chance to make this right.

"They offer it?" she asked. "I've been in the running for a long time."

"They offer it," I said. "And it'll be worth the wait."

"I knew it," she said. "I *knew* it."

We stopped hugging and both looked over at Benny, her arms crossed, eyebrows scrunched as she watched us both.

"You really hurt me," Benny said, fury in her tone. "I was preparing to never speak to you again, Charlie."

"I know," I said. I wanted to go to her, but I couldn't stand. Instead, I just thrust my arms out ineffectively. "Does it make it any better that I tried to leave *because* I love you so much? And love is hard for me, Ben. I am terrified of getting hurt."

"Charlie, we are all terrified of getting hurt. That's what you don't understand. That's what makes love special, because it's a risk. Not because it's easy."

"I see that now," I told her as sincerely as I could, desperate to have her believe me.

"Do you, though?" she asked. "How can I trust you? You're so afraid of being left, but you don't realize you leave people behind all the time. That's selfish. To do to others what you're so scared of having them do to you. You think you're the only person in the world who hurts."

"You're right," I said. "You're so right."

There was a tense silence, and I could almost see the energy battling between us, Benny wanting to soften and me wanting her forgiveness so badly it felt like my heart might actually explode inside my chest if I didn't get it.

"If you abandon us again, I'm done," Benny said resolutely.

"I won't," I said, certain of this in a way I couldn't explain. But I knew that I was not going anywhere ever again. I was going to love Mom and Benny so hard, to make up for lost time, to prove to them I was worthy of their forgiveness. "I promise you. I won't."

I held out my pinky finger, a callback to us as kids, making pinky promises that felt like sacred oaths. This was a vow. Earning Benny's trust back would take time, but I wasn't worried about that.

I'd do whatever it took.

Love stuck around.

Love got through the hard times. It was either love, or lifeless existence.

There were no other choices.

And you either loved 100 percent, or you didn't love at all.

Benny's mouth ticked into an almost-smile and that hint of her anger dwindling was enough to make me let out a sigh of relief.

She made it to my bedside and held out her pinky finger and we entwined them, shook once, kissed the spiral of our fists, and separated.

"One more thing," she said. "There's another person who you owe an apology to. He doesn't even think you want to see him. That man is crazy in love with you and I swear to God if you don't give you and Alex a shot, I'm not going to believe that you've changed at all."

I nearly shot to my feet. "Alex is *here*? WHERE? He didn't go to Chicago?"

"Charlie," Benny said gravely. "Alex has been here day in and day out. He hasn't left your side."

"Where is he?" I asked, panicked. "I can't lose him." I never imagined Alex would be here, never imagined I would actually get a chance to make *everything* right. Of course I didn't deserve it, but that didn't mean I wasn't going to try.

Benny gave me a real smile this time.

"Finally," she said. "You've come to your damn senses, woman."

48

Alex

Outside Charlie's door, I was pacing, deciding if I should just leave. I'd wanted to know that Charlie was okay and now I knew. What was keeping me here? She'd made it clear that she didn't want me back, that this was going to end. I had already felt foolish enough being by her bedside with Benny and Jackie, as if I were part of their family. Physically, I had been incapable of leaving until I knew Charlie was okay.

For so long, I had thought I was messed up forever, that losing my mom had broken me irrevocably. I understood Charlie's guardedness, because it was nearly identical to my own. Over the last few weeks of spending time with her, I'd tried not to fall. I'd tried so hard. I'd called friends, my dad, my grandmother, anyone who would pick up, and asked them to talk me out of having feelings for Charlie, but I'd looped back around. Every single person I talked to told me she sounded like someone I needed to fight for.

I'd never in my life been this bent out of shape over someone.

Except, of course, for teenage Charlie Quinn, back in high school, the girl I'd watched from afar, trying to get up the courage to talk to her. When I'd seen her at that party during our senior year, it took every ounce of bravery within me to approach her. My mom knew everything about Charlie Quinn. She'd been the one I talked to about every interaction. I'd texted her that night, told her that Charlie was at the party, and she'd resolutely encouraged me to take my chance.

Nobody I knew had a relationship with their mom like I did. Sometimes, even now, the ache of missing her felt so intense I thought about doing exactly what Charlie did—isolating from the world so I never felt that grief again. So I never had to get hurt. So I never had to love anyone enough that losing them would break me.

And I'd been like that for a long time, throwing myself into work, climbing the ranks, disappointing the memory of my mom who had told me, even with her last words, that there was nothing in this world more important than love.

"Don't let this break you," she had told me, frail and dying, trying to impart all the wisdom she had within the space of a few days.

For the past year, I'd been working fourteen-hour shifts at the restaurant in Malibu, begging the investors of the Chicago restaurant to bring me in early, to not let a month lapse between jobs. I'd been in LA trying to avoid anything that reminded me of my mom, which was, of course, impossible. Everything reminded me of her.

And then I saw Charlie in the dining room of Wavy and a bolt of lightning hit me, like suddenly I was alive again. Like I was my teenage self, getting up the nerve to talk to my crush. Like maybe my mom had sent her there, to give me a second chance with the only person that had ever made me nervous, had ever made my breath hitch in that unmistakable way.

In high school, Charlie had been complex, intense, studious, and she'd kept to herself. Her mom was like a mythic figure of Hollywood royalty, inhabiting the Magic House that everyone talked about. But, Charlie also had that magic. Everyone liked her, even if nobody really knew her. She was funny and sardonic and completely impervious to the peer pressure everyone else succumbed to. She was wholly herself.

But when I saw her in the restaurant, I knew something had changed her. She was slow to smile and, even when she did, it never quite lit up her face.

Despite her rule, I still thought maybe I could bring her back, maybe I could figure out a way to make her smile and keep doing that for as long as she'd let me.

But, she didn't want me—for longer than a month, at least. She'd told me so many times.

Suddenly, I got to my feet, intent on leaving. This was stupid, standing outside while Benny and Jackie had a family reunion. I felt like a fourth wheel, hanging on to people that didn't want me there.

Even though I knew the Magic House was just a myth, the night I made dinner, I'd desperately wished for Charlie to change her mind, to even consider the possibility that what we had was special enough to pursue.

A foolish cry into the void.

Walking away, I wiped my eyes dry. Sometimes you don't get what you want, like mothers who get to watch you grow up and a woman who loves you back. It was time to finally board that plane and get on with my life, to throw myself back into work.

Behind me, I heard a strong patter of running and I shifted to the side, thinking it was a staff member attending to an emergency, but instead I heard Benny's voice scream, "ALEX, WAIT!"

"What's going on?" I asked, dread piercing my chest. "Is Charlie okay?"

"She's good," Benny said. She was in front of me now, breathing hard. "She wants to see you."

I reeled back, stumbling to the wall behind me for support. "She does?"

Benny nodded. "Be prepared, though," she said, eyes wide. "She's like . . . very different."

My heart sank. "In what way? Is she okay?"

"I don't even know how to describe it," Benny said.

"Good different? Or bad different?"

"Good, I think." She shook her head, like she was shell-shocked about this development. "She said she experienced some sort of vision while in the coma. She saw her life twenty-five years from now and she's determined to change. I'm cautiously optimistic."

"Does she seem out of it?"

"No, that's the weird thing. She's clearer than ever. You know how sometimes you'd be with Charlie and she'd go someplace else? Did you ever see that? Like, she drifted off to a dark place?"

"Yes," I told her. "A couple times. I felt like I'd never reach her again."

"Well, now her eyes are bright. When she looks at me, it feels like she actually sees me, like she really loves me. It's bizarre."

"But, a good thing?"

"Maybe," Benny said, shrugging.

"You don't trust her," I remarked, less question, more statement.

Benny nodded slowly. "I love her so much, but I don't know if she'll ever change."

"Give her a chance. You heard the doctor. It's a miracle she survived. That can really change people."

"You were leaving," Benny said, as if she just noticed it. "You know, you don't have to come back. You can go. She may not be different. I can tell her you were gone already, if you want me to. I don't want her to keep hurting you."

Benny's words lingered and I considered leaving. I could walk away now and not take the risk of getting hurt by Charlie, not wait around to see if she had really changed. This could be my out.

Could I stand it if I let her back in and she rejected me again?

What would I regret more—walking away or going back? My mom had lived by the code of no regrets. She'd thrown herself at everything she ever wanted, with complete and total abandon. She had come from nothing and risen through the ranks of Hollywood, becoming one of the most influential producers. She had been purposeful and steadfast in her commitment to never leave any dream untouched.

When she was dying, she told me, "I wanted to do more, but I am full of all that I did. It's better to try and fail than to regret your own inaction." I was by her side constantly, soaking up every last bit of her wisdom before she left this world. Sometimes, I could still hear her guiding me, little whispers of encouragement.

In that moment, her voice came through clear as a bell, that dry wit of hers imploring, "This is Charlie Quinn we're talking about here, Alex! You know you can't walk away from her! Go. Don't even think about it. Just go!"

"Of course I can't walk away," I told Benny.

She smiled. "Good man," she said. "I would not have blamed you if you left, but I wanted to make sure you were coming back for Charlie and not out of some misplaced obligation."

"She really wants to see me?"

"She almost jumped to her feet when I told her you were here."

I felt almost faint with relief, but I didn't know what it meant. Maybe all she wanted was to apologize. Or, just to say bye.

But I'd regret not seeing her one last time, even if this was the last time.

And the only way I could think to honor the memory of my force of a mother was to live without regret. That was one of the only things she ever asked of me. Even if I loved Charlie without receiving her love back, at least I loved.

It was worth it just to be able to say I tried.

49

Charlie

It was as though hours passed between the time Benny went to get Alex and when the doorknob finally turned. I didn't know what I'd say to him or if he'd even be willing to talk to me, but then he was in the doorway, leaning against the frame, looking vulnerable in a way that had my chest aching.

"Alex," I whispered.

Mom left the room, knowing when to take a hint, and Alex moved toward me. Lying in the hospital bed, I had to let him come to me. I deserved his reservedness. Absolutely deserved to be the one yearning for him this time.

"Are you okay?" he asked. "How do you feel?"

"I'm a little sore," I said. "But I feel okay."

"Good," he said, seemingly relieved.

"Alex, I'm sorry. I'm so sorry."

"No, Charlie, you don't need to apologize. Really. I pushed you too hard. You were clear about your rule and I kept violating that boundary. You don't owe me anything. You were honest."

"Fuck the rule," I said. "I'm an idiot."

His eyes widened and the slightest hint of a smile played on his lips.

"Alex," I continued. "I had this vision during the coma and you had met someone else. You had a family. And I was so angry with myself for letting you go. I can't let that happen. I have a second chance and I'm not going to waste it. Actually, it's more like a third chance with you. I know this is impossible to ask, but can you stay? Can you not go to Chicago? Let's open a restaurant together. I'll bake bread and manage everything. I'm very organized and diligent! We can open it here in LA. Or, hell, we can go to Chicago. I don't care. Wherever you are, I want to be there. I don't know what will happen with us, but I know I lose you if I don't try. I want to take the risk. I'm so sorry I didn't realize it sooner."

No part of me felt afraid saying any of this. In fact, I felt nearly dazed with freedom that I was opening myself up, finally. Funny how you can think that the strong thing to do is to abstain, but the truth that I could see now is that the strongest people are the ones who keep getting back up, no matter how bruised and broken they've been.

"You're serious?" he asked. He stepped a little closer to me. Just the slightest amount, but I clocked it.

"I literally could not be more serious right now," I said, heart beating wildly. "I even have an idea for the name of our restaurant." I remembered it from the vision.

"I already have one picked out," he said, moving a little closer again. He was two feet away and I wished I could close the gap, wrap him in my arms, feel the warmth of his lips on mine again. I'd thought I'd never get that chance, that I was stuck in the future, that Alex had moved on and I'd been the one to set him free to love someone else.

Shivers erupted across my skin.

If the name he picked out was the same one from the vision, I would know for sure where I'd gone during that coma was somehow real, that it was a sign, a warning, a chance to do my life all over again, to love openly and wildly.

"Is it . . . The Perfect Bite?" I asked tentatively.

Alex doubled back, mouth open in shock, and shook his head in disbelief. Goose bumps erupted across my skin and that sparkly buzzing on the crown of my head magnified.

"How?" Alex asked, his voice shaking. He kept opening and closing his mouth, like he had no idea what to say.

Tears cascaded down my cheeks.

"Unbelievable," Alex murmured. "Then again, sometimes I swear I hear my mom's voice in my head, so I mean, anything is possible."

All I felt was a serene peacefulness, like someone who was standing in the middle of rubble, all walls broken down, knowing she would never need to reconstruct them again.

Walls only created regret, and I knew where that led.

Never again, I thought to myself. *Never again will I close myself off to life. Never. Again.*

"Something I need to know," I said into the silence we were existing in, both suspended in our collective bewilderment of all that had just transpired.

"Hmmm?" Alex replied. "Tell me."

"Alex Perry, will you let me love you? Can I try? I really want to love you. Even though I don't deserve it, can I cash in my third chance with you? I won't mess it up. I promise."

He froze, watching me, like he was assessing the truthfulness of what I was saying. I couldn't express more sincerity if I tried. Pleading with my eyes, I tried to convey all that I had seen, all that I knew now.

I'd tell him about Noah. I'd tell him everything, reveal every secret, and I'd ask him to reveal all of himself to me. I would not let any of these people fall through my fingers again, would love them so fiercely they'd get sick of me.

The alternative was hell.

He inched closer and my breath hitched.

"You just might be the love of my life, Quinn," he said softly. "So, my answer is yes. I'll stay. I'll go where you go. I'd regret it forever if I didn't."

I scrunched my eyes from happiness and relief and when I

opened them, they were blurry with tears and Alex was in front of me, close, his hand in mine now.

"Kiss me," I told him. "Please. I thought I'd never get to kiss you again. So, kiss me."

"Yes, Chef," he said, smiling, and my heart felt as though it may actually burst from my chest.

He leaned down, and his lips met mine, and they tasted so sweet, felt so warm, and there was absolutely no sense of hesitation within me.

When he finally pulled away, he whispered reverentially, "So it *is* the Magic House." He cupped my face with his soft hand. "I kinda wished for you. I didn't really think it would happen, but it did. Somehow, it came true. What did you want most?"

"Nothing," I said, thinking of the emptiness of before, when I realized I had nothing I wanted, nothing to really live for. "Actually, maybe that's not true. I think I wished for something to fight for. Something to want again. Something to love."

"And then you have a vision of what it's like if you never wanted again? Never loved again? Closed yourself off?" He looked a little awestruck.

"Wild," I told him. "I may have to concede to the Magic House."

He smiled. "You just might."

And then he leaned back down and kissed me again.

We stayed like that for a while, like two people who'd found what they thought was lost forever.

In that moment, I realized that you don't get the love without the risk of grief.

You don't get the laughter without the risk of silence.

You don't get the joy without the risk of loss.

I'd never cower in the face of risk ever again.

The risk was worth it. Every single time, it was worth it.

I'd say *yes, yes, yes* a million more times—live so heart wide open I'd never protect myself again.

That was the new promise I made, in a nondescript hospital room, surrounded by incredible people who were just waiting to love me.

I let them.

Finally, I let go and let them all the way in.

But, you know what was better than being loved by them?

Getting to love them back.

That was the real magic.

EPILOGUE
3 YEARS LATER (FOR REAL)

Jackie

"Does she win, Charlie?" Benny asked. "You know. You know if she does. You had your vision."

"Benny," Charlie said, laughing. "I'm not going to tell you."

"Come on," Benny implored. "It's the *Golden Globes*. Just tell us if she wins it."

Charlie shrugged. "I don't know. Maybe." Her face was impossible to read.

"Leave her alone," I said. Benny snapped a picture. I hadn't seen her without her camera in hand all day. She wanted to document every moment. "My girls are here with me and they're happy. I get to act every day and do what I love. I was nominated for a Golden Globe. I've already won, Benny girl. I'm the luckiest woman in the world."

I smiled so big my makeup artist had to stop working on my eyes for a moment.

"Sorry," I told her. "I'm just so happy."

Clara only smiled back. "It's a big deal," she said. "I'm doing waterproof mascara. I have a feeling you'll be crying a lot tonight."

I laughed. "Thank you."

There was a group of us gathered at Quinn Canyon while the "glam squad" that my managers had arranged did their magic on me. I was having a pedicure, a manicure, a blowout and updo, my makeup applied, and I could hear my stylist, Audrey, steaming the gown we'd borrowed from the collection of old Hollywood glamour, which fit the character I was nominated for portraying in *Starlet*. The dress was from the 1950s, as was all the styling around it. My hair was being set in large waves, and Clara was applying the perfect red lipstick for my skin tone.

This moment had been in the works for months, but also, for my entire life.

The press around *Starlet* had surprised everyone, except for maybe Charlie, who had a calm sense of knowing about everything these days. For years, I'd worried I had been too old to break into Hollywood, and then too stubborn to realize maybe my time had passed. But, something had kept me going. Something told me it was going to work out. That faith, even when I stumbled, just never faltered.

The public had embraced my role as Ingrid Curtis in a way that not a single Hollywood executive had expected, though. *Starlet* was a bare-bones production with a tiny budget that was not projected to be a hit. In fact, nobody in the industry really understood why it had been green-lit in the first place. It went against all of Hollywood's conventions. The story of a washed-up star who was no longer young and in-demand? A starring role given to an actress with hardly any notable credits to her name who was fifty-five years old?

Everyone expected it to fail.

We called it the "tax write-off" for the streaming service that distributed it.

But I gave it everything. I *became* Ingrid Curtis and inhabited that role as if my life depended on it. Every single person on the set of *Starlet* came ready to work. We were the underdogs and all we wanted to do was make eight episodes of something we were proud of. There's a power in having no expectations, no pressure. There's power in having everyone count you out.

There's a shared collective moment when you look around and go, "Nobody has faith in us, *except* for us."

By the end of those eight episodes, we were a family.

When the first season dropped six months ago, the cast and crew and I celebrated, expecting nothing. But by the next week, it had become the most streamed series of the year. It took off like a rocket. I *knew* it was brilliant and I had always known I had it in me.

Since then, it had been one big whirlwind. Forty years to my overnight-success moment.

The streamer threw money at us, demanded more episodes, and when it was nominated for eight Golden Globes, the pitch of *Starlet*'s success went from high to hysteria. I couldn't walk down the street without being stopped. My agents couldn't keep up with the onslaught of scripts sent my way, talk shows that wanted me as their guest, magazines asking for interviews and cover stories.

Jackie Quinn was a superstar.

It only took four decades for the world to finally notice.

Charlie came up behind me when the hairdresser stepped away to let my curls set and she hugged my shoulders. "I'm so proud of you," she said. "Win or lose, it doesn't matter. You're inspiring so many people, including me."

"I love you," I said. "How's the restaurant?"

"It's amazing," Alex said, appearing from the kitchen with a smile on his face. Of course, I already knew The Perfect Bite was doing incredibly well. It had become a destination spot up in Montecito. They'd made it through their first year and were booked up for the next six months. Alex's incredible cooking and passion and Charlie's bread-making skills and business acumen were a killer combination.

"We're having the time of our lives," Charlie said, and the way she looked up at Alex made me so happy I thought my heart might just beat itself right out of my chest. It was a look of total devotion.

But before they opened The Perfect Bite, they'd spent a year traveling all over the world on the cheap, staying in hostels and Airbnbs. I hadn't even known Charlie had wanderlust. They met me in Cannes when I was shooting some scenes for *Starlet* and we ate mussels and fries in the sunshine. I'd never seen Charlie so free, unburdened, and happy. Maybe knowing she was going to be okay freed me a little, too. When you have a child so stressed out, who thinks they need to carry the world on their shoulders, all you ever want to do is try to unburden them.

When they returned from traveling, Charlie got into therapy. She was doing so much better, but she had a lot to work through. I did, too, of course, and so I started seeing my own therapist. Then Benny followed. Triple Quinn was not perfect, but we were trying.

A year after Charlie's accident, Benny had, indeed, like Charlie predicted, gone on tour with Ravi. He'd been opening for a big artist across the world and Benny's pictures had revolutionized tour photography, and people to this day still give partial credit to Benny for Ravi's skyrocket to success. She was now one of the most in demand photographers in the business, going on tour with some of the biggest names in music. Benny and Ravi had a whirlwind romance that ended in horrific heartbreak for Benny—it caught her so off guard, but Charlie was there to catch her. She knew what it felt like to be destroyed by love, and she brought Benny back from the brink.

While Charlie was in that coma, I questioned everything. It was a dark night of the soul moment for me. I was certain I would quit acting, that I'd been stupid to pursue it for so long when it obviously hadn't wanted me back. Benny had told me about that text message from Ravi and she wanted to turn it down, wanted to take the safe route. We both sat in our personal hells, battling demons, wondering if Charlie had been right all along, that we'd been delusional, chasing impossible dreams.

But when Charlie came out of that coma, her steadfast faith in all of us, including herself, was so intoxicating we all got bolder. I would have turned *Starlet* down if it weren't for Charlie telling me to take it. My agents cautioned me against the role, told me that nobody was betting on it, that it might kill my career before it even took off to be associated with a catastrophic flop. I insisted on signing the contract against their advice. And Ravi's label didn't want to hire Benny. She had to plead her case, bet on herself, show up to the profession she didn't even know she was qualified for yet.

Charlie had pulled off miraculous things for us all. She had no idea how much we respected and loved her, and when Benny and I finally got to receive the full force of her love and faith, it was like a fire erupting in flames. We needed her.

In the end, Charlie made Benny and me better, not because she made us more cautious, but because she made us more well-rounded. She helped with every detail of my deals, organized my life, kept me on top of my finances, took my flighty sense of self and grounded it. The only way Benny could have received the offer to photograph Ravi was because Charlie had coached her on the interview, organized a load of agencies for Benny to approach, put together a killer portfolio, helped Benny with her schedules, and given her confidence that met up alongside luck and opportunity.

Charlie's pragmatism never left her, and we were all better for it. She softened while Benny and I became sharper. And Charlie allowed herself to concede to uncertainty, to let go of control, to let go of everything that had been weighing her down.

Ultimately, we *all* let go of our extreme positions and discovered middle ground, contributing our gifts and allowing help where we needed it. Benny brought her levity and hopefulness.

Charlie brought her levelheadedness and to-do lists. And I brought the permission to dream as big as we all wanted, the faith that everything works out the way it should. (Alex, of course, brought the food and somehow became the only person who could wrangle the Quinn women back into being allies, whenever we drifted.)

We all got better because of each other. We needed each other. We helped each other. That was the magic of Triple Quinn. That was the little family I built from nothing but hope and a steadfast belief that love was the antidote to all of life's ills. That, cliché as it is, love could truly conquer all.

Growing up, I never received the beauty of unconditional love. It was my promise to myself that if I were ever given the chance to bear children, they'd know love so fierce it would be undeniable. I would be the type of mother I never had, build the type of family I always wanted, break generational cycles, and live and love with total abandon.

Finally, I felt confident enough to say I had done that. I'd really done it.

A couple hours later, I walked the red carpet with Charlie and Benny at my sides, all three of us dressed in gowns, amazed at where life had dropped us. But the truth was, the joy wasn't new for me; even when I was rejected relentlessly as an actress, I had never felt lacking. Nothing had ever been able to steal my happiness for long.

The ceremony began and I genuinely didn't care if I won or lost the award.

But, I have to tell you, when my name was called as the winner, I pulled my girls into a hug, strode up the stairs proudly, and accepted with so much gratitude I thought I may actually faint from the weight of all my blessings.

I held the golden statue in my hands, tears of joy streaming down my cheeks and said, "This is for my girls, my Triple Quinn. This was always for you. I love you both more than words could ever express. You inspire me every day. It's the highest honor to be your mom. Thank you for choosing me."

Charlie coming back to us that day in the hospital was the happiest day of my life.

But this one—this was a very close second.

★ ★ ★ ★ ★